THE FIRST BOOK CELLAR MYSTERY

WALKER TEXAS WIFE

MELISSA STORM AND K.M. HODGE

WALKER TEXAS WIFE Copyright © 2016 Blue Crown Press. All rights reserved. You may not use, reproduce or transmit in any manner, any part of this book without written permission, except in the case of brief quotations used in critical articles and reviews, or in accordance with federal Fair Use laws.

ISBN: 978-1-942771-28-9

Editor:
Stevie Mikayne

Cover and Interior Design:
Mallory Rock

Proofreader:
Falcon Storm

PO Box 721
Union Lake, MI 48387

Walker Texas Wife is a work of fiction. Names, characters, places and incidents are products of the author's imagination, or the author has used them fictitiously.

To the friendship that was found amid the secrets.
To each other.

Stay up-to-date with the latest Book Cellar Mysteries and more by subscribing at:

* * *

www.MelStorm.com/subscribe

&www.KMHodge.com/subscribe

* * *

As an added bonus, you'll receive a free short story as our way of saying "Hey, thanks!"

CHAPTER 1
ANNABETH

ANNABETH King hated stereotypes, but knew she fit the hot-tempered Irish girl to a T. All morning she had been a powder keg waiting to go off.

An absurd discussion about the lyrics to *Don't Stop Believing* hadsparked the most recent fight between her and Marcus. In retrospect she knew the fight had had nothing to do with the song, the oppressive heat, or even the last two days spent traveling across the country. No, it had everything to do with the *incident* from nine months ago—the one they didn't talk about.

"Either slow down, or pull over and let me drive," she said, her shrill voice annoying even her.

Marcus, just as hotheaded, pressed down on the gas pedal making the orange needle on the dash hover at eighty-five. "Is this slow enough for you?"

As he erratically shifted lanes to navigate around the traffic, she grabbed hold of the *Oh My God* bar to keep from being thrown against the door. "You're going to get us killed. Pull over, and let me drive!"

"Can you even reach the pedals?" he growled, not taking his eyes off the road.

He fought dirty, always bringing up her height, knowing it would get a rise out of her.

Well not today!

Instead of shouting back an equally hateful retort, she bit her tongue until a small drop of blood welled at its tip. The acrid taste of it mixed with the sour words that she wanted to fire back at him.

Her lack of response seemed to calm Marcus as he dropped the speed back down. Out of the corner of her eye, she noticed the muscles in his chiseled jaw still twitched.

Their tempers had run hot from the very start, their vitriolic diatribes a kind of foreplay. But they were miles away from that now. As much as she hated him at that moment, she still found herself drawn to him; the longings from before had not been tempered by the *incident*.

His arms, she thought with a sigh, the thick muscular forearms and biceps that filled out the crisp white T-shirts that he always wore had been her undoing.

Even his smell left her intoxicated—a heady mixture of sandalwood and his own musk that made her mind wander to a much happier place and time. A time when she would have been tasting him instead of the bitter words that hung on the end of her barbed tongue.

Beside her, Marcus loosened his grip on the wheel and his breathing slowed. Without taking his eyes off the road, he slid his right hand onto her knee. His mocha colored hand stood in stark contrast to her almost translucent white skin. "I'm sorry."

His baritone voice, full of contrition, calmed her frayed nerves.

"Me too," she said, giving his hand a reassuring squeeze.

For a brief moment he took his eyes off the road and flashed her a wide, dazzling grin that melted away some of her resolve to hate him.

"You've been driving awhile. Why don't we pull over at the next exit?"

He gave her knee a quick squeeze then put both hands back on the wheel and worked his way over to the far right lane.

"Yeah, I could use a break."

They pulled into a Shell station to make the switch and top off the tank. After filling up the tank,

Marcus slid into the passenger's seat and held up his phone. "Morgan wants an update by tomorrow."

"No pressure." Annabeth sighed as she merged their truck back onto the highway. Being behind the wheel at least gave her a feeling that she had some semblance of control over her world. She finally relaxed enough to enjoy the drive.

The heart of Texas was not at all what she'd expected back when they'd first decided to pack up and leave Detroit.

"I know it's ridiculously hot out, but it really is a beautiful place," Marcus mumbled beside her.

Annabeth scanned the horizon as she drove up a steep hill that overlooked the breathtaking green and yellow vista. "The trees look like broccoli."

From the corner of her eye she saw Marcus smirk and roll his brown eyes.

"About earlier..." He rested his arm on the top of her seat.

Annabeth glanced at him. "It's all right. We're just tired. It's been a stressful week."

Marcus huffed "A stressful *year*, more like it."

He parted her hair with his fingers and began to rub the thick cords of tension at the nape of her neck. At his tender and insistent touch, she stopped breathing. It took everything in her to keep her eyes on the road and not let them slip closed.

Boundaries needed to be set, she thought as she

took a breath at last. His hand felt so good that she couldn't bring herself to tell him to stop.

"Yes, it has been a hard year for us, hasn't it? Though, the way I see it, things can only get better from here." She let out a deep sigh, relaxing into his touch.

"Your mouth to God's ears, babe."

As they pulled onto a deserted ranch road, they saw in the distance a small town up ahead—home.

"Turn right onto River Bliss Road. Your destination will be on the left," the GPS announced.

"Thank God," Annabeth muttered.

They drove past the quaint 1970's ranch style homes to the very back of the Peach Creek subdivision. Children were out playing on manicured lawns that looked too green to be real.

"All they need is a kid on a bike delivering papers and it could be a Norman Rockwell painting," she said with no small amount of sarcasm.

Marcus chuckled.

It had been a long time since she had heard him laugh like that.

"That's it, 1013 William Drive. Home sweet home." He pointed to the last house on the left—almost identical to the rest of the houses on the block. For better or worse, it would be their home for the foreseeable future.

As they pulled into the driveway Annabeth noticed a young Hispanic woman watering the lawn next door.

Marcus nodded in her direction, trying to be discreet. "Go introduce yourself."

She hated when he told her what to do. He knew this, but did it anyway. Just because she knew it was the right thing to do didn't mean she agreed with his bossiness. She slammed the door of the car shut. The pointed blades of grass poked at her feet and made a crunching sound as she walked over. The woman crouched down in the flowerbed that divided their properties.

"Hey, neighbor." Annabeth extended her hand in greeting.

The young woman looked up as she wiped her hands dry on the back of her white jean shorts.

"Oh, hi," she said with an easy smile as she took Annabeth's hand in a firm grip.

"I'm Annabeth, and this is my h-husband Marcus." She hooked her thumb in Marcus's direction, still a bit irritated at him.

"Hi, I'm Violeta, but everyone calls me Vi. Y'all need help unloading that truck of yours?"

"Sure, we can use any help we can get," Marcus called as he flashed a charming smile her way.

Vi's cheeks colored a faint pink. Her black hair curtained around her face as she looked down. He had that effect on women. It wasn't the first time his smile had left another woman a little knock-kneed.

Before Annabeth might have gotten jealous, or

at the very least shot him a look, but now she just felt numbed. She had perfected the art of hiding her feelings so well that even she didn't know how she felt about anything anymore. They didn't call her the Ice Queen for nothing.

When *Frozen* came out, some of her colleagues had thought it was funny to give her an Elsa mug to go along with the awful nickname. *And they wondered why I left.* A small voice in the back of her mind reminded her that she hadn't always been that way—he had been the exception.

Worrying her lip, a nervous habit, she fished out the house key from her pocket and jogged ahead of them. As she opened the door she felt a faint flutter of anticipation. This new beginning needed to be better than what she'd left behind in Detroit. It just had to be.

Behind her she heard Marcus's teasing tone and the girlish laughter of their new neighbor.

"Ever onward," she mumbled to the open house, steeling herself against the backlog of emotions that threatened to escape.

Annabeth put aside her growing troubles and took control of the unpacking process. Under her guidance, it only took the three of them two hours to unload the U-Haul trailer and unpack most of the boxes. She honestly couldn't believe that Vi had stayed the entire time to help. Their new home had come fully furnished so they just had boxes of clothing and other personal effects, but still.

Vi grabbed the last one marked *books* from the back of the truck. "Are you a big reader, Anna?" she asked.

Annabeth grimaced. No matter how helpful their new neighbor had been, she just couldn't have Vi calling her *Anna*. "Please call me Annabeth."

"Oh Jeez, I'm sorry, Annabeth," she said, her face turning a subtle shade of pink.

Damn it, this is why I have no female friends. She knew she came off as a bitch, but she honestly didn't know how else to act. They didn't have a *how not to be a bitch* class in school.

"Don't worry—it's silly really. Anyway, to answer your question, yes. I love to read. We moved here so I could get my Ph.D. in comparative literature. On the way down here I started reading *Gone Girl*. Have you read it?"

Vi clasped her hands together in front of her. "That's what our book club is reading!"

"Well, that's a coincidence, all right." Annabeth smiled as she locked up the moving truck.

Vi lingered nearby even though the work was done. "You have to come. We're meeting tomorrow night."

"I don't know..." Annabeth felt too tired to commit to anything except twelve hours of sleep in her new bedroom.

"Just think about it. We always have such fun." Vi carried the last box into the house.

"Well looky, looky, a new neighbor," called out a husky female voice behind her.

Annabeth turned around and saw a young woman about her age. The smartly dressed woman walked over to Annabeth with her dog in tow—a Pomeranian with a teddy bear cut and a bright pink rhinestone leash.

"Hi." Annabeth extended her hand. "I'm Annabeth."

"Pleasure to meet you Ms. Annabeth. I'm Brooke Fischer. I live two blocks down on Emily Street. You can't miss it. The HOA just awarded us the yard of the month for the third month in a row."

Flipping her long dark hair over her shoulder, she bent down to pick up her little dog and buried her nose in its fur. "This gorgeous little fur baby is Tiara. Say hi, Ti-Ti," she said in a baby voice as she made the dog wave hello.

Annabeth fought the urge to roll her eyes or spout off some sarcastic remark that would more than likely go right over Brooke's airy head. Not that she would have noticed. This woman only had eyes for her ridiculous-looking dog.

"Nice to meet you both," she said, with a forced smile that she was sure looked more like a scowl.

Before she could say another word, Vi walked over to them wearing a delighted expression. "Oh good you two have met! I hope you don't mind, Brooke, but I invited Annabeth to our little Drink and Gossip Club. You're not going to believe this but she's reading *Gone Girl*, too!"

"Well isn't that a coincidence? How sweet of you to invite our new neighbor, Vi. Annabeth, please don't feel like you have to join us. I'm sure you have loads to do. Just moving in and all," Brooke said with a smile as fake as her own.

"Actually, I'm looking forward to it. It will be good for me to get out. I've been stuck alone with only my husband as company the last few days."

Annabeth enjoyed watching her squirm. She hated women like Brooke, who looked down on her and treated her like a second-class citizen because she didn't wear Jimmy Choo's or get her nails done every week. Messing with Brooke would be a nice distraction from her complicated life.

"Of course," Brooke said. "I don't know if Vi here gave you all the particulars, but it's tomorrow night, 8:00 p.m. at the Book Cellar on Main." She put her dog back down on the sidewalk. "It's been just swell chatting with you ladies, but I really need to finish my five miles if I'm to stay on track for my half-marathon training schedule."

"Sure, of course, I look forward to seeing you tomorrow night."

"Likewise. Toodles, ladies," she said with a patronizing flicker of her hand.

Annabeth watched Brooke and her dog power walk around the corner, disappearing from sight.

"Isn't she just great? We've been friends for forever it seems," Vi said, almost gushing.

"Yeah, she seems very... nice," Annabeth answered.

"Well I better skedaddle as well. I promised my sister I would swing by and take her to the movies tonight." Her smile was so genuinely sweet that it made Annabeth want to protect her from all the horrors of the world.

Annabeth was not a hugger by any stretch of the imagination, but when Vi wrapped her arms around her and squeezed, she couldn't help but reciprocate.

"Thank you so much for all your help tonight, Vi. I guess I'll see you tomorrow. Have a good time at the movies."

Vi smiled. "No problem, what are neighbors for?"

Annabeth fought back the sudden build-up of tears.

What was wrong with her? She wasn't the kind of gal who got mushy.

"Goodnight, Annabeth." Vi made her way across the lawn to her lime green pickup truck and drove off.

"Goodnight," Annabeth said to herself, Vi already gone.

The sound of the front screen door opening and closing made her jump. She felt Marcus before she saw him. He came up behind her, tilting his head down to her level. The familiar and comforting feel of him up against her made her want to fall back into his embrace—leaning on him like she once had. But she wasn't allowed to do that anymore, so instead she stood there using the last of her energy to stop herself from doing what came so naturally.

"I know the last thing you want to do is to get into that truck again, but we have no food. I Googled what's around here—which is nothing, by the way. I did discover that there's a Jet's Pizza about 30 minutes up the road from here." His boyish enthusiasm made her smile.

Marcus raked his fingers over his coarse, close-cropped hair the way he always did when he was tired. He had done the bulk of the driving all day and had to be exhausted. But he knew she lived and died for pizza so of course he'd scoured the Internet for the closest pizza place.

"All right, but only if I can drive," she said with a wink.

Her heart raced and her breath quickened as he lowered his head a little more toward hers.

"Whatever you want, babe."

Annabeth's breath caught in her throat. His brown eyes glistened in his playful way that left her knock-kneed. For a split second she thought he might try to kiss her, but the moment quickly passed and he straightened to his full height again. The awkwardness returned, leaving her as frustrated and disappointed as ever. A part of her wondered if she actually would have let him kiss her this time.

They took the long drive through the Hill Country and back to the civilization of the big city in a comfortable silence. When she opened the door to the pizza place her mouth watered. They ordered a couple slices and two Diet Cokes. As much as they enjoyed the idea of small town living, there was something to be said about the conveniences Austin could offer.

The pizza was divine. So much so that she didn't notice right away that he was watching her eat. His eyes teased her—the same kind of teasing that had always led to trouble in the past, the kind she secretly ached for again.

"What's so funny?" she asked at last.

"The way you eat your pizza." He tried—and failed—to hold in a roaring laugh that snuck out in stops and starts. "You're adorable."

Annabeth wiped at her face in earnest before tossing the balled up napkin at him. "Shut-up."

Marcus shook his head with an amused smile while under the table her crossed legs bobbed up and down.

"Are you nervous about tomorrow?" he asked with a wink.

Stilling her leg she flushed again. "A little. I just hope that there are some students my age and not a bunch of teenagers."

Marcus huffed out a small laugh. "Anna, I have no doubt you'll do great. You just have to get your confidence back. We both do."

She had never felt self-conscious before, but now—after all they had been through—she found herself second guessing everything all the time. Instead of looking ahead at the challenge with excitement, as she once had, she feared failing and what that might mean. Hell, apparently she couldn't even eat pizza right.

"You know I go by Annabeth now. And what's so amusing about the way I eat?"

Marcus snickered as he drank the rest of his Coke in one big gulp. His tennis shoe tapped her on the side of the leg, making her look away to hide her hot red cheeks from him.

"C'mon. Let's walk off some of this dinner. It's almost cool out now," Marcus said, taking her by the hand.

As they stepped outside Marcus held tight to her hand. He had been right. It had cooled off.

Once they were out of earshot of the other couples and joggers, Marcus cleared his throat. "It's going to be different this time, Anna... *Beth*. I know I messed up, but I hope you can trust me when I say that I won't slip up again."

His intense gaze bore through her. She knew if she turned her head and met his eyes full on, she would be lost. So she stared straight ahead, hoping he couldn't see the sheen of unshed tears that were beginning to pool for the second time that night.

"I want to trust you and believe we could make it work, but I'm still not sure it's the best idea right now, given what happened last time. I need more time to figure all this out." She swallowed back the ball of emotions that threatened to choke her.

Marcus let out his breath in slow, even puffs through his parted lips. "I guess that's all I can ask of you, huh?"

Annabeth tugged her hand free and stopped walking. "I'm kind of tired. Maybe we should head back."

Marcus stuffed his hands in his pockets and looked away. "Sure, whatever you want."

"I can sleep on the couch tonight," she said.

Marcus shook his head emphatically. "Absolutely not! *I'll* sleep on the couch. I'm always up before you anyway."

"Right." Annabeth bit her lip and fought back the urge to cry.

"Give me the keys. I'm driving." He reached out his hand, the one she had been holding before.

She fished inside her shorts pocket and handed him the keys, their fingers brushing together in the exchange, creating a spark that she felt down to her toes.

He stalked off without waiting for her, his long-legged stride one she had no hope of matching even on her best day.

He wanted her and she wanted him, but that wasn't enough. They couldn't be together until she found a way to forgive him—forgive herself for what they'd done.

CHAPTER 2

SHOPPING list in hand, Vi weaved in and out of the aisles of the local HEB grocery store. Barring any unforeseen Joy crises, she planned to run a few leisurely errands then relax at home for her day off—though caring for her disabled adult sister meant that, in reality, she never had a day off.

Vi had been twenty and Joy twenty-four when their mother and stepfather had died in a car accident. Their bio dad had stepped out on the family early on, back when the doctors had first diagnosed Joy with a profound learning disability and autism. After nine long years she'd enrolled Joy in a group home.

On the hard days when she didn't think she could give any more, she would fantasize about what her life would be like if Joy had died in the car crash along with their parents. The thought shamed and thrilled her in equal measure.

What would Father Horatio think if he knew?

It would take more than just a few Hail Marys, she knew, to atone for such a fantasy.

As she pushed her cart down the cereal aisle, she let her mind wander to thoughts of her new neighbors. They were such a cute couple. She couldn't help but feel a small stab of jealousy over what they had, something so simple and yet so far from her own reach. They weren't overt in their affection for each other, but you could still tell they loved each other.

It had been so long that she had almost forgotten what it felt like to have a man kiss her, touch her, love her. She had read about how cells die and new ones take their place and how every seven years you have totally different cells than the ones you'd had seven years prior. It would be seven years next month since she had last been kissed.

How many non-virginal cells do I have left?

The vibration of her phone in her back pocket startled her. Her heart sank when she read Oaklawn Group Home on the screen. Back to reality, she thought with a sigh.

"Vi speaking." She paused in the aisle and ran her fingers through her tangled hair.

"Ms. Vi, I'm sorry to bother you so early, but your sister Joy is insisting that you plan on coming by this morning, and she won't do her chores because of it," Ms. Lockard, the group home owner, mumbled hurriedly.

Vi felt a flower of rage bloom in her gut.

Is it too much to ask for a Joy-free day every now and again?

"Put her on, Ms. Lockard. I'll talk to her," she said with a sigh.

"Vi, they want me to wash the dishes. We're going to the rodeo today. We're going to see Ricky ride the bull today."

"Joy, we aren't going to the rodeo today. I told you that last night. We can maybe go next weekend." Vi tossed a box of Mini Wheats into the cart.

"No, no, no Vi. We are going today. Today. Today!" Joy's voice got louder and louder.

"Joy, do your chores for this week and I will take you next Saturday. Okay?"

Great, now I have to go to the rodeo and see Ricky. Maybe I'll luck out and Joy won't hold up her end of the bargain.

"Promise?"

"Yes, Joy, but you have to do every single one of your chores, including the dishes." Vi turned the corner into the coffee and tea aisle and studied the art on each of the brightly colored packages.

"We can see Ricky? Promise we get to see Ricky?"

"Yes, Joy, we can see Ricky."

Her heart raced just saying his name. She hadn't so much as caught a glimpse of him in months and hadn't spoken to him in almost a year. She'd ignored his calls until one day he just stopped calling. But Joy loved him with a fierceness that couldn't be tempered. Wait a minute, Vi thought. She no longer heard her sister's characteristic frantic breathing on the line.

"Joy?"

"Ms. Vi, thanks for your help. Sorry again to have to bother you so early in the morning. Hopefully it will be the only time we'll have to call you today. One more thing since I have you on the line. We're going to need you to send us another two hundred dollars to cover some extra expenses for your sister, and I wanted to double-check that you were still going to be able to make those muffins for the bake sale next week?" Ms. Lockard had a way of asking for things that made it difficult for Vi to say no.

"No problem. Yes, I'll pick up the muffin mix now," Vi said, even though she knew she would just end up hitting Mitzi up for some muffins. "Thank you for everything you do, Ms. Lockard. Have a great day and don't hesitate to call if you need anything else." Vi rushed to end the call before Ms. Lockard could rope her into volunteering for any more special tasks.

In a huff, she rounded the corner and almost rammed right into another cart. She recognized in an instant the tall, muscular form standing before her, the sure, strong hands gripping the cart, and the dark, sparkling eyes.

Ricky.

The universe must truly hate her. Just seeing him made her mouth go dry. Why hadn't she at least combed her hair?

And despite her disheveled appearance, he'd recognized her, too.

"Violeta?" his smooth, syrupy voice vibrated down to her toes like a plucked tuning fork.

"Ricky." She patted down her messy hair, which he seemed to find amusing.

"It's good to see you, Vi. I was hoping I would run into you now that I'm in town."

Vi blushed. Seeing him again after such a long hiatus left her flustered.

"Yes, it's—good to see you too." Vi felt like such a loser. She couldn't even carry on a conversation with this man without stumbling over her words.

Ricky shifted their carts over to let other people by. His close proximity made her palms sweat. Of course, in contrast, Ricky seemed calm and unaffected.

"Are you and Joy going to come out to the Rodeo next weekend? I can get y'all some VIP passes."

Vi felt her cheeks grow hot. "Yes, Joy loves the rodeo. She's been talking about you nonstop the last few weeks. I think she has a little crush on you," she said, hoping to deflect the conversation away from herself.

Ricky smiled and tugged at the brim of his hat. "I hope she ain't the only one."

Vi looked away from him as she worried her bottom lip and twisted the end of her shirt around her pointer finger. "Ricky..."

"I'm going to lasso you in one of these days, Vi. You can't keep running away from me, not forever."

Vi looked down at her flip-flops, blinking back the hot tears that threatened to spill. She refused to cry in front of him.

"So, uhh, we'll see you next Saturday. For the rodeo."

Ricky reached for her hand and brought it to his lips. "It's a date."

"It's not a date," she said with such conviction that even she almost believed it.

Ricky let go of her hand and turned away. "You keep telling yourself that, *amorcito*."

Little love. He called me his little love. The familiar endearment sparked something in her that she was sure had died. As she stood there amidst the coffee beans and tea bags, she could almost feel Ricky's arms wrap around her, his lips… Just a memory. The past needed to stay in the past, she told herself.

WALKER TEXAS WIFE

She didn't look up until she had seen his boots turn the corner of the aisle. Only then did she wipe away the single tear which had fallen down her cool cheek. Vi tried to push him and his damn smile out of her mind.

And somehow she managed to keep it together until she got home and put all the groceries away. Only then did she shed her bitter, angry tears. For better or for worse, she had chosen this life.

Rather than mope around for the rest of the day feeling sorry for herself, she put on her favorite playlist and began to dance around the kitchen on the balls of her feet. When she danced she could shut out the world. It had been a long time, but her muscles recalled in aching clarity the turns and points. Sashaying across the room, she didn't notice her new neighbor Annabeth standing at the open back door until she started to clap.

Vi unhooked the old iPhone Brooke had given her last year from the portable speakers she had gotten from a swap group. The sudden silence that filled the room was jarring.

"You surprised me," she said, embarrassed by the flustered tone in her voice.

"I'm sorry. I didn't mean to startle you. I heard the music, and the door was open, so..."

Vi sighed. "It's okay. I guess I'm just not used to having other people around. Old Mrs. Tannerbone, who used to live next door...well...she tended to keep to herself."

"I'm sorry. It was presumptuous of me to just pop in without knocking." Annabeth's pale cheeks turned bright pink.

"Don't worry about it. Was there something you wanted?" Vi asked.

Annabeth reached into her back pocket and handed her a single key. "Yeah, I have a favor to ask. Could you please hold on to our extra key? I have a habit of locking myself out of the house."

Vi took the key and grabbed her own keyring, stringing it on. "Oh dear, I've done that myself a few times. Always on the go, and such. Once, my sister Joy locked me out and the fire department had to come and break into the house to let me back inside." She tucked a lock of hair behind her ear. "We'll just have to try and not lock ourselves out of our houses at the same time."

Annabeth smiled a tired smile. "Right... And I was just wondering what I should wear for tonight. For book club. Any tips?"

Vi smiled. "Oh, that. Just any old thing will do. We don't dress up...well Brooke does, but Brooke always dresses up. What you're wearing is fine."

Annabeth let out a nervous sigh. "Are you sure Brooke is okay with my coming? I got the impression she wasn't too keen on my crashing in on your group."

"Bah, don't mind her. She can come off a little much sometimes, but she's really a sweetheart."

"Okay. Did you want to go there together?" Annabeth asked.

"Absolutely!"

"Great, I'll go get cleaned up and be back in an hour. I promise to knock this time," she said with a goofy grin.

"Sounds like a plan." Vi watched Annabeth wave and walk out the back door, closing it behind her.

It might be nice having a friend next door. She never saw Brooke these days—their busy schedules were always at odds. The loneliness of her life had grown palpable. She couldn't really afford to eat at the Book Cellar this week so she made a quick sandwich and flipped on the evening news as she ate.

Just as the anchors were wishing everyone a safe evening, a loud series of raps sounded on her front door. Well, she did say she would knock this time, Vi thought with a smile. When she opened the door, Annabeth stood on her porch with her wild red hair piled high atop her head. She wore feather earrings, a bedazzled cowl neck sleeveless shirt, and dark blue designer jeans. On her feet were brown leather boots with elaborate swirls that matched the colors of her shirt. She looked beautiful. Even the freckles that dusted her nose looked perfectly planned and placed just right. Brooke was going to flip her lid when she saw her.

Maybe this wasn't a good idea after all.

"Is this not okay?" Annabeth scowled and looked down at her outfit.

Vi shook her head. "No, no. You look amazing. Let me just grab my bag and we can head out."

When they pulled into a parking spot in front of the Book Cellar, Annabeth gasped. "What a cool building!"

"Yeah, it used to be a bar. Some hipster type, who made it big in the dot-com days, bought it and converted it into a bookstore coffee shop. It's a great place to hang out. Not one of those establishments where they are too cool to have good customer service."

Annabeth laughed. "Okay, well that's good."

As they got out of the car and made their way to the entrance, a man standing inside the café tapped on the glass storefront window and waved. Jesse. Vi loved Jesse's easygoing nature, which often countered Brooke's dramatic high maintenance ways. It was definitely a good thing her two best friends balanced each other out so well.

Jesse met them at the door with a beer in hand and bussed their cheeks in greeting. "Well looky here, Vi brought a friend. The new neighbor, Annabeth King, I presume?"

Annabeth eyed Jesse suspiciously.

Vi leaned into Annabeth. "Jesse here is the *official* neighborhood gossip. He has a blog and everything."

Jesse put his hands on his hips and shot Vi an admonishing look. "You make me sound like those blue-haired ladies that hang out at Trudy's all day under the dryers."

Vi giggled. "You should check it out. You never know what you might learn. Last time I was there I heard that Ms. Habberdash's poodle Mimsy had a case of worms so bad that they had to call in some specialist to deal with it."

Jesse shuddered. "That's disgusting. Don't make me regret getting you a muffin, love." He handed Vi her favorite chocolate muffin with the sugar crystals sprinkled on top.

"Thanks, Jess." She eagerly grabbed the muffin and sank her teeth into its toasted top.

"Now, Ms. Annabeth, y'all are from Detroit, right?" He took a sip of his beer while awaiting her reply.

Annabeth's mouth opened in surprise. "How did you know that?"

Jesse shrugged. "I can't divulge my sources, but, suffice it to say, nothing gets by me."

Before Annabeth could respond, the door to the shop opened and in came Brooke. Every head in the place turned. Her long dark hair hung straight down her back and she wore a simple but elegant black dress. On her feet were black designer sandals with tiny gold jewels, and on her arm she carried a Coach purse, her

Pomeranian Tiara in tow. She always looked like she had just walked right out of one of those high-end catalogs. The ones Brooke wanted Vi to order from.

"Fashionably late as usual, I'm afraid," Brooke said as she flipped her hair behind her.

Vi caught Annabeth rolling her eyes.

Oh dear. She really hadn't thought this through.

"Let's grab our spot before some students take it," Vi said, anxious to get the night over with.

Out of the corner of her eye, she saw Jesse lean in and whisper to Annabeth. She was just able to make out his words over the din of the busy coffee house.

"I can't wait to find out what little secrets you have hidden away. I bet they're doozies."

CHAPTER 3
BROOKE

BROOKE was not a "take 'em as they come" kind of woman. She liked to approach each new day with a thoroughly detailed to-do list scrawled onto her favorite rose-scented stationary with her initials emblazoned across the top. BFF. Brooke Frances Fischer. The one—the only—BFF to the entire town of Herald Springs. Well, at least as far as they knew.

Everyone in the town—heck, in the state—loved Brooke and her tiny fur companion, Tiara. After all, what wasn't to love? In her prime, she'd been crowned Miss Herald Springs Teen Queen, and her beauty hadn't faded one lick over the years. Like the imported Chianti she kept plentifully stocked in her home's private cellar—and also, by special request, always on hand at the Book Cellar—Brooke had only gotten better with age.

At twenty-nine, she had her pageant title, a husband who was both handsome and wealthy, an adorable Pomeranian of blue ribbon blood...and then there was her business. While she only worked a few hours each week, her party-planning business was always in high demand. The Herald Chronicle had even named her Business Woman of the Year for three years running. Not that it was hard in this tiny Podunk town, but still—she loved seeing the look on Mitsy Grazier's face year after year as Parties by Brooke beat out her muffin bakery yet again.

Yes, Brooke had quite the glamorous life, one for which she preferred to hold the reins. Which is why it was so upsetting that Vi had invited a certain frizzy-haired stranger to their book club that evening.

Vi, her little Violeta, of all people should have known better. And there she was now, waving spastically at Brooke as she entered in her new D&G cocktail dress and Hermes sandals. Nobody dared tell her she was overdressed for a trip to the local bookstore. In fact, they'd probably all soon be buying cheap knock-offs at the local Target, but by then Brooke would have moved on to a bold, new fashion statement that was all her own.

Always keep them guessing what you'll do next, she thought to herself as Jesse pulled out a chair for her at the head of their table.

"Sorry, ladies and Jess." She settled Tiara on her lap, then shot an ingratiating smile toward the group. Indeed, it took work to stay at the top, even where your closest friends were concerned. "I didn't have time to read the book."

That much was true. She'd lost interest after the first few pages failed to grab her attention. Besides, she'd spent the better part of that morning lying in bed and Googling up a storm on her iPad.

Annabeth King had appeared in their neighborhood with no notice, seemingly out of nowhere, and Brooke knew better than to trust anyone without first doing her research. Hers had failed miserably when she couldn't so much as find a Facebook account for one Ms. King. There were a billion others, but not the red-haired ball of frizz she was looking for.

Vi chortled and took a bite from her giant chocolate chip muffin.

The new girl—the one with seemingly no digital footprint—rolled her eyes. Well, one way or another she'd dig up a bit of intel, especially since Vi seemed to insist on making the she-devil a part of their regular entourage. Everyone thought they were best friends with Brooke Fischer, but few actually were. Could she really trust this walking fashion disaster with such an important responsibility? Frankly, she doubted it, but she'd at least wait to see what she could find out before making any official decisions on the matter.

"That's okay, Queen B. We know you're very busy and important," Jesse picked up his eReader and pulled up his notes and highlights for *Gone Girl*. "We're happy to catch you up."

"Actually, I figured we'd use this opportunity to get to know a little bit about this stranger in our midst. Annie, is it?" She put on her biggest and brightest smile.

"It's Annabeth, and this *is* a book club, right? Let's talk about the book. Personally, I loved how Flynn didn't—"

"Yeah, we call ourselves a book club, because we meet here at the Cellar and occasionally will read a book or two." She let out a low giggle. "But really we're just a group of friends taking a quick break here and there to relax and knock back a few drinks. Isn't that right, Vi?" She turned to her best friend who was mid-bite.

Vi nodded vigorously and covered her mouth with her hand as she spoke. "Oh, yes. Like I told you, Annabeth, we're the drink and gossip club."

Jesse tucked his eReader back into his shoulder bag and drummed his fingers against his half-empty glass of beer. "Drinking and gossiping, my two favorite things. And tonight's topic of conversation is definitely you, my dear. Help us fill in the blanks, lest we should be forced to fill them in ourselves. And, believe me, you don't want that."

Brooke and Jesse laughed. Whereas Vi tended to be clueless about, well, pretty much everything, Brooke could always count on Jesse to have her back. She often thought of him as her gay best friend, even though he actually had a wife and two kids. But Jesse's knack for fashion, gossip, and blogging would have been too much to bear if she thought of him as a virile, manly man. At least gay was safe, right?

Vi stared at the surface of the table.

The bartender delivered a glass of Brooke's signature Chianti along with an almond biscotti for her pooch. He gave Tiara a quick scratch behind the ears before running back to the counter to help the waiting line of customers.

Annabeth turned red, whether from nerves or from indignation it was difficult to tell. "Not really much to tell. I'm Annabeth King, and I came to…"

"No need to be so nervous. We're all friends here." Brooke fixed her gaze on the newcomer, daring her to suggest otherwise.

"Thanks, but I'm not nervous. Like I said before, there isn't much to tell. My husband Marcus and I moved here from Detroit so I could go back to school to get my Ph.D. in Comparative Literature—"

"At U of A," Vi interjected with a look of pride on her beautiful but unkempt face.

"Yes, thank you, Vi. I'm going back to college for my Ph.D. I got a full scholarship and a TA job in the English Department teaching Freshman English Composition. Marcus was lucky enough to get a job at the university as a manager in the records department."

"Living here makes for quite the commute. Why aren't you living on campus?" Jesse asked.

"We've had enough big city living to last us a lifetime, and Austin seems like it might be a bit too weird for my tastes, especially if we were to live on campus with all the crazy undergrads. We heard about how Herald Springs was voted one of the best small cities to live in. So we thought, sure why not?"

"You just went for it, moving to some small town cross country, without doing your research, huh?"

"Research?" Annabeth laughed. "You make it sound like buying the best vacuum or something. It's just a place to live."

Jesse gasped. "Take it back, take it back now. HS is so much more than that. You'll see." He sipped at his beer, his eyes crinkled in a mischievous smile.

"Jesse's right. How could you suggest buying a vacuum is more important than buying a house? Unless you didn't buy it outright. You're not…" She paused to let the disgusting revelation sink in amongst the group. "Renters, are you?"

Jesse shuddered while Vi rolled her eyes.

"No, we bought. And that's not at all what I meant. I—"

Brooke held up a hand. She'd heard enough. "It's fine if you are. I mean, who are we to judge? On behalf of Herald Springs, we welcome you, regardless of the circumstances that brought you here."

"Yes, welcome to the town," Vi gushed.

"You done good choosing HS as home. You'll see," Jesse added.

"Umm, thanks, I guess. Would it be okay if we talked about the book now maybe?"

Brooke leaned back in her chair and let out a breath she hadn't realized she'd been holding. She wasn't exactly sure she liked Annabeth. Not yet anyway. But at least she knew this woman was no threat to her long-held position of Herald Springs's social ruler.

Still, something was definitely off about Annabeth King, and Brooke fully intended to find out what that something was. Oh, how she loved a fun new side project.

CHAPTER 4

ANNABETH

VI hugged Annabeth goodnight on the narrow strip of grass that divided their two properties. They'd stayed late after Jesse and Brooke had gone home. The Cellar's funky blues band paired well with their beers.

Vi had told her all about her mentally disabled sister, her work at a domestic violence shelter, and how she hadn't been on a date in years. Unlike the nosy bitch, Brooke, Vi had never once asked any personal questions or pried in any way into Annabeth's past.

"Goodnight, Annabeth. Don't forget next Saturday you're coming with us to the rodeo," Vi said with a teasing smile.

"I wouldn't miss meeting Joy for the world." Annabeth felt a little tipsy as she stumbled over the prickly grass to her front door.

It took Annabeth a minute to steady her hand and unlock the door. Once inside, she kicked off her boots and tiptoed down the hall to her room. As her eyes adjusted to the dark she noticed a familiar form lying on her bed. *Marcus.*

Drunk and tired, she was caught off guard when he pulled her down onto the bed with him.

What the hell?

"Why are you in my bed?"

"Mmm..." He hummed as he drew her up against his bare chest.

"*Marcus*—" she warned, but he cut her off.

"No funny stuff. I promise. The couch is killing my back. Have pity on a man."

"Fine, I'll sleep on the couch then." She tried to sit up, but Marcus's strong forearm hooked around her waist and held firm. A game of tug of war broke out between her head and heart.

"Stay." His husky voice weakened her defenses.

"Marcus..." She wet her lips with a quick sweep of her tongue. She knew her disheartened protest wasn't going to sway him.

Her heart's plea won her over at last. For the first time in months, she dropped down her guard. He seemed to notice the shift in her attitude and became bolder. His finger traced lazy circles on her bare arm, making gooseflesh break out next to the freckles on her upper body.

"Anna," he said, his breath tickling her neck. "I miss you."

Annabeth felt her chest tighten as a swell of emotions washed over her tired body. "I miss you too."

She wasn't sure if it was the darkness or the alcohol in her system but she felt uninhibited enough to voice the question she had wanted to ask him dozens of times over the last few months. "Do you ever dream about it?"

She felt his body tense against her. "Yeah, all the time. Even when I'm awake."

His words struck a chord in her and she soon found herself twisting her body until they were nose to nose. The close proximity made her breathless. She had to fight with herself to stop from further closing the gap between them. Forget about the past and lose herself in him.

Marcus looped his arm around where her shirt had started to ride up.

"Do you? Dream about it?" His bowed lips pursed and his brow furrowed.

Annabeth swallowed hard to keep herself from crying. "Yeah, sometimes," she said, her voice just above a whisper.

Marcus tucked the loose strands of her hair behind her ear. "Morgan called while you were out."

Her chest prickled with fear. "Oh?"

"The appeal was rejected. We're still in the clear."

Annabeth let out the breath she didn't know she'd been holding.

Marcus regarded her with a look of surprise. "Did you think their appeal was going to be accepted?"

"Shouldn't it have?" she asked, looking directly at him.

"No, Anna. They were right in rejecting it."

"But a girl died because we—" Annabeth said, choking on her words until Marcus cut her off by putting a finger on her lips.

"We did not kill that girl. Get that straight in your head. You can't keep carrying around the guilt for a crime you didn't commit."

Annabeth sighed. "If we had been paying attention, she might not have died."

Marcus tightened his hold on her so that she rested her head on his bicep.

"We don't know that, and if she hadn't died we wouldn't be here now." He soothed the back of her neck where a knot the size of Texas had been building over the last year.

His words sounded more like a justification to get them off the hook. Even in the dark she could sense him looking at her, trying to read her.

His firm hand slid up and down the leg of her jeans, sending a shiver down her spine. When his nose touched hers he pulled back. "Why don't you go get cleaned up. Brush your teeth. You smell like beer."

Embarrassed, she felt a shy smile creep across her face. "Sorry."

"Wait. Did you have a good time?" He loosened his hold on her.

"Yeah, actually. I met another neighbor, Jesse."

"Oh and what's she like? Same as that bitchy Brooke?"

"Well, *he* is a very handsome and intriguing man. Not bitchy at all."

Annabeth smiled knowing she had his full attention now. He had never acted jealous before, but the precarious nature of their current relationship changed everything.

"Tell me more. Should I be worried?"

Annabeth giggled as she fished her phone out of her pocket and pulled up Jesse's blog.

"Yes, but not for the reason you think. He's this town's local gossip columnist. Here's his latest blog. He already knew our names and where we came from." She worried her lip and handed her phone over to him.

Marcus read out loud portions of the blog post.

> *Speaking of things that go great with chili, seems we've got a couple of new arrivals in Herald Springs this week. Make sure to stop and say hello to Marcus and Annabeth*

King. They just moved here from Detroit. He's taken a job in the records department at the college while she's doing the whole grad school thing. Think they'll be much competition for Brooke this spring at the neighborhood cook-off, or will her chili once again reign supreme? Let's hope for their own sakes, they're not too good in the kitchen...

Sighing he handed her back her phone. "What do you think?"

Annabeth stretched her leg so that it brushed up against his. She had been thinking about the Jesse situation all night.

"It would be wrong to just disregard him as small potatoes. We'll need to be careful, but it's too late for that conversation tonight. I'm going to go freshen up." She slipped out of bed and went to the master bath to get ready for bed.

The emptiness of the room greeted her when she stepped out of the bathroom a few minutes later. Down the hall she could hear the faint sounds of his snoring coming from the living room.

Disappointment and loneliness shared the room with her in his absence. But she'd ruined any chance at a light-hearted romp when she brought up their horrible past.

That night she dreamed of it. She awoke soaking wet and gasping for air. She wondered if, after everything was said and done, she would ever be able to let it all go—or if it would stay with her for the rest of her life. A small price to pay for the life that was taken.

CHAPTER 5

VI loved her job as an advocate at the Lighthouse Crisis Center, but the hours sometimes wore on her. That night she had the overnight on-call shift. At 3 a.m. a call came in from the hotline that a woman had requested help. When she worked late hours she would sleep in street clothes. This allowed her to be out the door five minutes after the call came in.

When Vi found the young woman waiting on the side of the road, her heart broke. Dressed only in a man's white T-shirt and light cotton shorts, she looked like a little girl wearing her parents' clothing. As it turned out, she hadn't been too far off. The girl was only eighteen and three months pregnant to boot.

It was after eight by the time Vi got her situated in the shelter.

She had just enough time to shower and get dressed to be on time for the 9:30 Mass at St. Paul's. If she didn't go today she would have to try and sneak in a weekday service, which never worked out. And skipping it altogether was out of the question. Even in her rebellious teen years she'd never missed church. Ricky liked to tease her about her strict adherence to the Catholic attendance code. As a traveling bull rider he was almost never in town to attend church.

But even if she wanted to, she couldn't bail. Father Horatio was depending on her to take him after the service to visit with her Abuela Rose, who was in a memory care nursing home. Every Sunday after the service, Vi would take him to visit with her and give her Communion.

Before she walked inside the church, she shot off a text request to Mitsy Grazier to order a last minute batch of her famous chocolate muffins with the sugar sprinkled on top. She hadn't had enough time to make some for the group home's annual fundraiser bake sale. Brooke would flip her lid if she knew that Vi was giving business to her archrival, but desperate times, desperate measures, and all that.

"Ms. Vi, don't you look lovely this morning?" a familiar voice called out, causing her to turn on her heels.

Ricky.

Just the sight of him gave her unholy thoughts. He had on a cream-colored hat and a blue button-down dress shirt that looked freshly pressed. His green twill dress pants hugged him in all the right places. *Damn!*

"We seem to be running into each other a lot lately. When did you start going to the early service?"

Vi tried her best to avoid his heated gaze, but she was no match for Ricky. Never had been.

Ricky's hand bumped against the back of hers. One of his fingers hooked her hand and brought it up to his lips for a quick kiss. "Since I found out the most beautiful woman in town went to this service."

"Ricky..." Vi pulled her hand away from him in a half-hearted admonishment.

Dipping his head down until it was level with hers, he whispered, "I also know you can't run away from me here. You sure force a man to get creative in his wooing."

Vi's hand went up to the St.Rita medallion around her neck—a nervous habit.

"Ricky," she said, a plea against his unrelenting advances.

"It's just church," he said, quietly enough so none of the nearby busybodies could hear. "I can't very well bite you with Father Horatio in the next room." A teasing twinkle lit his eye as he held out his arm.

Vi laughed, despite herself. "All right then." She slipped her arm around his firm bicep and allowed him to escort her to a waiting pew.

True to his word, he had been the perfect gentlemen. He put the kneeler down for her and, after prayer, cupped her elbow to help her up.

During the giving of the peace, he gave her a chaste kiss on the cheek, but it still made her heart dance a wild *cha-cha-cha* that was hardly appropriate given their circumstances. His smell and the familiar feeling of his bristled cheek against hers ignited the spark of a million different kisses from the past.

"Peace be with you." His incendiary whisper turned the fire inside of her into an all-out blaze.

Vi's breath caught in her throat as she inhaled him again. Being around him like that was dangerous. She needed to get away, she thought as she turned to the others in her aisle.

"Peace be with you, Maria," she said to the woman on the other side of her.

Afterward when everyone was once again in their seats, he leaned over and whispered in her ear, "You forgot me."

That was the problem, she couldn't forget him. The memories of his touch and kiss had been branded into her memory. She had to stay strong, though, because her intense love for him was the very reason she'd pushed him away. He deserved a family, a life of peace and happiness, none of which she herself could offer him.

"Peace be with you, Ricky," she said at last.

When the service finally ended, the parishioners, who had stayed after Communion, stood around outside the church chatting. Ricky followed Vi through the double doors and into the sweltering heat. They walked in silence under the shaded canopy of a top-heavy oak tree. His fingers played with the brim of his hat as he seemed to be searching for the right words to say.

"I don't suppose you'll let me take you out for coffee?" he asked at last.

His request wounded her. He wasn't making it easy on her at all. But before she could officially turn him down, Father Horatio arrived before them, wearing a bright and knowing smile.

"Ricky, it's so good to see you again. It's been too long."

Ricky pinched the brim of his Stetson and placed it back on his head. "Thank you. It's good to be back again."

"Are you just in town for the rodeo?" Father asked.

"Yes. It's my last one. I'm giving up bull riding."

What? He loves the rodeo.

When they were kids he'd told her time and again that he was going to die a bull rider. Why would he be giving it up now at the height of his career? What would he do for money in the meantime? Did he already have a job lined up? He was horrible with money—did he have enough cash to get by?

She watched as he stuffed his calloused hands into his pockets. He always did that when he was nervous.

"Oh? What are your plans?" Father asked.

Vi looked at Ricky, eager to hear his explanation for giving up the one thing she knew he loved above all else.

"I'm not getting any younger so I thought it might be time to settle down. Get a stable job and find me a nice girl to marry."

Father Horatio slapped Ricky on the back. "That's wonderful, *Mijo*."

Marry. The word stabbed and twisted her like a knife in her gut. A wave of panic washed over her. Did he mean her? Another woman? Even though it was what she said she wanted for him, the thought of him being with another woman was too much. When she realized both men were looking at her, her face grew hot. She needed to redirect the conversation—quick.

"Forgive me, Father, but we should really be going."

"*Sí*," Father said as he shook Ricky's hand and leaned in. "I look forward to hearing more about these plans of yours." He eyed Vi with a conspicuous grin.

Ricky's hand brushed against hers. "So I guess coffee is out for today, but are we still on for next weekend? I was able to get you and Joy VIP passes. I even got tickets to hear that band you like. You know Marmalade Sunshine?"

Vi nodded, awestruck that he had thought to get tickets to the band that they had seen on their first date ten years ago. His brown eyes searched hers for answers she just couldn't offer. Swallowing hard, she looked away from him.

"Yes, we will be there. Thank you for the passes. Joy will be tickled pink."

"I'll see you then." Rick kissed her on the cheek, lingering a little longer than was proper.

"Give Abeula Rose a kiss from me." Ricky winked.

Vi watched him as he walked away. Why couldn't he just take the hint and leave her alone? She had told him countless times that she didn't have the time or the energy for another relationship. Caring for her sister and her aging grandmother while holding down a full time job kept her busy enough. Besides, why would he want to share that responsibility with her, when even *she* didn't want it? No, she loved him too much to rob him of a normal life with the family she knew he dreamed of having someday. But apparently for him, that someday was *this* day.

Father Horatio touched her arm, bringing her back to reality. "You look tired, *Mija*."

She nodded distractedly as Ricky got into his truck and drove away from the church, away from her, again.

Father Horatio followed her gaze. "Maybe you wouldn't be so tired all the time if you asked for help. Let someone in."

"Does having Mitsy make the muffins for the bake sale count?"

Father laughed as he stuck his hands into his pants pockets. "Maybe a little, but still I worry about you. It's not right for you to shoulder all these burdens alone. Especially when there is someone who seems willing and able to share in the journey with you."

"I'm sorry to make you worry, Father. There is no need to be. I'm fine. I just had a long night at work."

"If you insist." He studied Vi as if waiting for more, but when she failed to respond he spoke again. "I'll drop this for now, but promise me that you will think about what I said?"

Vi looked away from him to hide her glassy eyes. "I'll think about it."

"Good. Well, let's go then. We don't want to keep your Abuela Rose waiting."

Vi swallowed hard. It had been an emotional day. As she fished her keys out of her bag she got a text from Brooke.

> *"What all do you know about this Anna chick? When I was out walking last night with Tiara I saw her husband, what's-his-name, asleep on the couch. Are they fighting? I told Jesse and he thinks there is more going on with those two than meets the eye. We need to do a little digging. Meet me Monday at the Cellar at 9."*

Below the message was a meeting invitation from Brooke that linked to her phone's calendar app.

Vi clicked accept and dropped the phone back into her purse. She didn't have time for both Abuela and Brooke right now, a realization which confirmed her decision to stay as far away from Ricky as she possibly could.

Vi felt herself being pulled apart into a million little pieces. Here a piece for Brooke, there a piece for the women at the shelter. The biggest piece of all, of course, went to her sister. But what happened when there were no more pieces left to give? Would Vi just disappear completely?

CHAPTER 6

BROOKE

BROOKE groaned and tossed her iPhone across the long, mahogany table before sinking back into her plush dining chair. Why wasn't Vi answering? Vi *always* answered.

Of course, she knew her best friend had a life outside of her, but she still struggled with feeling rejected by the one person she could generally depend on to be there for her. She waited a few more minutes, tapping her French-tipped nails on the table. A quick glance toward her phone confirmed that her message had still gone unanswered.

She'd run out of options. It was time.

WALKER TEXAS WIFE

She tore into the package with quivering hands and stared the cruel piece of plastic down, as if she could intimidate it into delivering the result she wanted. She'd be a good mother, right?

Of course, she would.

So then why did getting from point A to point B prove to be so difficult here? Things always came easy for Brooke, because she *made* them happen. And she'd been dutifully following her fertility diet, taking her folic acid, and even following the old wives' tales about the best, most effective sex positions. So what was the deal? They'd been trying for months now, and nothing. She doubted this test would be any different than the others, but still she had to take it to know for sure.

So she took the test, then waited. Those three minutes felt like pure and utter agony.

Brooke tried not to think about how this result had the power to change her entire life, but here she sat again—month after month—waiting for confirmation of what she already knew to be true.

She squinted at the results window, and, as expected, it remained hopelessly empty. Just like her womb.

Still.

Again.

Always.

No longer a surprise, just a heartbreaking reality.

Tiara jumped up onto Brooke's lap and gave her a kiss on the chin.

She smiled and scratched the tiny dog's head. "Hi, baby." The only baby she'd ever have at this rate.

Tiara wheezed excitedly and wagged her tail like a tiny, off-season jingle bell.

The thunderous sound of the garage door opening boomed in Brooke's ears. He'd come home early, ever the optimist that this would be the month she'd greet him with good news.

"Brooke?" Brian called as he stopped at the coat closet to hang up his jacket.

"I'm back here," she answered from her place on the hallway floor.

A moment later, he came into view. Brooke couldn't bring herself to look up past his knees. She didn't want to see that pained expression she knew all too well. Couldn't they just pretend for a little while longer?

"I take it the test was negative."

Brooke nodded and buried her face in Tiara's fur.

He stooped down and wrapped his arms around her.

"Next month, then. We'll get it next month."

For Brian, each cycle was a new opportunity to become parents, but for Brooke, each negative pregnancy test felt like another baby they had lost before they'd even had the chance to meet it.

She put on a smile for his benefit. "Yes, next month. Absolutely. Anyway, Vi just called a few minutes ago. Says she needs my help with something or another. You know Vi. Can't do anything without me."

Brian stood and helped pull Brooke to her feet. "Tell Vi that I need time with my wife sometimes too." He kissed her on the forehead. "I'll be here. Waiting."

She grabbed her purse, phone, and Tiara's leash, then left just as the sound of the nightly news began to flood the living room.

She'd nearly made it out the door when Brian called after her again. "Brooke, when will you be home?"

"Oh, just a couple hours." She ground her teeth, should have claimed she needed more time for her invented outing.

"Maybe when you get home, we can go have dinner at Genova's." A statement, not a question.

"Sure, I'd like that."

"Okay, you two lovely ladies have fun with whatever it is you're up to. Fill me in on the details over dinner, okay?"

"Okay." Brooke hovered at the door for a moment to make sure the conversation had truly ended.

It hadn't.

"Wait, you can't leave without a kiss." Brian jogged over to her and saddled her with a deep, full-contact kiss. "Maybe after dinner, we can try to—"

"Bri, I've gotta go." She kissed him again before he could finish the sentence she definitely didn't want to hear. "Love you. Bye."

Finally, she'd managed to escape, even though she'd accidentally agreed to dinner in the process. She hated being around her husband on days like this, but it wasn't as if she could say no either.

At least her alibi hadn't been a complete and total lie. If Vi wouldn't answer her texts, Brooke would find some other way to make herself heard. She knew her best friend's schedule well enough by now to know she'd be able to find her at her grandmother's nursing facility.

Abuela Rose had become so senile she didn't even know Vi was there half the time, but that didn't stop Vi from dutifully visiting each and every week.

And she also knew that if she confided to her friend what was really happening at home, she'd drop everything to be there for her. She'd wrap Brooke in her arms and sway back and forth with her, just as she so often did for Joy, for the girls at the shelter, and any other hopeless case she came across.

She let herself fantasize about being taken care of by her friend, but soon she reached the nursing home and had to push all such thoughts far from her mind.

"You are strong. You are powerful. You are in control," she said, eyeing herself in the rearview mirror as she spoke her daily affirmation.

WALKER TEXAS WIFE

After applying a fresh coat of her signature Ruby Woo lipstick, she tucked Tiara under one arm and her Kate Spade bag under the other, then marched into the old folks' home like she owned the place.

Confidence, as always, was key. She smiled at the orderlies and patients as she clacked through the halls in search of Vi and Abuela. Her practiced pageant wave came in handy as various residents called greetings to her, but she just pointed at her wrist and shook her head to indicate that she just didn't have enough time to stick around for a chat. Nobody knew that her beautiful social performance was just that, a performance.

Inside she was dying just a little bit more every day. But she refused to let anyone know that there was anything wrong with her marriage, life, womanhood. As far as anyone suspected, Brooke led the perfect, charmed life, and she planned to keep it that way—even if that meant hiding her pain away from her best friend in the process.

"B-Brooke? What are you doing here?" Vi stood before her, still dressed in her overly formal church attire.

"You didn't answer my texts. I was worried about you, honey."

"But you only sent them an hour ago, and you know I visit with—"

"I just needed to make sure you were okay. I mean, how was I supposed to know that Anna—whatever—didn't have you hogtied in her basem—"

"Brooke, shh!" Vi hissed and pushed her out into the hall. "You're going to scare Abuela with all that crazy talk. Besides, how could you even say such a thing? Annabeth is nice, and it's not really fair for you to be so suspicious of her. Can't you just give her a chance?"

Decision time. She could either shrug off the whole Annabeth thing and move on, or she could take it up a notch. Well, the answer to this little dilemma was obvious.

"I'm telling you, something's not right about those two. Didn't you see my text?"

"So her husband sleeps on the couch. So what? All couples fight... Well, except you and Brian that is." Vi smiled apologetically, having not the slightest idea how right she'd actually been.

Brooke heaved a big, dramatic sigh. Theatrics were often the best way to get through to Vi. Something about her Spanish blood. "I just... Well, I have a feeling, okay? *Please*, Vi. I need you to help me with this."

"Fine." Vi gave in with a slight eye-roll. "What exactly did you have in mind?"

"Well, we can start by breaking into their house."

CHAPTER 7

ANNABETH

BEEP, Beep, Beep. The grating sound of her phone's alarm startled her awake. It was the first day of classes at the University. Where had the weekend gone? Annabeth hated mornings and everything they stood for. Mondays were the worst—a form of lawful torture that left her bitter and angry at the world, at least until she had her coffee.

Coffee made everything better.

Marcus reached over her to snatch the noisy cell from the nightstand and toss it out of reach before she could press snooze. "Good Morning...time to get up, sleepy-head."

His familiar teasing made her smile. "There is nothing good about mornings," she said, speaking directly into her pillow, which felt like heaven right about now.

Annabeth felt the bed shift as Marcus lifted the covers and joined her. Goosebumps rose along her spine and arms as his deft hand slipped under her tank top, rubbed the muscles of her lower back, then inched up along her side. His rough hands stopped just shy of her naked breasts. The light touched tickled her, causing her to squirm and giggle. How easy it would be to skip class and stay in bed all day with the sexiest man alive—at least to her.

"Anna-banana." He teased her as his nose pushed aside the hair covering the back of her neck. "Mmm...you smell good. Good enough to eat."

When his teeth nipped the sensitive skin at the base of her neck, she let out an involuntary gasp. Annabeth shifted underneath him until she was on her back with his warm, minty-fresh breath on her face.

He smiled wide and nudged his nose against hers.

Something about that simple gesture brought it all flooding back—the reason they had moved to Texas and why she needed to shut down his advances sooner rather than later.

"We need to get going." She put both hands on his chest and pushed him away.

His teasing smile fell away as she put space between them.

A part of her enjoyed seeing how her actions had hurt him.

Marcus's full lips flattened and formed a thin line as he pushed off the bed. "Yeah, aren't you teaching this morning before your classes?"

Annabeth slid out of bed and grabbed the clothes she had set out the night before. "Yeah, at 8:00."

"You'd better hurry up then." The underlying irritation in his tone came across to her loud and clear. "By the way, coffee is already made. You'll have to grab something to eat at school, though."

This is never going to work. We can't even get through the first fifteen minutes of the day without fighting.

Slam. She shut the bathroom door behind her with such a force that it rattled within the frame. It didn't help the situation, but it made her feel a little better—for the moment at least.

A soft rap sounded on the door. Why couldn't he just take a hint?

Annabeth splashed cold water on her face. She tried to ignore him, but the knocking only grew louder, more persistent.

"What, Marcus?"

He opened the door without looking at her and held out her phone. "Your phone's buzzing."

"Thanks." Annabeth took the phone and watched out of the corner of her eye as Marcus closed the door without another word.

She had two new text messages.

> Mom: *Miss you, sweetheart. Hope to hear from you soon. I know you're probably busy with work, but just a short note to let me know you're still alive would be nice.*

Annabeth shot her back a quick text.

> *I miss you too, Mom. I'm working, but very much alive.*

The second message was from Vi.

> Violeta: *Good luck at your first day of class!*

Another sharp knock at the door made her jump.

"Jesus Christ, I'm hurrying as fast as I can!"

She could hear his deep sigh in response, but honestly she didn't care.

He was right, though—they needed to get out the door soon if they wanted to make it there on time.

I hate when he's right, she thought.

In less than five minutes, she threw on a pair of jeans and her favorite band T-shirt. The best part of going back to school was the wardrobe change. Gone were the stuffy pant suits and skirts.

She then tied her hair up in a bun and slipped into her comfy bright green ballet slippers. She knew Marcus hated to be late, but making it anywhere on time had always been a challenge for her.

Marcus stood at the door with both of their coffee cups. He looked like he was wound tighter than an eight-day watch. "Ready?"

Annabeth could feel the heat of his irritation and underlying rage, which only added fuel to her own heady emotions.

She slung her bag over her shoulder and snatched the keys from the hook by the door. "Yes. And *I'm* driving."

She was out the door and into the driver's seat before he could protest.

* * *

THEY had arrived at the University of Austin with only five minutes to spare. Maybe living in the suburbs and commuting wasn't the best idea. The morning had been one disaster after another. It had taken her longer than she thought to find the first class, causing her to be ten minutes late. Then she hadn't been able to get her PowerPoint to work. By the time the tech guys got it fixed, it was too late. The students were far too engrossed in their laptops and phones to want to discuss the syllabus. The whole experience had been mortifying.

The excitement over going back to school had dissipated before she even made it to lunch. As she walked across campus to the English Department, she began to wonder whether or not she was out of her depth.

Maybe I'm just too old to start over, she thought.

After all, for the last six years, all she had read on a regular basis was the pile of reports that littered her desk at home and at the office. When she'd turned thirty a few months back, she'd given up hope about completing her degree. She really did love her job and the solitary life that came with it, but after the incident, everything had felt wrong. This opportunity had not given her the break she'd thought it would.

She'd already finished her third cup of coffee by the time she finally stepped into the lounge for the English Department. The dank room looked like it hadn't been decorated since the 1970s. Exhausted and irritated, she slumped into one of the overstuffed sofas that smelled like stale cigar smoke. She tried not to think of how dirty it was and relaxed for a moment. Her eyes slid closed and she let out a deep sigh.

WALKER TEXAS WIFE

A smooth, baritone voice startled her. "Rough day?"

Annabeth's heart jumped and her eyes flew open with a start. Too much caffeine coursed through her bloodstream. Before her stood one of the most handsome men she had ever laid eyes on. He looked to be about her age, a little on the short side but not too short. His jet black hair fell across his forehead in a styled-bed-head kind of way. He had light brown skin, coal black eyes and a charming smile that showed off his perfectly straight white teeth. She couldn't help but smile.

Damn.

Oh, crap, it was her turn to talk now.

"Yeah, you could say that," she said, as she regained control of her vocal chords.

The man extended his hand and flashed a dazzling smile that made her feel a little faint. "My name's Fernando. I'm a Ph.D. candidate. Teach Intro to Poetry. You?"

Annabeth sat up to shake his hand. "Annabeth. I'm getting my Ph.D. in Comparative Literature, and *attempted* to teach English Composition to a bunch of mindless drones and attend two classes of my own."

Fernando chuckled as he sat down beside her. "I know the first week is always the hardest. The Freshmen suck. I want to throw every single one of their phones out the window."

Annabeth let out a deep, low sigh. "You're telling me. I mean, what's the deal? Paying hundreds of dollars to learn something, only to spend the whole class surfing social media. It makes absolutely no sense. But then again, I paid my own way through school, so I get the importance of a good education."

Jesus! She was babbling. Her cheeks flushed with embarrassment. If Fernando noticed, he was at least kind enough not to mention it.

The corners of his mouth turned up into a flirty smile. "Would you like to get a cup of coffee, *Professor* Annabeth? I promise I won't look at my phone. I can fill you in on all the ins and outs of the department. I feel like I've been here forever."

Before she could answer him her phone bleeped. *Marcus.*

"Speaking of phones," she said, holding hers up to check the message.

> Marcus: *"I know things are weird between us now, but I've been thinking about you all morning. I hope your class went well. We can celebrate tonight with a couple of beers. Maybe catch some of the Tigers' game on your iPad. I downloaded the MLB app, so we should be good to go. Text back. I worry about you."*

Annabeth shot a quick text to let him know that beer and baseball were always a good idea and that she was having coffee with a colleague but would be ready to go home within the hour.

"I'm sorry if I've been presumptuous. Surely, a beautiful woman like yourself must already be taken," Fernando said, peeking over her shoulder.

Annabeth dropped her phone back into her bag and twisted her wedding ring off so it fell in as well. The clink of it hitting her keys sounded like a thunderclap.

"Actually, I'm unattached for the moment and would love to have an electronic-device-free coffee with you." Annabeth couldn't help but smile when she looked at this gorgeous man.

Fernando stood and held out his palm to help her up. His hands were smooth, unlike Marcus's, which were thick and calloused from working in his Dad's repair shop all through high school and college.

"Has anyone every told you, Anna, that you have a beautiful smile?"

Annabeth's skin prickled. *Why does everyone insist on shortening my name?*

"Call me Annabeth, please. If you wouldn't mind." She held her breath, hoping he wouldn't take offense.

"Your wish is my command, Annabeth." He lifted her left hand up to his lips.

A wave of guilt washed over her as his lips grazed the spot her wedding ring had been only moments before. Even though the ring was nothing more than a meaningless symbol, she still felt in her heart the pinprick of unwarranted contrition.

"Where would you like to go?" His inky black eyes twinkled down at her.

"I heard my students talking about some Toad place on the Drag. How about there?"

Fernando's dazzling smile showed off his perfectly aligned white teeth. "Frog and Toad, huh? Brave choice." He squeezed her dampened hand.

"I'm up for it, if you are." She tried hard to keep her tone light and flirty.

"*I* am up for anything. Lead the way, m'lady."

Annabeth breathed out a laugh as she tugged him by the hand out of the building and onto the commons. The sudden exposure to the bright Texas sun caused her to squint. Then she remembered the sunglasses that rested on the crown of her head and pulled them down.

Now finally able to see clearly, she noticed a familiar cabby hat coming up the path, growing closer, closer. Of course, on a campus that stretched two miles wide and boasted fifty-thousand-plus students and faculty, she would manage to run into the one person she would rather avoid.

Marcus.

Her hand went limp within Fernando's. How much of their flirtation had Marcus just witnessed?

Shit, shit, shit.

CHAPTER 8

DOUBTS about Brooke's plan played in Vi's mind like a broken record.

She did love and admire Brooke. Sometimes when things were too much she would catch herself imagining what it would be like to have her strong, capable, *normal* friend as a sister instead of Joy. Of course, Brooke wasn't perfect by any means. Her overactive imagination and anxious, high maintenance attitude sometimes wore Vi down, but, more often than not, she added a dose of comic relief to an otherwise depressing life. She always meant well...

This new scheme was up there as one of her more insane missions. When Brooke made a case for her ideas she tended to lay it on thick and heavy. This time was no different.

"They live next door to you," her friend had insisted. "Don't you want to know what kind of a person is just a stone's throw away from where you sleep at night?"

And while Vi didn't think that Annabeth and Marcus were bad people, she could see some logic in Brooke's argument. Better to be safe than sorry. The Kings *did* seem to be hiding something. Although she and Annabeth had spoken at length the night before, Vi knew virtually nothing about her or her past.

Brooke won her over in the end, like she always did. Vi just couldn't say no—a defenseless satellite caught in the orbital pull of Brooke's gravity. They agreed to do it the next day while Annabeth and Marcus were out.

While she brushed her teeth, she ruminated over her choice to once again follow along with Brooke in another of her crazy schemes. Each time, Brooke managed to twist her delusional ideas into something that sounded completely reasonable, and each time Vi followed along. Past exploits flashed across her mind like a bad chick flick. Like the time Brooke had convinced Vi to put laxatives in Mitsy Grazier's coffee just before the big bake-off. Mitsy missed the whole thing, and in her absence, Brooke took first place.

They certainly made a special pair, a textbook case of *Folie à deux*, a madness shared by two, a rare diagnosis she'd learned as part of her social work training but hadn't understood until she'd fallen in with Brooke. *Folie à deux*. How else could she explain to herself her rationale for doing what they were about to do?

Vi picked up her phone and shot off a quick text to Annabeth, wishing her good luck on her first day of teaching. She felt like a hypocrite. When she heard Annabeth's truck pull out of the drive, she sent a second text message, this time to Brooke to let her know the coast was clear. No backing out now.

A few short minutes later, a knock sounded at the door. Say what you wanted about Brooke, but the woman was always punctual, no matter what the circumstances.

Vi had to stop herself from doubling over with laughter at the sight of her bestie dressed all in black like some TV cat burglar. If that wasn't funny enough, poor Tiara was likewise dressed.

Brooke gave her a quick once-over before her face pinched in disgust. "Is that what you're wearing?"

Vi looked down at her navy blue T-shirt and ripped thrift store jeans. "What's wrong with what I'm wearing?"

"Don't you have something black?"

This was nothing new to Vi, who had grown accustomed to Brooke's unintentional rudeness.

"I'm not changing, Brooke."

"At least put your hair up. We don't want to leave any DNA fibers behind as evidence. Don't you watch TV?"

Vi rolled her eyes, but complied with her friend's wishes and pulled her thick black hair into a high and tight bun. When she caught her reflection in the mirror, she remembered her days as a dancer when her hair was always up. No sense thinking about that now. She would need to stay sharp in order to keep Brooke from going too far with this latest escapade.

Brooke perked up. "Perfect. Let's go!"

There was one thing left to discuss before they left and she knew Brooke wasn't going to like it.

"Tiara stays here."

Brooke's face scrunched up into a pout.

"Brooke, we can't afford for her to piss all over the rug or worse, run off and hide. Leave her here."

Brooke sighed like a petulant child. "Oh, all right."

She put Tiara down on the stained cement floor. "I'm sorry, baby, but you need to stay here at Auntie Vi's house. I will be right back. Don't you worry."

Now that they got that little detail out of the way, they made their way outside. The long walk across the yards seemed to take an eternity. Every little sound made Vi jump. When Ms. Haberdash walked passed with her dog, Mimsy, Vi paused mid step.

Oh, God. I'm going to have a heart attack!

Brooke pinched her arm hard and scowled at her.

There was no need to worry. Ms. Haberdash gave them a perfunctory nod and kept on going about her merry way.

Brooke pinched her again making her yelp.

Jesus, Mary and Joseph, that hurts!

Vi took the hint and started walking again.

When they finally made it to the back door and out of sight, Vi let out a sigh of relief. Of course, it didn't last long. Before she knew it, Brooke had pulled a glass cutter out of her bag.

Where the hell did she get that?

Vi grabbed her hand right before she cut into the glass pane that ran the length of the back door.

"Brooke, I have a key."

Brooke straightened her spine and narrowed her eyes at Vi. "They gave you a key? You didn't give them one, did you?"

Vi shifted her weight from one foot to the other. "Yes, she gave me their spare in case she locked herself out, and, no, I didn't give her mine."

Brooke didn't hesitate a moment longer. She snatched the key out of Vi's hand and unlocked the door. They both stood paused in the doorway listening for an alarm. Vi let out a breath.

"Are you ready?" Brooke's wide-eyed excitement worried Vi. Nothing good ever happened when Brooke was in one of her manic states. They had gotten this far, though, so they might as well finish what they started.

"I don't think I have a choice at this point."

Brooke stepped inside and looked back at Vi who still hovered outside.

"C'mon. Don't just stand there like a deer in headlights. Get in, and close the door."

Vi, ever the good soldier, stepped inside and closed the door behind her. The echo reverberated through the sparsely furnished home.

"I should give them my decorator's card." Brooke pulled on a pair of black leather gloves as she looked around the house. "I honestly don't know how anyone could live like this."

"What exactly are we looking for? Please don't tell me we just unlawfully entered my neighbor's home to ridicule her decorating taste."

Vi watched over Brooke's shoulder as she riffled through the mail on the kitchen counter. All junk. "Let's check the bedroom first."

Vi followed behind Brooke as they crept down the hall to the master bedroom. The home's layout was similar to her own, only reversed.

Brooke pushed open the partially ajar door with the tips of her gloved fingers.

The bedroom sheets and blankets lay askew— half on, half off. All Vi could see were Annabeth's things. So where did Marcus keep his stuff?

While Brooke rummaged through Annabeth's belongings, Vi turned around and went into the office space across the hall.

What she saw saddened her. Brooke had been right. Marcus's clothes hung neatly in the closet. On top of the computer desk was a small leather travel toiletry bag, a large pile of papers, and scribbled in legal pads. Two folded blankets and a pillow sat off in the corner. She remembered Brooke saying she had seen him sleeping on the couch.

Vi's mind tried to come up with logical reasons behind why they would sleep in separate rooms. Maybe he snored.

Brooke popped her head into the room. "Whoa! See, what did I tell you? Not the happy little couple that you thought they were."

Vi sighed.

"Hey, look at this." Brooke showed her the opened notebook she'd been reading. "He has a list of women's names, their ages and where they live. Look here. There are different countries listed next to each of the names."

Vi shivered. These were things she couldn't unknow. "Brooke—"

Before she could say anything more, two photographs of young women fell out from between the paper and fluttered to the floor.

Vi bent to pick up the pictures, holding them between her thumb and index finger. The girls looked to be about eighteen or nineteen.

Vi felt a wave of nausea roll over her when Brooke started taking pictures of the notes with her iPhone.

"Why in the world would he have all this information on these young girls? Do you think Annabeth knows?" Brooke's eyes widened as she continued to take snapshots of the notes and photos. "I can Google all this later."

They needed to get out of there—and fast. Vi shoved the pictures back between the papers and tugged hard on Brooke's arm.

"We've seen enough. Let's get out of here before someone catches us." Vi swallowed back the bile that was creeping up her throat.

Of course Brooke was like a dog with a bone. "Just a minute. I want to get some more pictures of these notes."

Vi couldn't wait another moment longer. She turned on her heels and bolted from the room. She was halfway across her front lawn by the time she vomited up her breakfast on her azaleas.

Brooke came charging across the yard. "That's disgusting, Vi. Go lock the door. I put everything back where it was, but I might not have gotten everything perfect."

Just then a police car came rolling down the street with its lights flashing. Vi's heart thundered in her chest, then everything went black.

CHAPTER 9
BROOKE

BROOKE pulled her gloves off finger by finger in a slow, seductive fashion. She could flirt her way out of anything, and she would prove it.

Meanwhile Vi sucked in a sharp breath beside her before buckling at the knees and falling to the grass in the Kings' front yard. Such an amateur.

"Afternoon, ladies." The officer smiled and craned his neck toward Vi to get a better look. "Say, uh, is she okay?"

"Thank goodness you're here!" Brooke cried. "Everything *was* fine. We were just planting some fresh azaleas as a nice housewarming surprise for our new neighbors, when—wham—Vi toppled over headfirst into the garden. Not before losing her lunch first, I'm afraid. You know that danged flu has been making its rounds." She shrugged and shot a sympathetic look toward her friend.

"My, my, my..." The officer shook his head and looked Brooke over from head to toe before glancing back toward Vi. "It certainly is a good thing I just so happened to get called over to this house. Looks like you could use a pair of strong arms and a sturdy back."

A practiced smile spread across Brooke's face. Her charm had become so second nature. She no longer needed to remind herself to smile, to brush her fingers up against the officer's arm as she talked with him, to add that special lilt to her voice that made her seem all damsely. Men liked that, a fact Brooke knew all too well.

Together they pulled Vi to her feet and walked her over to a lawn chair on the Kings' front porch.

"Can you stay with her while I go inside and get her a glass of water?"

"It would be my pleasure."

Brooke felt the officer's eyes on her as she sashayed straight through the Kings' front door. She also heard a low moan come from Vi, but thankfully she could peg anything out of sorts on the poor creature's obvious delirium. Besides, they still didn't know *why* the officer had shown up when he did, and she needed to put on a good show, just in case they needed a proper alibi for later.

She handed Vi a bottle of Evian, surprised at Annabeth's good taste.

The officer smiled at her chest, hooked on her material charms. Time for Brooke to set things straight.

"So what brings a *strapping* officer of the law to our quiet little neighborhood?"

He inhaled lustily before continuing. Men were so easy, so very easy.

"Seems it was a false alarm. The Kings' security system picked up an unplanned entry onto the property, but I can see now it was just two kind neighbors giving them a bit of a welcome celebration."

"Oh no, you didn't think we'd…?" Brooke let the question linger as she dropped her eyes to the ground then looked up at the officer beneath a veil of thick eyelashes.

"Of course not, uh, ma'am. We just have to make sure is all. No harm done, but still I will have to report our chat. Procedure and all."

He walked back in the direction of his car while punching numbers into his handheld device.

Was he suspicious? What was the code for breaking and entering?

Brooke ran after him and, when she caught up, pushed the device down to his side, bringing her arm so close to the crotch of his pants she could feel the itchy fabric brush the hairs on her arm.

"Oh, please, officer! Don't ruin our surprise! Vi and I have worked so hard to make the Kings feel welcome, and this will only worry them. I want them to know how much we—how much *everyone* in Herald Springs—are truly glad to have them here. Will you help us with our friendly little ruse?"

Back on the porch Vi began to pant like a panicked pooch.

Keep it together, Violeta, she mentally reprimanded her disappointing sidekick.

If this were a superhero movie, Vi would have already been killed by the villain, leaving Brooke to charge forth on her own. Instead, Brooke was always having to think on her feet to make up for Vi's many shortcomings. Lucky for her, she had catlike reflexes, and—some might also say—nine lives of her own to play around with.

A charged silence passed between Brooke and the officer, Vi's rhythmic panting something of a metronome backdrop. *Tick tock. Tick tock.*

Finally the officer gave a friendly chuckle. "Tell you what, I'll do you this small favor. If you'd do one for me."

"Oh, you will? Of course, of course. Anything you want, just name it." Brooke tried to mask her disgust by making her voice extra high pitched and girly.

Please don't let it be a sexual favor. Please don't let it be a sexual favor.

"Your number," he said with a lascivious smile. "If you would."

"Oh, is that all?" She giggled, then recited Vi's number for him as he clicked the digits into his cell phone.

A jarring screech cut Brooke short, as a distress call came through on the radio. The officer's brow furrowed. He repeated the number she'd given him, smiled, and jogged back toward the car.

"Is—is everything all right?" Brooke asked, panic clutching at her throat.

"Gottaskeedaddle to the other side of town. Seems we've got a robbery in progress. No time to lose. You ladies have a great afternoon. And don't worry, I'll have the alarm company turn off the alarm on their end. Your secret is safe with me." He pulled away with an exuberant wave back toward the women.

"You've got some balls," Vi said between sips of Evian. "Some balls, all right."

Brooke shrugged. "You wanna talk about big balls? When I grabbed his computer thingy, my wrist found itself in a rather unfortunate spot. And let's just say I'm not the only one with some major *huevos*, my friend."

Vi frowned, apparently not amused.

"Hey, I got us off, didn't I?"

"Yeah," Vi said. "And probably him too. Later tonight, that is. But why'd you have to go and give him my number? A horny cop calling day and night is the last thing I need."

Brooke bristled. How could Vi be complaining now when Brooke had just single-handedly saved the day?

"Violeta, calm down. Everything's fine. Besides, that whole ordeal gave us at least one new piece of evidence to add to our dossier."

"Our dossi-what?" Vi teased.

Brooke answered anyway. "Our fancy-ass case folder. The pictures of all those girls, remember? Those two hardly seem like the type to be into anything *that* perverted in the bedroom. I bet she just lies there, while—"

"Brooke! Get to the point!" Vi fanned at herself then took another sip of water.

"Well, you're no fun. My point is people don't just keep records like that without a reason, and usually a reason like that? Totally sinister. Well, at least that's my guess anyway. I've never run into a real-life criminal mastermind before, at least not that I know of. Although—"

"*Brooke!*" Vi shouted again. "Seriously, stay focused. Tell me what exactly it is you're suggesting."

"Well, for starters, that I was right about these new neighbors of ours."

Vi waited for Brooke to continue. When she didn't Vi took a slow breath, then said, "Okay, so then what do we do next?"

"We write this all down so we can further study the evidence, figure out what's really going on here."

"And?"

"Why do you think there's an *and?*"

"With you, there's *always* an *and*. Just tell me what it is already, Brooke."

Brooke narrowed her eyes at Vi. "*And* we're going to have to go deep undercover in order to properly continue this investigation. Meaning we've got to make this Anna chick one of our very best friends, get her to invite us in of her own accord, see her and Marcus up close, learn the truth once and for all."

"I admit we found some strange things in their house, but I bet you there's a good explanation for everything. If we just asked, I'm sure—"

"Out of the question!" Brooke shouted. "You trust way too easily, Vi, and one of these days that's going to be your downfall. You can mark my words on that. Luckily, I'll be here to rescue your ass as per the usual. Now, let's go inside, make Tiara her lunch, and then get to work. We've got a lot to do."

CHAPTER 10

ANNABETH

ANNABETH stifled a yawn behind the back of her hand.

Oh, my God! Will he ever shut up?

For the last twenty minutes, Fernando had been talking nonstop about his dissertation—and for the life of her, she couldn't figure out how someone that good looking could also be so dull. His words ran into each other, long strings of sentences laden with three syllable words that were apparently meant to impress her, but just made her want to close her eyes and fall asleep. It was the kind of act she might have fallen for ten years ago. He was so into himself that he didn't even notice she was bored to tears. At least he was pleasant to look at.

Fernando's phone alarm buzzed, stopping him mid-sentence in his impromptu Proustian lecture.

"Shit! I'm late. I've got a meeting with my advisor. He wants to go over my thesis. Very important."

Fernando pushed back the chair and fumbled for his bag.

"I'm sorry. I hate to run. I guess time just got away from me. I find that happens a lot whenever I am in the company of smart, beautiful women like yourself." His black, velvet smile made gooseflesh break out on her bare arms.

Fernando pulled out his wallet and tossed a copy of his business card at her. "Call, email, text—hell *Snapchat* me. I would really like to see you again. Somewhere that they don't serve the drinks out of recycled paper cups."

Annabeth picked up the card and glanced at it. It was for a sound engineering business. Interesting... She smiled, returning her gaze to him. "I might take you up on that."

Fernando touched her hand and smiled—though the smile didn't reach his eyes. "Until then, my dear."

Annabeth was taken aback when he took her hand and raised it to his warm lips.

The sound of her heart's rapid beat hammered in her ears. She found herself holding her breath. Something behind his coal black eyes gave her pause, though she couldn't say what.

She let out a slow easy breath and admired his perfectly shaped ass as he walked away.

As much as she didn't want to deal with Marcus, she shot off a quick text to tell him where to meet up. He was her ride after all.

He surprised her by walking through the coffee bar's door less than two minutes later. Oh great, she thought, he looks pissed.

Marcus grabbed the chair across from her and plopped down into it. He regarded her with a scowl, his arms crossed over his broad chest.

"What's the matter with you?" *And how much did you see earlier?*

Marcus wet his lips with a quick sweep of his tongue. "Who's the guy?"

Jealousy did not become him. The man she had fallen in love with had been strong and confident and never would have worried about competition. What had become of that man?

"A Teaching Assistant in my department. He wanted to fill me in on the ins and outs of the English Department. He also knows a lot of other TAs so he's kind of important for us to know." Annabeth couldn't believe she had to justify her actions, least of all to him.

Marcus leaned in closer to her with his arms resting on the small table—an intimidation tactic that she knew all too well.

"You let him touch you. Kiss you."

Annabeth let out a slow breath. She didn't want to fight. "It was my hand. He kissed my hand."

Were you spying on me the whole time?

Annabeth shook her head in disbelief.

How dare you accuse me of impropriety!

Marcus dropped his voice to a harsh whisper. "That's how it starts. You don't know men and how they think. He wants to sleep with you and will do everything in his power to make that happen. Trust me on that."

Annabeth let out a light chuckle. "It doesn't matter what he wants. It only matters what *I* want. And you gave up your right to have a say in whom I spend my time with."

Marcus's eyes narrowed as he leaned away from her. He tipped the chair back, balancing on the two back legs. "So I guess it would be okay, then, for me to use the number I got today from Shelley in the Marketing Department?"

Annabeth took short breaths as she tried to temper her hurt feelings. She couldn't let him know how much every second of this exchange was digging the knife in deeper. "Of course. If that's what you want to do. I have no hold on you."

Marcus brought the chair back down onto all fours. Annabeth was pleased to see a surprised expression flash across his face. He had been angling for a fight, but had failed to goad her into one.

"Well, now that we got that all straightened out, let's talk business since that's why we're here." Under his breath, he added. "Not to play house."

The bitterness and guile behind the words he chose were not lost on her. The ever-widening chasm between them was far and deep. She was beginning to give up hope of ever making it back to the other side. It pained her to think that he might never have any desire to get back to where they were before the incident.

"What were you able to find out?" Annabeth straightened her back and avoided his eyes—it was just easier that way.

Marcus reached into his messenger bag and pulled out a notebook. "I looked up all the information I could find. Some of the girls that we identified in our profile have either gone back home or now have family living in the area that we didn't know about, which precludes them from being possible targets." Marcus pulled out a few sheets of loose leaf paper. "I narrowed the list to two girls. One is working in my department and the other is in the class you taught this morning. Her name is Amy Rangel. She's nineteen and her family is from Mexico. She's here on a student visa. Her parents are dead. She has a brother and an elderly aunt in Puebla. She has no friends and belongs to no clubs."

Annabeth nodded as she thought back to all the students in her class—a sea of young, attractive faces. They needed to go forward with this despite the nagging doubt that echoed daily inside her mind about whether or not she was up for the job.

"Do you have a photo?"

Marcus pulled a printed off black and white copy of the young girl's school ID photo. She was beautiful. A slight tremor rippled through her arm as she reached for the photo. Flashes of the other girl—the one they lost—flashed through her mind.

I can't go through that again, she thought.

"Are you all right?" His voice was laced with concern. When his familiar calloused hand covered hers, she felt a wave of warmth spread up her arm and pool inside her core. It had always been so easy between them, and now, long after they had ended things, it was hard to shut it down. He seemed to sense the shift between them.

His hand slid from hers, and he looked away. "Sorry."

Annabeth wet her lips. This war between them wore on her daily. With each passing day she realized how much she too was to blame. It was time to step up and be the bigger person.

"Me, too."

Marcus's jaw twitched. His downcast eyes seemed to be avoiding hers. "What do you have to feel sorry for? This is all my fault."

No matter how much he insisted the blame was his alone, Annabeth knew better. Things didn't happen in a vacuum. It was never just one person's fault when it came to matters of the heart. She had played a part in the destruction of their relationship. Everything had started to unravel between them well before the incident. It just made for an easy scapegoat—blame the incident and each other.

"Marcus..." Annabeth reached across the table for his hand.

He glanced away from her, but not quickly enough to hide his glassy eyes. "Anna, *no*. Let's just go home. I don't want to get into all this again. Not now."

He grabbed both their bags and got up to go. "C'mon. It's been a long day. Let's just put it to rest already."

Sooner or later they were going to have address the elephant in the room. Not tonight, but soon. It wasn't a conversation she looked forward to having, but she didn't see how they could move forward if they didn't. Not talking is what had led to the incident in the first place, after all.

They couldn't afford to relive the past.

CHAPTER 11

VI tossed her keys on the counter and slumped into her kitchen chair. Her face still felt hot. The aftertaste of vomit had stuck with her, too.

Why did I let Brooke talk me into another one of her ridiculous schemes?

Self-loathing washed over her as she laid her cheek down on the cool Formica table. She loved Brooke like a sister, but, just like a sister, she sometimes hated her in equal measure.

Beethoven's *Fifth Symphony* ring tone started to play. Her sister, the real one, was calling.

Let it go to voicemail. Joy can wait for once. I'll just close my eyes, just for a minute.

As her eyes slid closed and she started to doze, a sharp knock at her back door shook her from her reverie. Vi lifted her heavy head to see a friendly pair of eyes looking back at her through the glass. Marcus.

Vi pushed away from the table and stood up on wobbly legs.

Uh… I don't feel so good.

Marcus's broad smile greeted her when she opened the door. "Hi, sorry to bother you, but Anna and I were wondering if you didn't want to come over for dinner?"

Vi felt the room spin like she was on an out-of-control carnival ride. She had always hated those spinning ones. Give her a roller coaster any day. As Marcus stood waiting for an answer, beads of sweat started to fall down her forehead, blurring her vision.

"Are you okay?" His strong hands reached out to stabilize her. Just like the Disney Movie heroes Joy was so obsessed with, he swept her off her feet and carried her over to the sofa.

A look of concern flashed across his handsome face. "You're burning up!"

Such a sweet man, she thought. But no, that wasn't right, she remembered. The pictures and statistics of young college girls had been all over his spare bedroom. He was up to something, and it sure didn't look good.

Vi wasn't one to make snap judgements, but what she and Brooke had found while snooping was pretty damning. She wanted to ask him, to make him explain himself, but no. She couldn't do that without outing her and Brooke and their junior sleuthing expedition. They weren't Nancy Drew and company, after all. *They* could go to jail for heaven's sake.

Unaware of the guilt that wracked Vi's mind, Marcus continued to do his best to make her comfortable.

"I can make you some soup," he offered, after pulling off her shoes and placing a fuzzy blanket on top of her. His charming smile caused her heart to skip a little as did his caring nature. It was so nice to be taken care of for once.

I can't take advantage of his good graces. I can take care of myself. I have for this long, after all.

"I'll be fine. I just need some rest." She forced an exaggerated yawn.

Maybe if I close my eyes, he will leave.

"All right. Get some sleep." His rough, calloused hand brushed her fever-damp hair away from her forehead. "But either Anna or I will be back to check on you later, okay?"

She listened as he rifled through her kitchen, poured a glass of water, and put it down beside her along with a bottle of ibuprofen. The echo of his heavy shoes clomped across her worn linoleum floor, and soon the rickety back door wedged shut with a tired groan.

And Vi fell fast asleep.

The vivid fever-induced dreams that followed were surreal and frightening, causing her to awaken with a start. Her clothes clung to her damp skin, and she was out of breath. The shrill sound of her phone's ring tone made her head throb.

What? What time is it? Where's my phone?

She groaned in pain as she tried to sit up. Everything hurt. *Can't I just die in peace?* Flipping her phone over, she saw several push notifications lit up. Five missed calls from the group home meant that she would have to put her impending death on hold.

A sharp knock at the front door startled her.

Seriously, can't everyone just leave me the fuck alone?

Vi laughed a little at such a ridiculous thought. Ugh...it hurt to laugh. The knocking grew more persistent.

Vi stumbled to answer the door. There, standing on the worn welcome mat, was Joy herself with a self-satisfied grin on her face.

"Joy? What are you doing here? You're supposed to be at the home."

Her sister shrugged and pushed past her into the house like it was no big deal.

Not now. Not now. God, why does it have to be now?

"Joy, I asked you a question."

WALKER TEXAS WIFE

Joy walked with purpose into the kitchen. "Make me square pizza. The square kind."

Vi stood under the kitchen archway blinking.

Am I dreaming?

"Me pizza!" Joy plopped down at the kitchen table like she still lived there.

And Vi's legs moved of their own accord. Like a robot she went through the practiced motion of making a Joy-approved pizza—bending to Joy's whims, no matter how ridiculous. She didn't have the energy to argue that day.

Instead, she dutifully put the pizza in the oven and, of course, burned her hand in the process. Her cellphone started to ring as she ran cold water from the faucet over the burn.

Joy jumped up to get it and handed it over without answering. "*Your* phone is ringing. *You* should answer it."

Vi took the phone from her sister and turned off the tap.

"This is Vi."

The sound of Mrs. Lockard's anxious voice filled her ear. "I've been trying to reach you for the last hour. Joy is missing—"

"It's okay, Ms. Lockard," she said, interrupting the other woman. "Joy's here."

"What! How did she get there?"

Vi knew she really must be sick because that question hadn't even occurred to her.

"I don't know. She just got here. I'll bring her back tomorrow."

"It would be better if you brought her back today. We can't let her think that she can just run away. Staying with you would just reward her behavior."

Vi sighed and rubbed her aching head. Mrs. Lockard was, of course, right. "I can't today. I'm, umm, unwell," Vi said. The words felt like gravel in her mouth. She hated saying no, especially to Ms. Lockard.

"Oh, dear. I'm sorry to hear that. I'll send Henry to fetch her then. Don't *you* worry. She'll be gone in a jiffy."

"All right. Thank you." Vi ended the call and slid into the chair across from Joy.

There was no point avoiding the inevitable. "Joy, how did you get here?"

Joy twisted her shirt collar and chewed on the frayed cloth. "I want it now, Sissy!"

Vi reached across and tapped her sister lightly on the arm. "Joy, look at me."

Joy looked up. Her eyes zeroed in on the bridge of Vi's nose. Joy had never once met her eye-to-eye.

"What, Sissy?"

"How did you get here?"

Joy twirled out of her seat and started to dig through the pantry. "The bus. The 354 and the 721."

Wow, she did that all by herself!

Vi shook her head. She couldn't very well have Joy wandering around town without anyone knowing where she was. She could get hurt.

"You can't just leave without telling someone, Joy. Everyone was worried."

Joy poked her head out of the pantry. Her arms were filled with snacks, which she promptly arranged within a book bag she had brought with her, clearly just for this purpose.

"Why? I came home. I'm hungry."

"They have food at the home, Joy."

Her sister shook her head and flapped her hands against the side of her thigh—a tell-tale sign that she was getting agitated. "It's dog food. I want pizza."

Vi sighed. "Joy, they do *not* give you dog food. I know you may not always like what they have for you to eat, but you can't just run off every time you want pizza. Next time call me and I can bring you something okay?"

Oh shoot, the pizza.

Vi jumped out her seat and ran to the stove to pull out the anchovy and pepperoni pie before it burned. She cut it into three sections just the way Joy liked it. "Here you go. Remember tiny bites. It's hot."

Joy snatched the food from her and ate it like it was her last meal.

"I guess you really were hungry." Vi made a mental note to talk with Mrs. Lockard about Joy's diet.

Before she could think a minute more on the subject, there was another knock at her door.

What is this? Grand fucking central station, today?

This time Annabeth was the one who had come to her door.

"Hi, sorry to bother you. Marcus said you were a little under the weather. I made you some soup." She held up a Tupperware dish full of what looked like chicken noodle soup. "It's my mom's recipe."

Without even asking to be let in, Annabeth walked past her to put it in the fridge. "Oh, hi. You must be Vi's sister." She extended her hand to Joy, who just ignored her.

"Say hello, Joy," Vi said.

Joy continued to eat her pizza and only mumbled a barely audible "hello" in return.

Vi sighed. She was too tired and sick to deal with all this.

"Go lie down," Annabeth urged. "It's okay. I'll take care of everything."

If only! I'd marry the woman on the spot if she promised to take care of everything.

She really was sick if she was actually fantasizing about marrying her already-married neighbor just so she could take a nap...

CHAPTER 12

BROOKE

ONCE the officer had left, Brooke hurried home, worried that her husband would catch her in her cat-burglaring gear. And even though she felt sexy as hell, the last thing she wanted was to deal with his questions. Brooke could outsmart pretty much everyone, except her top-notch attorney husband. After all, professional arguing was kind of his job—and the fact that she and Tiara could buy pretty much anything and everything their hearts desired... well, that said it all.

Anyway, her fears proved to be completely unfounded, given that he had to work late. *Again.* He'd been so attentive when they'd first started dating, but now? Now she spent more nights by herself than with him.

And she kind of liked it that way to be honest.

Neither of them were the same people they'd been when he had first introduced himself in their college philosophy class all those years ago.

"If you ask me," he had said, leaning across the aisle. "That Descartes was full of crap. 'I think, therefore I am?' Please. Screw thinking. If you don't *do* something, then you can't *be* anything. Hi, I'm Brian."

She'd rather liked the Cartesian argument, but chuckled with Brian all the same. Besides, she liked the way his hazel eyes captured the light that filtered in from the high windows of the lecture hall.

After class, he'd invited her to a party his pre-law frat was throwing to welcome everyone back for the spring semester. She'd shown up with her girlfriends and without a bra. A quick bit of digging online had told her everything she needed to know about Brian Fischer. His old money brought with it important connections, ones she could take advantage of. Brooke knew her assets (thus the absence of a bra) and she knew her aspirations. She was going to make something of herself, the way her mother never had. And at this point she had only two years left to make the next phase in her life plan a reality—graduating from college with both a BA and an MRS.

It wasn't hard to fall for Brian.

He had all the right words, all the right moves, and all the right ideas. Brooke had never been in love before, but she was pretty convinced that the fluttering feeling in her chest and the dizzy feeling in her head amounted to that thing called *amore*. When he asked her to marry him on the eve of their graduation, she of course said yes and jumped headlong into planning the perfect wedding, one worthy of the future Mr. and Mrs. Fischer.

That, of course, was when she discovered what love was really all about. Only the effervescent feeling of bliss wasn't about her groom, but rather the excitement of weaving layer upon layer of intricate details together to construct a truly beautiful evening for them and their guests.

"Parties, huh?" Brian had laughed when she told him about her dream of opening up her own event planning boutique. He insisted that she volunteer at the junior league instead—the way so many of the partners' wives did. She needed to make important connections for *his* career and *their* future.

And she did as he said, at least for a few years, all the while begrudging him for it. When Brian made partner—the youngest in the firm's history, *hooray*—she told him she was done with the token board positions. That she was finally going to make *Parties by Brooke* a reality.

Brian shrugged, but said nothing to discourage her. She could see the condescension in his eyes and could feel something important in the foundation of their marriage begin to shift.

Why could Brian have his dream, but not her? They danced around each other for another couple years in a beautiful, but passionless, tango.

Finally, Brooke couldn't take it anymore. She'd seen what divorce had done to her mother—landed her and young Brooke on state assistance, gotten them both disowned from the family, led her to drown in booze.

Brooke would *never* let that happen, not to her.

Besides, men like Brian Fischer didn't come along every day, and she needed his influence to help with her business, just as he had needed hers. It wasn't as if he was mean to her. Just cold, making her worry he planned to discard her now that she had helped him reach his goals. After all this effort, she could still end up like her mother—alone, penniless, and swollen with alcohol.

No, she refused to let that happen. That's why she'd come up with the perfect plan late last year...

"Let's have a baby," she said, and Brian's eyes lit up with such joy, she knew immediately she'd made the right call. Maybe passion could be a part of their marriage after all.

He took her then and there, and honestly it was the best sex of her life.

That was more than six months ago, and though they still dutifully timed her cycles and experimented with various old wives' tales, the failed attempts were beginning to wear on both of them. Brian worked harder, longer hours at the office and came home exhausted and irritable. Brooke no longer enjoyed their lovemaking the way she once had. She could feel him slipping away again…

Should she give it all up? Go back to supporting his career and put hers on hold while she worked on making herself once again into the wife that Brian needed?

Brooke poured a glass of her favorite Chianti and swirled it gently to unlock the bittersweet aroma she loved. When the dry liquid hit her tongue, she imagined it soaking up all the wrong words she'd said to Brian when they'd fought over breakfast. It had been such a stupid thing, really. She'd forgotten to wash his lucky boxers despite multiple reminders over the course of the week, and now he'd had to go to court without them. How had it slipped her mind anyway?

She'd make it up to him when he got home. Pour him a nice bath and perfume it with her favorite lavender vanilla blend, give him a massage, and… Yes, that would do nicely.

Now she just had to wait for him to come home, discover her sweet, little surprise, and take her like he meant it. Until then, she'd just have to keep herself busy. And her old friend Google would make the perfect companion.

Signs your neighbor might be a pedophile, signs your neighbor is a serial killer, is my neighbor into freaky sex stuff? And just in case, *Annabeth King, Marcus King, the Kings of Detroit*—none of her searches bore fruit exactly, but now her suspicions were more alive than ever. Was it possible the Kings were kinky pedophile serial killers? Maybe amateur porn producers? Certainly there was no normal explanation for the evidence she and Vi had uncovered.

Speaking of… Brooke's phone buzzed on the countertop beside her. *Check on Vi,* the notification read.

"Oh, shoot," Brooke mumbled to herself and then, because she hated to let such a good vintage go to waste, downed the remaining half of her glass. Some things were more important than a good decant, and Vi was definitely one of them. The strange vomiting-fainting spell from earlier that afternoon worried her. The fact that she'd managed to forget it, even momentarily, spoke volumes about how much more worried she was for her marriage.

Just keep swimming, she reminded herself. Though she'd never admit it, the crazy blue fish from *Finding Nemo* had become something of a role model for her. And ever since she'd secretly ordered the movie on Pay-Per-View, she'd heard Ellen Degeneres's cartoonish voice in her head, reminding her to keep going, no matter what the circumstances.

"C'mon, Tiara, baby," she called, grabbing up her dog's rhinestone leash. "Let's go see Auntie Vi."

They jogged the few blocks to Vi's house, then let themselves in through the front door.

"Hello! It's me and Ti!" Brooke pushed into the living room. Vi was probably in bed, sleeping off the anxiety from that morning. Unless she was really sick, in which case...

"Who's T?" a very non-Vi voice asked.

Brooke jerked to her left and saw the pedophile porn killer weirdo herself, standing there heating soup over the stove. Vi's stove.

"Oh, Anna, you scared me!"

"Queen B! Queen B!" another familiar voice called, and before she knew it, Joy bounded into her arms and saddled her with a huge hug.

"Joy-Joy! It's good to see you! How is your sister feeling today?"

"She's mad at me, because I ran away." Joy's lower lip jutted out for a second before her entire face transformed back into a carefree smile. "But now I made a new friend. Have you met my new friend Annabeth?"

"Yes, we've met." Annabeth didn't look up from the soup she was stirring.

"Where's Vi?"

"Sis isn't feeling too well," Joy said between bites of garlic bread. "So Annabeth sent her to bed."

"Oh, I see." Brooke waited for a few beats. "Well, it looks like you two have everything under control. Thanks for keeping an eye on her, Annabeth. See you tomorrow, Joy-Joy?"

"Nope, they're coming to take me back tonight." She frowned, and Brooke gave her another hug.

"That's too bad. We'll have to have a girls' night out some other time. Agreed?"

"Okay, but only if Tiara can come too."

"She wouldn't miss it for the world."

Tiara gave a little bark as if to agree, then the two of them headed back out the front door, and straight into...

"Oh my gosh, sorry!" Brooke sputtered, then looked up and saw... "M-Marcus! Hi!"

He placed a strong hand on each of her shoulders to steady her. "Good evening, Brooke. I was just coming over to see if Anna was still here. I hadn't seen her for a few hours, and figured..." He laughed.

Did she sense a bit of frazzled nerves beneath his cool demeanor? Ooh, she could use this opportunity to do a little more investigation into the peculiar Kings. After all, men had always been far easier for her to read than women.

The door creaked open behind her, and a cloud of red frizz stepped out onto the porch. Somewhere within all that hair, Annabeth King stood watching, listening.

But Brooke refused to let the woman unnerve her. Instead of acknowledging Annabeth, she put on her signature smile and spoke directly to Marcus. "Oh, hey, can I ask you something?"

"Shoot." A smile spread from ear to ear on Marcus's face, which was actually quite handsome now that she was really looking at it for the first time. Then again, she'd always found herself enamored of that sizzling tall, dark, and handsome combo. And Marcus was so tall, so dark, and so handsome. Yum. How had icky Annabeth ever managed to land *him*?

Ah well, the Lord giveth, and Brooke could taketh away if she damn well pleased. Now she was doubly motivated. Step one, get some intel. Step two, get under Annabeth's skin. She didn't *actually* want to steal her man, but neither of them needed to know that. Now did they?

"I…" She let her eyes linger on his lips as she thought of the best way to play this encounter. "I was wondering if you and Annabeth might be able to help me out. You see, a couple of our volunteers for the annual autism gala canceled on us, and it's sort of last minute, but I was just wondering if… maybe… well." She gave her best imitation of a true blush, and Marcus, of course, ate up the entire bumbling damsel act.

"Say no more, Brooke. Of course, we'd be happy to help. Isn't that right, Anna… Annabeth?"

"Oh, thank you, thank you, thank you!" Brooke gave him a huge hug, making sure to press her breasts up against his chest as she did. "You're a lifesaver!"

Now *he* was the one blushing. "Aww, it's nothing really... I'm—I mean, *we're*—happy to help in whatever way we can. Just tell us what you need."

"Well, we need a new bartender, an MC, and somebody to run sound, of course—"

Annabeth stepped forward and held up her hand. "Umm, I think I might know someone who can help with sound. That is, if *my* suggestions are welcome."

"Of course," Brooke said. "Thank you, Annabeth. *Thank you, Marcus.*" She leaned in and kissed him on the cheek, then jogged away with a flirty, little wave.

She reached home at the same time as Brian. The garage door thundered open just as she was unhooking Tiara's leash. Brooke fluffed her hair and prepared to meet her husband with a hungry kiss. After all, hadn't she just resolved to try harder to bring the warmth back into their marriage?

Brian shuffled into the kitchen without even looking at her.

A sinking feeling landed in the pit of her stomach. "Babe? Is everything all right?"

"What do you think?" he asked through clenched teeth.

WALKER TEXAS WIFE

"C'mon, don't be like that, baby." She wrapped her arms around him from behind and attempted to press a kiss to his cheek.

He pulled himself away so fast that Brooke fell forward and had to catch hold of the table to keep from falling. "Honey?" Her voice shook with fear. She hated that.

"What's the matter? Didn't get enough play from that fucking nig—?"

"*Don't* you dare go there, Brian. *Nothing* is going on."

"It's too late to play dumb. I saw you flirting with that, that... *man* outside his house. The whole neighborhood saw!"

"Oh, you mean, Marcus, that was just—"

"I don't need to hear your explanation," Brian growled.

His voice lowered several notches. "Just don't let it happen again, or..."

"Or what?" Brooke asked, afraid of what the answer would be.

Brian shook his head, and his features rearranged themselves into a placid expression. "Nothing, babe. Sorry, I overreacted."

"Should we at least talk about this?"

He stretched his arms overhead then gave her a quick kiss on the cheek. "Nah, I'm exhausted, and it'll be another early day in court tomorrow. Speaking of which, would you mind running my lucky boxers through the wash before heading to bed?"

Brooke nodded and made her way to their second floor laundry room. Somehow she had a feeling that if she didn't get this one simple thing right, there would be hell to pay. She just wasn't sure who would have to pay it.

CHAPTER 13

ANNABETH

ANNABETH caught herself grinding her back teeth, something she was prone to do when under a lot of stress. Brooke's little stunt with Marcus had pushed her to the limits of her patience. It had irked her even more that he had seemed to fall for it hook, line, and sinker. The last thing she wanted to do was help Brooke with her gala, but she couldn't very well say so in front of Marcus. She'd just look petty.

It's for a good cause, she reminded herself.

Even though it was getting late, she needed to get out of the house. A swim would do the trick.

Annabeth snapped the hair tie off her wrist and pulled her hair up off her neck. She missed the

Olympic-sized pool back home where she'd swum almost every morning before work to help manage the stress of the job and her ever-complicated personal life. Now it had been two weeks since she'd been in the water. The tension inside her was nearing critical levels. Between her disastrous day at class, her argument with Marcus, and dealing with Brooke, she knew she needed to swim. *Now.*

It took her less than five minutes to change into her sleek one-piece suit and a sheer black cover-up.

With a towel under her arm, she set off on the five-minute walk to the small pool in the back of their subdivision. As she walked across the street, the heat from the blacktop seeped through the thin rubber of her flip-flops. Like walking on the sun, she thought.

The pool had two designated lap lanes. It wasn't Olympic-size by any means, but it *was* serviceable. She carefully tucked her hair underneath her swim cap. Years of exposure to harsh pool chemicals had done a lot of damage to her hair and scalp, so now she religiously wore her cap even for a quick dip. The comforting smell of chlorine filled her nostrils as she padded across the cement to the pool—dropping her things on one of the lounge chairs.

A relieved sigh escaped her lips as she dove into the lukewarm water. Her arm rose and dipped down. Her fingertips sliced through the water, propelling her forward with each scoop. Right, left, right, left, she rotated her shoulders back and forth until her fingertips touched the wall. Annabeth tucked and rolled in the water so that her feet met and she pushed off the side wall. The thrill of shooting through the water sent happy little endorphins through her veins. Ever since she had been a little girl, swimming had been her drug of choice.

After she rounded out her fifth lap, she paused at the ledge to catch her breath.

"Bravo," a voice called out from the far end of the pool.

Annabeth turned her head to see Jesse standing at the end of the pool, clapping. His adorable little ponytailed girls bookended him. They were both clad in matching Hello Kitty pink suits and water wings.

"Wow!" the oldest girl exclaimed. "You're a good swimmer!"

"Thank you." Annabeth smiled at the girls as she adjusted her swim cap.

"Go ahead and jump in girls. We only have an hour today. No complaints when it's time to come out, either."

"Okay, Dad."

The girls broke out into a run for the shallow end of the pool. Jesse cupped his hands over his mouth and shouted, "Walk!"

The girls halted their running and instead speed walked the rest of the way into the pool. Jesse rolled his eyes as he slid into the lane beside Annabeth.

His snoopiness made her nervous. She didn't want all her hard work to be put to ruins by some bored house husband. She had done a little research and had discovered that his blog was quickly becoming an Internet phenomenon. Even though his main audience was stay-at-home moms—most of whom not-so-secretly wished he was their husband—he could still cause any number of problems for her and Marcus.

Still, she'd take his warm, friendly presence over Brooke's scolding frigidity any day—even on a hot one like this.

"My girls were very impressed with your laps. So am I. You been swimming long?" He tipped his head back into the water and slicked back his wet hair.

Annabeth thought about his question carefully before answering. She knew very well that the best, most believable lies were the ones that had a kernel of truth to them.

"Yes," she said at last. "I was a lifeguard in high school and college."

Jesse looked away from her for a second. He blew little bubbles in the water and looked over with a smile at his girls who were splashing each other, then twisted his body back toward her. His large eyes squinted against the late afternoon sun.

"You never swam competitively?"

"No," she said without missing a beat.

"You're pretty good," he said, pointing out the obvious as he seemed so often keen to do. "It's hard to believe that you wouldn't have been on a swim team or something."

Annabeth had been a very competitive swimmer growing up and had even tried out for the Olympics, missing the time trial by a tenth of a second. Her event had been the women's 200-meter freestyle. Her real name was all over the Internet with pictures of her as a young girl and woman standing on podiums all over the U.S.

She couldn't tell him that, though. If he knew her past, he would know her secrets. She couldn't afford to have him snooping around and messing everything up for her.

She shrugged in a way she hoped looked natural. "I don't like competition. I just did the lifeguard gig because it was easy and paid really well."

"Hmmm." Jesse seemed to consider her answer as he treaded water with ease. "So I guess you wouldn't want to race me then?"

Annabeth met his challenging look head on. "No, not really."

In actuality she wanted nothing more than to swim against him and win. Anything to wipe that smug, self-satisfied grin off his face.

No wonder he and Brooke were so tight. They were both annoying as hell.

For the life of her, though, she couldn't figure out why Vi was friends with *either* of them. She seemed so sweet and unimposing. But how much did Annabeth actually know about any of her new neighbors?

She pushed any thoughts of making Jesse eat her watery dust out of her mind and swam over to the ladder on the side of the pool. "I should actually get going. I have a busy day ahead of me tomorrow."

He smiled with a knowing look behind his eyes.

What does he know?

"Have a good night, Annabeth," he said before diving underneath the water.

She watched with interest as his broad arms and shoulders sliced through the water with a measured ease and speed.

Annabeth wondered for a moment if *he* had swum competitively. She let the thought go and wrapped her towel around her, securing it at her breast.

Her phone blinked blue, letting her know she had a message. It was from Fernando. A chill ran down her spine, though she wasn't exactly sure why.

> *Annabeth, tell your friend I am free to send up the sound equipment for the event. I was hoping your message would be an invite to go out, but I guess getting me a gig is second best. A bunch of us from the department are*

going out Friday night. I hope you can make it.

Annabeth lifted her eyes just in time to catch Jesse as he broke the surface and shot a quizzical expression her way. His easy smile put her ill at ease. The less time she spent around Jesse the better.

Fernando, however, was a different story. As much as she wanted to avoid him as well, *he* was necessary for her to move forward with her mission.

Text me the info. I'll try to make it after my book club, she texted back.

Her flip-flops clapped against the cement as she we walked out of the community center and toward home. A block away, she saw two cop cars parked in front of a two-story stone house.

Annabeth walked with purpose toward the police.

"Excuse me, officer. Is everything all right?"

"Ma'am. We're just here about a suspected robbery."

Annabeth scrunched up her nose, trying to look cute and innocent. "Oh? I just moved in down the street. Should I be worried?" She tilted her head to the side and bit her lip.

The officer gave her a slow once-over before he cleared his throat and gave her a syrupy sweet smile. "Tell me, what street do you live on, ma'am?"

"William Street."

The officer rested his hands on his hips and puffed out his chest. "A car *was* dispatched to William this morning, but it was a false alarm. Don't you worry though, we'll catch the folks responsible for this nonsense. Just give us a call if you see anything suspicious."

"Well, thank you, officer. I appreciate all you and your men do to keep us safe."

"My pleasure, ma'am," he said with a grin. "You have a good night."

"You too." Annabeth let out a deep sigh as she continued on her walk.

Trouble seemed to follow her wherever she went. She had been foolish to think otherwise. This wasn't a new start in a new place. No, this is just where they'd run to escape from their problems.

CHAPTER 14

Vi took in a long, deep breath. Three days of being cooped up with a nasty case of the flu had been three days too many. Nobody had time to be sick in this day and age—least of all her.

Her boss had told her she could take the whole week off, but she couldn't stand a minute longer in bed. She was ready to get back to work and being her useful self. She didn't want to disappoint her clients at the shelter. They needed her.

She also needed a break from Brooke who had been over nearly every day to "take care of her". When all she really wanted to do was gossip about the neighbors and speculate about the reasoning behind the stuff they had found in Marcus's room.

I'm not sure which is more taxing, Brooke or the flu. It was too close to call.

When she arrived for duty, the Lighthouse Crisis Center's waiting room was already full. Vi knocked on the Plexiglas window for Rosa, the receptionist, to buzz her in. As she always did, she greeted Vi with a big friendly smile.

Rosa had been a kindergarten teacher for over thirty years, and when she retired, she got a job at the Center as the full-time receptionist. She was the perfect person for the job—everyone's stand-in-grandmother.

"Hey, Vi. It's great to have you back. How are you feeling?"

Vi moved her magnet into the *in* slot. "I'm still pretty tired, but what can you do? There are always more bills to pay."

Rosa handed her an intake file. "Room #1 is open. She, uh... she used to volunteer here. She seemed pretty upset, so I took her back to wait in private. All the other advocates are in with clients, and this one asked for you by name." Rosa flashed Vi a sympathetic smile. "You picked a helluva day to come back to work."

Vi's shoulders slumped as she read over the paperwork the client had filled out. A gasp escaped her lips when she got to the middle of the questionnaire— her reason for requesting services.

Rosa nodded. "Yeah, I know. She was pretty adamant about not wanting to involve the police. An EMT brought her in. She was in a car accident. And, well, you'll hear the rest soon enough..."

Vi hugged the file to her chest and said a silent prayer for the young girl in the other room. In their small town, they were used to the garden variety domestic disputes, but sex trafficking? This was definitely a new one. She needed a few moments to brace herself before proceeding in to talk with her newest client.

"Is she hurt?"

Rosa shook her head. "The EMTs cleared her. She's pretty banged up though."

"Okay." Vi hesitated. She would be lying to herself if she said she wasn't afraid of making a mistake.

I can do this!

She played the mantra over again in her mind, trying to psych herself up.

"You'll do fine." Rosa smiled at Vi, giving her the boost of support she needed to get moving.

It didn't matter how many intakes she had performed in the past, she always worried about saying or doing the wrong thing. Knowing the girl behind the door didn't help, either. Ideally, an advocate would pass off on cases where she knew the person, but in a small town like Herald Springs, everyone knew everyone.

But sex trafficking? How could...?

You're stalling, Vi!

She took a deep breath and twisted the doorknob. There. Just like pulling off a Band-Aid.

Vi gave the girl a quick glance before she dropped her gaze back to the client file. The irony of how often she'd drilled in to Joy the importance of eye-contact was not lost on her.

"Hi, Anjali. I don't know if you remember me or not. My name is—"

Anjali looked up at her with almond shaped dark brown eyes. "I remember you, Miss Vi."

Vi felt herself get flustered, of course she remembered her, she had requested to speak to Vi directly. Though Vi couldn't for the life of her understand why she would pick her over the other far more talented and seasoned advocates on staff.

Mother Mary, give me strength!

Vi sat down on the chair across from Anjali, whose upper lip was split and the side of her face swollen. The memory of Anjali from two summers ago flashed before Vi's eyes. She had been an energetic and happy young woman, eager to spend her time helping others despite her full course load at the University of Austin.

One day last fall she hadn't shown up for her volunteer shift. Vi remembered that the volunteer coordinator had been surprised since Anjali had expressed such an interest in the work despite her parents' insistence that she study engineering instead of social work.

Vi shook her head to break apart the memories of how vibrant the girl had been in the past. It seemed this new version of the girl shared only a name with her former self.

Vi exhaled slowly. "Umm, on your intake form you checked that you feel your life's in danger and that you are seeking shelter."

Anjali rocked back and forth—a comfort seeking motion that Joy often did when anxious. "I am needing a safe place to stay until I can get a ticket back to India. This is the only place I could think that might accept me."

Vi watched as the young woman's cupped hands shook in her lap. She looked thinner, gaunt almost.

Drugs.

Vi knew from her training that the pimps used drug dependency as part of their power and control over the young women.

"Can you tell me about what happened?" Vi asked.

Anjali looked down at her hands.

"We were all of us on our way back from the hotel. A big truck cut us off and there was a terrible crash of metal and squeal of brakes. Many in our van were injured, but not me. The police came, and our driver—the one who was in charge of keeping us together—he was not conscious and could not stop the cops from talking to us.

"The other girls were too frightened to say anything, but I knew if I didn't take this chance, I would never get away from them. I don't know who was driving that truck, but I think maybe it was a god sent to protect us, to deliver us to safety.

"So I made my voice quiet and asked the police to arrest me. It was the easiest way I could think to get away, especially since the other girls refused to say anything against them, and I... I was so scared. It was like a strength from outside of me had taken over, that same god who had been behind the wheel of the big truck.

"There was a woman officer and she seemed to catch on faster than the men. She pushed me against the police car and put handcuffs on me. She told them something about drugs and carted me away. She said I didn't have to talk unless I wanted to, then she brought me here. And I can't leave, not until it's time to return home. They will be looking for me. If they suspect... Well, they would kill me. Like they did the last girl who tried to run away."

Anjali pulled a pack of cigarettes and a lighter out of her pocket and lit up. Her hand continued to shake as she took a long drag. "It's all my fault. I trusted too easily." She shivered and spoke under her breath. "I practically invited them to steal me away."

Walker Texas Wife

Vi leaned in closer to the girl, mirroring her body language. "Anjali, what happened to you isn't your fault."

"Isn't it?" She laughed bitterly, then took a long drag of her cigarette. "I was raped so many times that I lost count. Businessmen from all over the world...they...used me like a tissue. If I hadn't gotten into that car none of that would have happened."

Vi's chest tightened at the thought of what Anjali had been through. As a seasoned advocate, she knew the last thing this girl needed was her pity. Instead, she let her body naturally reflect Anjali's posture back to her. It always amazed her how easily the words and mannerisms came to her in the moment.

"I know you feel responsible for what happened to you, Anjali, but it wasn't your fault. The men who did this to you, it's all *their* fault. They were in the wrong, *not* you. I am very sorry that you went through this. I want to help you in any way that I can to make sure that you stay safe."

"I escaped," she said under her breath. "They don't like it when girls get away. They're going to look for me. I've made them a lot of money."

Vi leaned in toward the girl to make sure she caught every word. Her heart ached at the thought of what Anjali had been through.

"How many other girls are there?"

Anjali looked up at Vi. "Enough to make them very rich." A look of fear washed over her swollen features. "I don't want to talk to the police. I just want to go home. I can't go back to them. They *will* kill me." Tears streamed down her cheeks.

"All right." Vi handed Anjali a tissue. She hated the idea that there were other girls out there, but she needed to focus on this one who was sitting right before her—that was her job.

"Let's get you settled in at the shelter and call your parents. Have they heard from you since...?" She wasn't sure how to finish that sentence. Luckily, Anjali didn't need for her to.

"Yes, every week as a matter of fact. He made me call them—never Skype—to lie. They think I am still in the school. They even sent me a monthly allowance, but he took it every time."

Vi stood at the door. "You don't have to tell them anything you don't want to."

"They can't know. My life will be as good as over. No one will agree to marriage with a girl who..." Her sentence broke apart into a fit of sobs.

"We're going to take this a step at a time. First let's get you some clean clothes and a room. Okay?"

Anjali nodded, swiping at the corners of her eyes with the crumpled tissue.

It took Vi a whole shift to get Anjali situated at the shelter and to call her family. They seemed happy to hear from her, but voiced their extreme displeasure in her request to come back home.

Vi wanted to intervene, but Anjali held her finger to her lips and shook her head. By the end of the call, they had agreed to purchase Anjali a ticket to come home for a week in October for her cousin's marriage festivities. Although it was still a month away, at least it would be a start.

* * *

Vi trembled the whole drive home. The pressure of keeping it together proved almost too much. When she pulled up to her home she saw a familiar truck parked in front.

Ricky. What is he doing here?

She watched in her rearview mirror as he walked toward her car. Vi got out and slammed her door shut.

"Ricky?"

His eyes narrowed in a look of concern. When his large hand touched her arm, the last of her resolve crumbled. Ricky reeled her in and held her up against his broad chest. The familiar beat of his heart grounded her.

A sigh escaped her lips as he combed his fingers through her hair and tipped her face up to his. She didn't even bother to try and stop him when he dipped down to kiss her. It had been too long. Seven years too long.

Vi wrapped her arms around his neck. She needed to feel loved, alive. Especially after the day she'd just been though.

Ricky pulled away, his thoughtful eyes examining hers.

"Hey," he said, rubbing slow circles over her back with the tips of his fingers. "What's wrong?"

Vi fought the urge to let him back into her life. The loneliness she felt was palpable. "*No sé,*" she said.

"Don't know or don't want to talk about it?" he asked with a knowing smile.

"Both." She returned his smile with a lopsided one of her own.

When they had broken up all those years ago, she had said it was because she needed to focus on caring for Joy. Each passing year it became harder to keep him at arm's length. It didn't help that he never fully left her life. It had been almost seven years since they'd broken up, but he still hung around like he was waiting for her to change her mind. Even when he was gone for months on end to various rodeos, he would send her postcards or trinkets for Joy.

"I just had a bad day. I'll be fine, Ricky."

A sad smile floated across his face. "*Fine?*" he repeated under his breath, then reached up to push her hair behind her ears. "I miss you, Violeta."

His words strummed the chords of her heart. I miss you too, she wanted to say. But she loved him too much to pull him back into the everyday hell that was her life. Ricky deserved so much more than what she could offer.

Of course, before she could utter a word, her phone rang.

Joy, always Joy.

The reality of her situation washed over her and she stepped back to answer her phone.

"What's wrong, Joy?"

Through the corner of her eye she could see Ricky's shoulders slump. His beautiful full lips formed a long thin line. But the sound of Joy's anxious babble brought her back to the present and reminded her once again why she and Ricky just couldn't be together.

"Joy, the rodeo is Saturday. This is Thursday. I'm not coming tonight."

She did not have the patience to deal with her today. Not after all she'd already been through.

Ricky swooped in to her rescue and snatched the phone from her hand. "Hey Joy-Joy. Yeah it's Ricky. I miss you too, *Mija*. She was sick, *huh*?" he said, looking straight at Vi with questioning eyes. "Yeah, I can watch after her for you. Love you too. I'll see you in two days, all right? Okay, Joy-Joy, goodnight."

Ricky ended the call and handed the phone back to her. Before she could say a word he stole a short, sweet kiss from her. "You should get some sleep, too."

Vi let out a shaky sigh, "Ricky—"

He placed a finger on her lips to silence her. "Goodnight, Violeta."

"Goodnight, Ricky."

She knew he wouldn't leave until she was safe inside so she unlocked her door and went in. As it closed behind her she fell back against it.

I will not cry; I will not cry.

CHAPTER 15
BROOKE

BY the time Brooke woke up the next morning, Brian had gone. He'd meticulously made up his side of the bed even though her half of the covers were still wrapped into a tight ball at her knees. On his pillow lay a note written out on Brooke's own BFF stationary.

> *Dear Brookey B,*
>
> *I'm sorry for being such a jealous jerk lately, and especially for last night. It's just that I love you so much, and I'm so afraid of losing you to some other guy that, sometimes,*

I forget to treat you like the queen that you are.

I don't know if you can forgive me, but I'm hoping this fresh breakfast will provide a start. Muffins are on the dresser, Champagne for mimosa is in the fridge. I'll try to be home early tonight.

Love,
Brian

P.S. Thanks for washing my lucky boxers. You're the best!

Her husband's racist outburst the night before was not the first thing Brooke wanted to think about upon waking up, but that was Brian for you—always making things about himself, spinning them to make *him* look like the good guy. Especially when he wasn't.

Stop being such a bitch. He's gone out of his way to make it up to you.

She took a deep cleansing breath and padded over to the dresser to grab one of Mitsy's famous banana nut muffins—the low cal version, she noticed with a scoff.

Tiara came running into the bedroom, the tiny bell on her collar jingling. "Good morning, Princess Tiara." Brooke bent down to scratch the little pom between her cute teddy bear ears, then bit down into the muffin with more hunger than she'd realized she had.

The sticky sweet taste of banana turned her stomach, and she had to force the soggy bite down her throat to avoid throwing up. Normally she loved Mitsy's muffins—of course, she'd *never* admit that to Mitsy—but something was definitely off about this batch. She thought about feeding the rest of it to Tiara, but what if the muffins made her delicate canine tummy sick, too?

Maybe I'm coming down with something, just like Vi. Crap! Best not to chance the mimosas, even though they sounded so good right about then. She put on a smile for the tiny fluff ball that was watching her with rapt attention.

"What should we wear today, girl, *huh?*" she asked in a baby voice as she led the way toward her massive walk-in closet.

"Today feels like a day for Marc Jacobs, wouldn't you agree?" She pulled a flirty sundress from its hanger, hoping its playfulness would help deter whatever ailment was nipping at her heels. As she was doing up the zip, her cell began to play Icona Pop's "I Love It".

"Ugh, I really need to change that." She let the call go to voicemail and moved on to apply her morning face.

The cell rang again, inviting the played-out pop group into her room once again.

"Definitely changing that." She sighed and raced over to the nightstand to pick up her phone before it could direct the caller to voicemail a second time.

"Parties by Brooke."

"Brooke? Brooke? Oh thank God," a woman greeted her frantically between gasps for air.

"Who is th—?"

"It's me, Kim. Kim Lockard. I'm sorry to call so early, but we have a big problem!"

Brooke braced herself for whatever revelation of crisis was sure to follow. Director Lockard had been pretty hands-off when it came to planning the annual autism gala, so for her to be this worked up about it...

"Everything's gone to hell," she confirmed.

"Now, now, I'm sure it's not—"

"Oh, it is! The Gables just went up in flames. Can you believe it? In one fell swoop, we've lost our venue, staff, caterer, everything. And with less than a week until the gala, I'm afraid we're going to have to postpone—."

Now it was Brooke's turn to interrupt. "Kimberly, calm down. I've got this." Then as an afterthought, "Was anyone hurt in the fire?"

"No, thank God. Are you sure it's doable?"

"Of course. I can call in some favors and get us back on track in no time."

Other than the sound of Kim's breathing slowing somewhat, the other end of the line stayed silent. Brooke rolled her eyes. She wished the woman would just take her word at face value rather than making her explain herself over and over again.

"Trust me, the gala will be a success. I promise we can make this work. I do this for a living remember? I'm not some inexperienced volunteer. Let me handle this. I'll have a new location, caterer, staff, all the bells and whistles in place before you can bat an eyelash."

Kim took a long, deep breath on the other end of the line.

Brooke imagined her pinching her sinuses as she so often did whenever something was vexing her.

"You're absolutely positive?" Kim asked at last.

"One-hundred percent. Let me go get to work. I'll call you later tonight to give you a progress update."

"Oh, Brooke. You're the best board member we have, and I know you'll do a great job. You always do. This fire just has me frazzled. Let me know when you've secured a new venue. Thanks again. I've gotta go. I have a million fires to put out this morning. Oh dear, maybe that wasn't the best choice of words. Ugh...... thanks again! Bye."

"Bye." Brooke put down her phone and stretched. The gala had always been one of her easier volunteer jobs. As the board chair for the finance and fundraising committee, she had prided herself on always bringing in more money each year than they budgeted. Losing the venue a week before the event was going to require some serious work, but she could pull it off.

Brooke shook her head to rid herself of any lingering concern, threw her hair into a messy bun, and headed out to fix the disaster that had landed firmly on her plate.

Just keep swimming. Just keep swimming.

She had a lot of work to do, but first things first, she needed a venue and quick. Thankfully the Book Cellar had the perfect room to host it and the owner owed her a favor.

Heck, they could even clear the businesses on either side of it for the night to open up a few extra dance floors. More dancing meant more fun for the party-goers, and more fun meant larger donations.

She slipped on her bluetooth and called Allen over at the B.C. It didn't take much coaxing to secure the space for the gala. He even volunteered to do the legwork needed to clear out the back patio that overlooked the Hill Country. With a little finagling he even threw in some bar tables and chairs for the back. There would be enough room to fit all the guest as well as another portable bar.

She would have to make a lot of calls today. Part of her job involved volun*telling* the Herald Springs elite to help make it happen.

While she made her calls, she decided to take a brisk walk into town to at least fit a little bit of exercise into her day. Besides, the fresh air always had a way of jumpstarting her brain in the mornings.

And as she rounded the block, she found Annabeth at the curb grabbing a heaping pile of junk mail from her mailbox.

"Howdy, neighbor," she said with a wave.

Annabeth nodded and raised her chin, something Brooke had never seen a white person do before, but she was from Detroit originally and married to a black man to boot.

She's so... weird.

That was really the only word for Annabeth King. Weird. Really fucking weird. Oh, yeah, and possibly a porno pedophile serial killer, but Brooke *did* need all the help she could get.

It's not like she'll bring her personal drama into working the event. No, this one's as closed off as they come. The perfect last minute lackey.

"Wait," she called as she raced to close the distance between them.

Annabeth's eyes narrowed as she turned around to face Brooke with an irritated look on her face. "What?"

"So you remember that gala I told you and Marcus about? The one for Joy's group home?"

Annabeth folded her arms across her chest and pursed her lips. "Yes. Did Fernando get in touch with you?"

Brooke nodded as she felt her pulse point in her wrist.

There goes my target heart rate.

"Yes, thank you! I actually am in kind of a bind and could really use your help. The venue burned to the ground last night."

Annabeth's jaw dropped. "Oh no, was anyone hurt?"

"Everyone's fine, but the last minute location change is going to really put us behind schedule. The home really needs this fundraiser, too. They just lost one of their grants......anyway, long story short, I could really use your help."

Annabeth shoved the stack of mail beneath her arm and gave Brooke a nervous look. "Sorry, I have a lot of work for school, and I don't—"

No, she's not getting out of it this easy. Besides, it was time they properly inducted little Annabeth into how things worked around here.

Before Annabeth could turn to walk away, Brooke grabbed her wrist and made the other woman look at her head on. "Look, I wouldn't ask if it weren't important. I really need you. Please don't say no."

Annabeth let out a long sigh. "All right."

"Thank you!" Brooke squealed and gave Annabeth a hug, realizing too late that she'd crossed an invisible barrier the two kept erected between them. She drew back and arranged her features into a more neutral expression. "We'll talk more about it at book club later tonight. You are coming, right?"

"Yes, I just loved how the main charac—"

"I can't talk now. I'll shoot you an email later with all the details." Brooke turned on her heel. "Thank you! You're a lifesaver!"

CHAPTER 16

ANNABETH

ANNABETH slung her messenger bag over her shoulder. Even at eight o'clock at night, the heat of the day strangled her. Her flip-flops clapped against the hot asphalt as she crossed the street to the Book Cellar café.

Annabeth checked her phone and spotted a new text message from Fernando.

Hope to see you downtown tonight.

The idea of spending time with Brooke again made her want to gouge her eyes out with a dull butter knife, but Vi had come over that afternoon and asked her with those big puppy dog eyes of hers, and she just couldn't say no. It turned out she had a soft spot in her bitter heart for her sweet little neighbor.

The bell above the door clanged as she walked inside. The cool air blasted her face. God, that felt good. The white noise of the patrons mingled with the classical music playing through the kitschy 1950's speakers that hung on the wall. Through the chatter and violins she could hear the distinct sound of Vi's giggle. Following the laugh like breadcrumbs, she found her and the others gathered around a large round oak table with a dozen or more glass bowls containing a votive and clear beads.

Brooke had ribbon trailing around her to the ground. In her left hand she held a glue gun. *Wow.* Who would have thought she'd do such a menial task when she had so many minions she could pawn it off on.

"Oh, goodie! Another set of hands." Brooke flashed a half-smile.

At the same time, Vi's face lit up as she jumped from her seat, nearly knocking over several finished centerpieces.

"Violeta!" Brooke exclaimed in a voice much deeper than the one she normally used.

But Vi ignored her friend's warning and proceeded to squeeze the life out of Annabeth. "I'm so glad you could come! We're working on the centerpieces for the gala. It is going to be *so* amazing this year. I just know it will be the best yet. Brooke is really outdoing herself!"

Annabeth smiled and maybe blushed a little, too. She would never admit it out loud but she liked Vi's Pollyanna-esque attitude much more than she thought she might.

"I'm happy to help."

Brooke gave Annabeth a hateful look, but said nothing.

A warm hand touched her bare arm.

"Good evening, ladies. My, my y'all been busy." Jesse pulled out the chair between her and Brooke and sat down. "Sorry I'm late. Heather had to work tonight. Had to get a sitter in order to come on out here."

Annabeth caught the quick sideways glance between the decided King and Queen of Herald Springs.

Was that a blush? Does the Queen Bee have a crush on the local gossip? Oh the scandal!

Annabeth tried to push away her bitter thoughts—she hated to descend to their level. This wasn't high school after all.

Jesse drank down a large mouthful of beer and leaned back in his chair so that it balanced on the back legs. He shot her a knowing glance that made her wonder if he could read minds. Either way, his gaze made her uncomfortable.

"How are your girls?" she asked.

He gave her a slow, almost cautious smile. "They're great. It's always an adjustment getting back into the school routine. Oh, you know what? They were talking about you this morning. They want us to do a swim race." Jesse pulled out his buzzing phone.

Annabeth bit her bottom lip. She didn't like the idea of him and his girls talking about her.

Can't he just let the whole swimming thing go?

"Is that right?"

Jesse grumbled something under his breath as he looked at his phone. "Excuse me, ladies. I need to take this."

Annabeth followed him with her gaze as he got up and walked over to an empty corner of the café.

Brooke's sharp voice sliced through the air between them. "You swim?" she asked—almost an accusation.

"Y-yes." Annabeth started to fill the empty bowls with the beads and votives.

Vi looked up from the box of finished decorations. "Oh? Jesse is a great swimmer. He swam in college and won a bunch of awards. Did you swim in school, too?"

Annabeth felt her skin grow hot despite the air conditioning. "No, I never swam competitively. I was just a lifeguard."

From several yards away the sound of Jesse raising his voice reached their table. His shoulders were hunched and his back stooped. He had begun to pace. Annabeth caught snatches of his conversation.

"Honey, I… No, no, of course not. I didn't mean…"

Brooke stared after him with a worried look. Apparently forgetting the project at hand, because— "Ouch!" she cried. She shook her hand out as the hot glue gun clattered to the table.

Vi rushed to her side to examine the burn. "Oh, no! Are you okay?"

Brooke brushed her off with an eye roll. "I'm fine. Just lost my grip is all. Get back to work."

Annabeth glared at Brooke. Why did she have to be such a bitch?

"*Your* money, right. Perhaps we should talk more once you've calmed down. Bye." Jesse ended the call and stalked back over to the bar. He came back to the table and finished off his first glass of beer before sitting down with his second.

"So what's my job, Queen B?" He forced a smile onto his face.

If Annabeth had blinked she would have missed the quick look of sympathy flash across Brooke's normally pinched features.

"Actually, I've got the perfect job for you. I'm having trouble with the pre-registration page. Would you mind looking it over and see if you can't get it working again? You're so good at that kind of thing."

Brooke batted her lashes. The woman really could lay it on thick.

Annabeth rolled her eyes. Definitely time for a topic change.

"Hey, I wanted to ask you guys... I ran into a cop the other day on the way back from the pool, and he said there was a false alarm on our street, Vi. Do you know anything about that?"

Annabeth caught a quick glance between Brooke and Vi.

What's that about?

"Oh that. That was the day silly Vi was out of her mind with fever and forgot her alarm code. It was really rather comical. Wasn't it Vi?"

Vi's eyes stayed trained on arranging the bowls within the box. "Yeah. It was really embarrassing."

Jesse smiled across the table at her with a thoughtful expression. "It's okay, Vi. You have a lot on your plate. But, hey, I'm glad you're feeling better."

Vi looked up from the decorations and smiled back sweetly. "Me, too. Thank you again for the soup and, umm, elderberry syrup. It really helped."

"One of the hippy mamas at the preschool raved about it. I was skeptical at first, but that stuff really works." Jesse finished off his second beer as he pulled up a page of HTML code on Brooke's computer. "Ah-ha! There's your problem. If we take out this line of code and put *this* in instead, your reg page will be as good as new."

Brooke beamed. "I knew you would be able to fix it! Thank you!"

The alarm on Annabeth's phone went off, reminding her of the meeting she'd scheduled. "I'm sorry. I'm going to have to go. I'm supposed to meet up with a couple of colleagues for drinks in Austin. I'll see you tomorrow at the rodeo, Vi." She got up from her chair.

Vi nodded with a smile as she tallied up the decorations. "Make sure you park in the paid lots instead of on the streets. They're a little safer. Austin isn't like Herald Springs, but you're from Detroit so I guess I don't need to tell you all of that."

Annabeth flashed Vi a quick smile. It was sweet that she worried, but it wasn't like Austin was dangerous like Detroit. "You sound like Marcus. Don't worry about me, Vi. I'll be fine."

Brooke raised her eyebrows and rolled her eyesbefore putting her attention back to hot-gluing ribbon to the glass. Annabeth wanted to slap the smug look off of Brooke's face, but refrained from living out that particular fantasy.

In a huff she turned to walk away, only to have a hand reach out and grab hold of her, pulling her back. Jesse. He paused for a second.

"Your bag."

Annabeth snatched her messenger bag and slung it over her shoulder.

God, how embarrassing.

"Thank you," she murmured as she left the café in haste. She didn't want to be late for her meeting with Fernando, and she *did* want to get as far away from Brooke and Jesse as she could.

* * *

FERNANDO stood outside waiting for her, smoking a cigarette as he leaned casually against a utility pole. The busy Austin downtown street was bustling with college students celebrating the end of the week. They made Annabeth feel old.

Fernando—her man of mystery—was a nice distraction. Strong, dark and handsome—he'd make the perfect charming villain.

When he noticed Annabeth approaching, he strolled over and surprised her with a kiss on the cheek, missing her lips by a hair. His coal black eyes remained fixed on her lips as if he wanted to kiss her again. She couldn't help but feel his charm. Would she turn him away if he made a move?

He wet his lips and flicked a bit of ash onto the pavement. "Do you smoke?"

She shook her head. "Quit five years ago."

Fernando chuckled. "You're stronger than I am. Fridays are my busy day so it's nice to unwind at the end of the week like this. Stupid smoking ordinance makes it a little hard, though."

His eyes raked over her body. A feeling of self-consciousness washed over her and she crossed her arms over her chest.

"I know what you mean. It *was* a hard week for me too."

He took a deep, indulgent drag then snuffed out his cigarette against the bar's brick exterior. "Let's go inside."

His fingers brushed her bare arm causing gooseflesh to break out alongside her freckles. A shiver rippled through her as he leaned in and whispered in her ear, "I'm glad you're here."

She swallowed hard. Why was her mouth so dry?

Unaware of her frazzled nerves, Fernando guided them deeper into the crowded bar. Half the English Department had shown up early, and *half of them* were already half in the bag.

Her breath hitched when she spotted the student Marcus had told her about—the one that fit the profile. That she had been doing a shitty job keeping an eye on. She'd managed to follow the girl around a little after class, but had lost her somewhere on the quad when some annoying douchebag skater guy had run her over.

Amy sat among a group of drunken revelers singing along to an old Willie Nelson song. She looked prettier and younger than she did in her photo. Her thick black hair was pulled back in a low pony. She had on a tight purple U of A shirt and a pair of shorts that looked more like the volleyball shorts she used to wear in high school.

Annabeth pushed through the group and pulled Amy away. "Hey! You're in my Comp 101 class, aren't you?"

"Yeah, I *love* your class! Let me buy you a drink!" Amy exclaimed with a youthful enthusiasm that Annabeth had never possessed—not even in her twenties.

Wait. How was she going to buy them drinks? Wasn't she just a freshman? Nineteen years tops?

Amy strode right up to the bartender and flashed what Annabeth could only assume was a fake ID.

Fernando elbowed his way through the crowd and stood by Annabeth's side.

"You two know each other? *Interesting.*" Fernando looked from Amy to Annabeth and back again.

Annabeth shrugged. "She's a student of mine. Wait, how do you two know each other?"

He snaked a possessive arm around Annabeth's waist. "We met at the mixer last week. The one you didn't go to. She's into Proust."

A moment passed as she debated grabbing his arm and flinging it away from her, but he only pulled her closer.

"Dance with me."

She leaned away from his sashaying hips. "No, that's really all right. I don't dance."

He gave her an exaggerated frown and came closer, continuing to dance against her. "What *do* you do?"

She felt her smile unfold a little at a time. He was nothing if not persistent. There was a time when she would have easily fallen for this kind of game. The benefit of age and wisdom allowed her to see his actions for what they were. A pick-up. Even though she had no intention of going home with him, a little harmless flirting wasn't going to hurt anyone. Anyway, he did seem to know everyone and he could be a good resource for her.

"I do *lots* of things."

He crept closer so that the length of him pressed against her, making her head spin. It didn't help that he smelled good enough to eat. His breath on her ear made her heartbeat quicken.

"Call me Fin. Everyone does."

Damn, he is good at this.

"Why Fin?"

"Because I'm a shark. All you see is the fin, until it's too late." He laughed, then nipped at her earlobe with a predatory growl.

Annabeth gasped, but her shock seemed to please him.

Amy danced over to them with three beers.

A teenager just bought me a beer.

Amy handed one to Fernando and another to Annabeth.

The DJ transitioned into the Hill's *The Weekend* and Amy's whole face lit up. "Oh. My. God! I love this song!"

"Me, too." Fernando redirected his gyrating hips toward Amy, circling her just like the shark he claimed to be. He must have noticed Annabeth's glance. He may have been creepy, but damn, he was hot as hell. It had been a long time since she had been with anyone. The unmet need grew with each passing second.

In one smooth move, Fernando pulled Annabeth up against his hard chest. "Just one dance."

Amy moved on to dance with a more age-appropriate partner, and Annabeth gave in to his inviting body that pressed against her with intent. His lips grazed her neck, making her gasp. Her heart beat in time to the music that snaked out from the speakers, and she just couldn't say no.

Eh, what could it hurt?

CHAPTER 17

VI

Vi toed the fairgrounds' dusty path with the tip of her leather boot. Her pearl-buttoned shirt, tight jeans, and belt with the wide buckle had her looking every bit the part of a stereotypical Texas woman. Her heart hammered in her chest in anticipation of seeing Ricky do what he did best—ride bulls. Some women got weak in the knees over fire fighters, some for Highlanders in kilts, but Vi only had eyes for her cowboy.

As much as she looked forward to seeing him again, she also dreaded it. Joy, on the other hand, had been a ball of uncontrollable energy from the moment she'd picked her up. The entire morning, Vi and Annabeth had tried to keep Joy busy with the many different attractions and games, but all the distractions in the world couldn't keep Vi's thoughts from returning to Ricky and the kiss they'd shared the other night. It had awakened something inside of her that she'd thought long since dead. The ache of wanting was more than she could bear.

Vi leaned against the metal rail post and watched as Joy rode a chestnut horse on a circular track. The rest of the riders all looked to be no older than seven, making Joy stick out like a sore thumb.

"You okay?" Annabeth appeared at her side with a couple bottles of local brew.

Vi tipped her hat down further to shade her eyes from the relentless glare of the noonday sun before grabbing one of the ice cold bottles and taking a long, hard chug. "Mmm, yep. I'm just fine."

Annabeth smiled into her bottle. "Sure, uh-huh. *Fine.*"

Vi hid her eyes underneath her hat.

Annabeth looked around the rodeo with a smile. "Marcus would really get a kick out of all this."

Vi took a quick drink of the beer. The bubbles tickled her nose. "Yeah, it's too bad he couldn't come."

Annabeth's already white face seemed to become paler. She broke eye contact to study the weeds that grew up along the fence posts. "Yeah, he lives and dies for football. U of M is playing this afternoon so he'll be glued to the couch for a while. There's no moving that man when there's a game on."

Annabeth's phone started to play an old Uncle Kracker song about eight mile and Heaven. "Sorry, I have to take this." She turned on her heels and walked a yard away from Vi. "Hi Mr. Morgan. Did you get my report?"

Joy came bounding over to Vi. "It's time for Ricky!"

Vi glanced toward her watch. Sure enough, it was time to head over and grab their seats. Annabeth ended her call and walked back over to them. "Sorry 'bout that."

"Sissy, it's time. We're going to miss it." Joy stared anxiously in the direction of the arena with the frayed collar of her shirt between her teeth.

"I can't wait to see my first bull ride!" Annabeth smiled.

As they neared the arena, she spotted Ricky standing out front talking with the director, hands on his hips, a serious look splashed across his handsome face.

"Ricky!" Joy took off at a sprint. Much to Vi's horror, she ran—arms flapping—right toward Ricky who hugged her tightly to him. He was the only one she would let hug her.

God, she's so embarrassing! What people must think? A grown woman acting like a seven-year-old.

Chuck, the director of the rodeo for the last twenty years, leaned down and kissed Vi on the cheek.

Walker Texas Wife

"It's so good to see you, shug. You're just getting prettier and prettier every time I see you."

She pushed him away playfully. "Oh, Chuck!"

"Well, who is this stunning creature?"

Annabeth blushed the color of her hair.

"Chuck, you old flirt. This is Annabeth and she's married. Also, she's new to Texas so be nice."

He took Annabeth's hand and kissed it. "Welcome to Texas, ma'am. Any friend of Vi's is a friend of mine."

Annabeth laughed.

Thank God she had a good sense of humor.

Ricky extricated himself from Joy's clutches and stepped forward to greet Vi. His soft lips brushed her cheek, sending shivers straight down her spine.

"Hey!" She gave him a quick sidelong glance before making introductions. "Ricky, this is Annabeth King. Annabeth, this is Ricky."

"Nice to meet you, Annabeth." His teeth gleamed white against his finely tanned skin. After tipping his hat toward the women, he led them up to the gate.

"I roped off a little VIP seating area for y'all right here. If you were any closer you'd be in the ring."

Always the showman, Vi thought with no small measure of pride.

"I got us some tickets to the concert after the competition. Chuck said Joy could help with the horses in the stables. Give you a break."

Ricky's thoughtfulness left her aching. As much as she hated to ask for help, she couldn't really say no to an offer like that, especially when he was dressed in full regalia. He could ask her to run away with him right then and there, and she might actually consider it. The skin-tight jeans alone made her want to take him out behind the stables. Like the good old days, she thought as she bit her lip.

The three of them sat down in the front row with Joy on the end. Annabeth leaned in and whispered, "Details. I'm going to need details."

Vi elbowed her in the ribs. She hadn't thought through having to explain the complicated nature of her relationship with Ricky.

"Seriously, Vi, he's hot!"

Vi ignored her comment and just watched Ricky whispering to his bull. His strong, broad shoulders flexed and his strong thighs hugged the bull. It was about to begin.

The announcer started into his spiel, but Vi didn't hear a word. Her eyes and ears were trained on Ricky. She watched as he waited in the chute.

He wrapped his hand in the rope and looked up at her, tipping his hat yet again. She held her breath as he nodded to the gate hand. The chute opened and out they went like a shot. The crowd cheered all around her, but she sat there holding her breath for the longest eight seconds of her life. Not until she saw that he was okay did she breathe again. She craned her neck to see past the mounted men who escorted him toward the exit gate.

"That was amazing!" Annabeth exclaimed.

"He did good Vi-Vi. Did you see him? He did *good.* He'll do even better the next round." Joy announced matter-of-factly.

But Vi couldn't answer, not yet. There were still two rounds to go. She knew she wouldn't be able to relax until she knew he had come out unscathed.

When the second and third rounds had been completed, Joy and Annabeth were on the edges of their seats, waiting for the final score. The enthusiastic MC announced that he had placed first with a score of 90 out of 100. The crowd leapt to their feet and cheered for their hometown boy.

Ricky finally made his way through the well-wishers to sweep Vi off the ground and spin her around. Before her feet even touched the ground, his lips captured hers and she welcomed the invasion.

Dear God, why did I ever stop kissing him?

The awkwardness of Joy and Annabeth waiting beside them broke the spell and he let her go.

"You did such a good job, Ricky." Joy stood stiffly and spoke in a monotone voice.

"I need a victory hug." Ricky scooped her up into his arms.

Annabeth tugged on Joy's arm. "C'mon, Joy. Chuck is going to show us the stables."

Joy squealed. "Yay! I love horses!"

"All right, then. Lead the way." Annabeth followed a very happy Joy toward the stables where Chuck and the stable hands stood waiting.

Without a moment's hesitation, Ricky took one of Vi's hands in his, using the other to tug her hard up against him.

The familiar earthy smell of the rodeo mingled with his own natural musk, and when he leaned down to kiss her, all her objections melted away.

Sense memories from their early days played out in her mind: their first kiss on the Ferris wheel at the county fair, the night he'd gifted her the pearl necklace, the final kiss before...

No, this isn't right.

She pulled away with a shy giggle.

Ricky slung his arm over her shoulders and guided her toward the stage where the bands were playing. "I couldn't believe it when I saw that Marmalade Sunshine was playing this year at the rodeo. I just had to get tickets."

"Our first date," she acknowledged, even though it pained her to think of their early days.

The band had already begun to play the first song of their set by the time they made it through the entrance. Ricky didn't waste a second pulling Vi into a soft, swaying dance.

"I meant what I said at church. I want to be done with all this. I want to settle down and start a family with a good woman. I'd like that woman to be you, Violeta."

"No...Ricky—"

But he cut her off with a long, luxuriant kiss that left her trembling. "I knew you were going to put up a fight." He chuckled. "Just hear me out, would ya? The ranch that wants to take me on as a manager can't put me on payroll until the new year. Thankfully, Chuck was able to book me all the way up until Christmas. But then I'm done with bull riding for good."

Vi squeezed Ricky a little tighter.

He's leaving.

Even though she knew it was only for a few months, she would still miss him. And so would Joy. It always took them a couple of weeks to adjust to him being gone.

His nose brushed against hers before he kissed her again. He certainly wasn't going to make this easy.

Vi broke the kiss and laid her head against his firm chest for the last time.

"I'm giving you an ultimatum, Violeta. We're not getting any younger. I love being with you but I can't keep waiting for you to come around. I'm tired of being alone. I want you, but I can't force you to choose me.

When I get back at Christmas, I need you to know for certain if you want me to stay or go. Okay? If you tell me to go, that will be it. No more of this limbo nonsense." Ricky's intense eyes sought hers out.

I can't look at him. If I do, I'll say yes.

Instead of meeting his gaze, she listened to the rhythmic beat of his heart. He was right. She needed to cut ties with him completely. This half-together, half-not was killing them both. It certainly wasn't fair to Ricky, who deserved so much better than this.

I need to let him go, even if it kills me.

"Violeta?"

She lifted her head off of his chest and kissed him. It was a kiss goodbye. She didn't need time to think it over. She had made up her mind years ago.

"Goodbye, Ricky."

Without another word she turned on her boot and walked away. Ricky called out after her but he didn't follow. She had a feeling that he was done chasing after her.

When she made her way over to Annabeth and Joy at the stable, she was sobbing. The grief of letting him go was more than she'd anticipated.

I did the right thing. She said it over and over again in her mind like a mantra. *Maybe if I say it enough times, I'll believe it, too.*

Annabeth came running when she saw Vi. "What's wrong?"

She choked back a heaving sob. "We broke up. For good."

Annabeth's jaw dropped. "What? I don't understand."

"It's better this way. He wants a wife and children, and I can't give him that."

Annabeth followed Vi's eyes to Joy and a look of sudden understanding dawned on her petite features.

"You're afraid you might have a child like Joy."

Vi looked away as a rush of shame washed over her; her terrible secret had come to light. Even though she loved Joy the best she could, Vi just couldn't fathom adding to her burden.

"I just can't go through that again. I won't. It's already cost me too much."

"Sissy. This one is called Pinky. I'm hungry Vi. I need to eat now." Joy's hands flapped and her eyes darted around. She was winding up for a meltdown.

Vi wiped away her tears and bit her bottom lip. Annabeth's comforting touch helped ground her. She closed her eyes and tried to come up with something to be joyful about, but came up empty.

This is what the rest of my life is going to be...

For better or worse she was married to being Joy's caregiver.

"All right Joy-Joy. Let's go eat."

CHAPTER 18

BROOKE

EVERYTHING is shaping up perfectly. The Book Cellar is a great venue, Brooke typed into her phone. She held back on adding *Just like I said it would be.*

Kimberly's reply came back almost immediately.

> *Do they do full catering or allow outside food?*

Where was the gratitude? Brooke had to work extra hard to keep her response upbeat and friendly.

> *Yes, they have a full-scale catering service AND they also allow outside vendors. Mitsy Grazier volunteered just this*

> *morning to do her famous desserts. We are all set!*

Brooke had to bite her tongue earlier this morning too when talking to Mitsy. She couldn't accuse her of serving expired banana nut muffins then beg for a favor, after all. She'd died a little inside needing to go to her biggest rival for help, but ultimately the success or failure of the gala would fall firmly on Brooke's shoulders and no one else's.

> *It's going to be the event of the year. We're going to make up the Book Cellar with all our decorations! It will be fabulous!!!*

Maybe if she included enough exclamation marks, Kimberly would finally get the point.

> *How do you plan on letting people know to go to the Book Cellar? Everyone's expecting it to be at the Gables.*

Okay, one last response, then Kimberly was going to have to find someone else to bother for a while. Brian would arrive for their big night out at any moment, and they'd both promised to put work aside for the evening.

Everyone on the list has been personally notified of the changes and I've put an article in the Herald. You'll get sympathy donations out of it. Just you wait and see. Try and relax and have a good evening. I've got this in the bag!!!!!!!!!!!

She'd fill the entire screen with exclamations if it meant Kim would finally shut up and listen for a change.

The waiter came by with a bottle of house Merlot—not her favorite Chianti, of course, but it would do in a pinch—and topped up Brooke's glass.

"Thank you," she said, then flipped over her phone to glance at the time: 7:20.

Brian was already twenty minutes late, and he had *promised* to be on time. Made a huge deal of how they'd both been working too hard lately, that he missed her. She scrolled through her call history and dipped a piece of bread in Genova's famous herb and oil blend. Nothing.

Couldn't he at least call to say he was running late?

She shot a text off to Brian.

I'm at Genova's. Where are you?

Then added a heart emoji to show she was in good spirits. The wine was helping with that.

Another text came in from Kimberly, and she forced herself to ignore it.

"More bread?" the waiter asked returning to her side.

"Oh, no, I've got plen...ty." Crap, she'd actually managed her way through an entire mini loaf without any help from her garbage disposal of a husband. She shrugged and offered a goofy smile so the waiter would leave her alone.

Seven-forty rolled around, and still no word from Brian. What the hell? This whole night out had been his idea. He said he wanted to apologize for that thing that had happened the other night—his unfounded jealousy over Marcus, she assumed.

Well, she wasn't going to beg for his attention, thank you very much. She'd already been waiting for nearly an hour. More than enough by her standards.

A fifty should do it, she thought, plunking a single bill down onto the table to help cover the wine, the bread, and the time she'd held onto the table. Her head spun from standing too quickly, and she had to grip onto the chair to balance herself.

"Everything okay, Ma'am?" the perky-breasted hostess asked.

Ma'am? When the fuck did I become ma'am?

Before Brooke could stop it, her eyes squinted tight of their own accord, her mouth spread out into a straight, flat line. She'd done enough playing nice today. Now she was angry. Really angry. Like she wanted to smash a few plates or something... Preferably up against Brian's head.

Vi. That's who she needed. Vi annoyed her sometimes, sure, but she never made Brooke angry. Not like this. Vi would know what to do to help re-center Brooke, get her to focus on other things.

She drove quickly from one end of town to the other, making it back to their neighborhood in record time. When she pulled up to the curb outside of Vi's house though, everything was dark.

The clock's dash read 7:52. Too early for bed. Then what...? A fog had settled over her brain, which made finding thoughts much more difficult than they otherwise should be. At last she remembered...

The rodeo. Shoot.

Of course Vi's one social outing would fall on a night when Brooke desperately needed her guidance. What was she supposed to do now?

Well, she wasn't going home, not if she could help it. Brian's excuses would have to wait for a new day or at least a few more glasses of wine. She thrust the car into park, then turned off the ignition. She'd walk the long way through the neighborhood, clear her head. Maybe she could find a way to slip into her house and grab Tiara without Brian noticing, if he'd even made it home yet, that was. For all Brooke knew, he was in bed with some perky-breasted paralegal or even that same hostess who had so casually referred to Brooke as an old lady.

"Ma'am, my ass," she grumbled.

"What about your ass?"

A large blue SUV had slowed to a crawl beside her. Jesse hung from its open driver-side window.

"Because anything that involves your ass, I surely need to be hearing about."

Brooke laughed despite herself.

Jesse frowned. "Tough night?"

"Something like that."

"Hop in, toots." He put the vehicle into park then reached over to unlock the passenger door for Brooke. "It sticks sometimes," he said with a twisted up smile.

Brooke sank back into the leather bucket seats. She exhaled, letting out all the anger one molecule at a time as she took in the gentle presence of her oldest friend in the neighborhood. Because of his swimming habit, Jesse always smelled faintly of chlorine—just enough to make him smell extra clean. That, mixed with the scent of grape jelly and whole wheat bread, made the smell quite nice, and—although she'd never tell him—quite *domestic*.

She hated being a housewife, and *she* only did it part-time. She couldn't imagine how emasculating and suffocating it must be for Jesse to do the whole stay-at-home parent thing all day every day.

"Better?" he asked, his eyes planted firmly on her, the car still idling at the curb.

"Loads. Thanks."

"Do you want to talk about it?"

"Not especially. Anyway it's no big deal. Just lots going on with the last minute changes for the gala, and Brian......" She let her voice trail off. How had she intended to finish that sentence?

Brian has been extra angry lately. He scares me. I think he may hurt me.

It was ridiculous. Besides, what could Jesse do?

"...has been working a lot lately," she finally finished.

Jesse's face fell. "I can relate. I spend more quality time with the damn cat than my wife. Sometimes I wonder if we'd still be together were it not for the girls, you know?" His knuckles tightened on the steering wheel, turning a splotchy mix of red and white from the uneven pressure.

Jesse slapped the wheel, startling Brooke, but when she looked over at him his smile had returned, the one that had a way of filling up whatever room he stood in. "But enough about that. Hearing about my problems isn't going to fix yours, is it? How about instead you let me take you back to the house and fix you up some liquid happiness à la Jesse Abrahamson?"

A shiver ran up Brooke's arm. "That sounds perfect. Thank you."

Back at Jesse's, he set her up on the sofa with an afghan, then headed over to the kitchen to work on the snacks he'd promised.

A rich, spicy smell filled the sprawling ranch, winning out even over the girls' finger paints, glue sticks, and glitter that were spread out over every square inch of the nearby kitchen table.

Brooke's mouth watered. "Mmm. What is that?"

"An Abrahamson family secret. They brought it over from the old country. A very big deal."

Hardly any time passed before Jesse was back at her side, sitting close and pulling the afghan over to cover himself, too. He handed her a glass of steaming red liquid.

"Hey, are you coming down with something? It's like a billion degrees out. You shouldn't feel this cold. Maybe you've caught that same bug Vi had."

She waved a hand dismissively. "Oh, don't worry about me. I'll be fine. Hey, where are the girls tonight?" She inhaled the rich, pungent aroma and let it clear out her sinuses.

"Sleepover, thank God. I love my daughters, but, man, is it good to have a break sometimes."

She chuckled.

"C'mon, try it already." He leaned into her chest and pushed her wine glass up toward her mouth.

Brooke shivered again despite the warmth that surrounded her. She tittered, awkward in the moment, then let the hot liquid flood her mouth. It was heaven in a glass.

He watched her carefully the whole time. "Well?"

"Oh, Jesse. It's delicious. Please tell me how to make it."

He laughed and stretched out like a cat happy in the sun. "No can do. But I can make it for you any time you want. Just come on over, and I'll whip up a batch. Deal?"

At that same moment, Heather burst through the door, her arms over-encumbered with a heaping stack of manila folders. "Jesse?" she called into the house without looking up from her phone. "A little help?"

Jesse leapt up and raced to his wife's side. "Hi, honey." He pecked her on the cheek and took the files from her. "Bad day?"

"You could say that again. Simmons completely dropped the ball on our new account, and somehow I got stuck with picking up all the pieces. What an idiot. He never should have been promoted to corporate. If I had a—"

She stopped suddenly, her eyes locking on Brooke. "Oh, hello, Brooke. I didn't realize you were over."

Brooke sensed a storm brewing in the Abrahamson household, and she had never been a fan of sudden changes in weather. "I was just going actually. See you at book club, Jesse."

She was so flustered, she took the glass of mulled wine and the afghan with her.

CHAPTER 19

ANNABETH

THE street lamps illuminated only part of Annabeth's path, leaving fear-inducing pockets of darkness along the way. Mondays were full days for her with her last class letting out at 9:00 p.m. Her professor had wanted to talk to her about her paper, so when she left, she was forced to walk to her car by herself. She recalled Vi's warning and Marcus's constant concerns about her walking alone after her classes let out. He'd offered to pick her up several times, but it seemed so silly. Tonight, though, she felt like a Jack-in-the-box right before it pops out.

The sound of her boots on the cement sidewalk echoed down the long deserted street. Annabeth squared her shoulders and walked with purpose. Her skin prickled.

I should have asked someone to walk with me.

Her breath quickened and her heart thundered as she approached a dark alley.

I'm being silly. Nothing is going to happen to me...

A rush of air teased the back of her neck making her yelp. Annabeth slowed her pace as she tried to calm herself. Just as her heart was starting to calm, an arm shot out of the darkened alley and wrapped itself around her chest and shoulders like a snake. The sharp blade of a knife pressed against her carotid artery, breaking the skin.

"Gimme your wallet, your watch, whatever jewelry you have. I don't want to have to hurt you, girlie girl." The man's voice sliced through her. He meant business.

Eight years of self-defense training went out the window in an instant. Annabeth couldn't move—paralyzed with fear.

I need to do something.

Her brain screamed at her body. The blade pressed deeper into her neck making her choke.

"Your wallet." His fetid breath on her neck made her gag.

I need to get away. What am I supposed to do to break free? His thumb.

Annabeth reached with her free hand and grabbed the thumb and yanked it back—hard. His grip on her loosened. While she yanked his thumb she used the heel of her boot to crush her attacker's foot.

"Ahh...Fuck!" The man cried out as he doubled over.

Annabeth brought down the hard point of her elbow on her attacker's skull, and he dropped his grip.

RUN!

She turned to flee and his hand reached out and grabbed her leg, sending her crashing down hard on the street.

Blinding pain shot through her body. Her right arm, which she'd used to break her fall, was now useless. Sprained? Broken?

"You little bitch!" The masked attacker rose from his spot on the ground.

He limped toward her with frightening speed.

Annabeth's breath quickened, and her heart raced. She tried to get up. Pain...God, so much pain. All she could do was inch away in a frantic crab walk. But it wasn't enough...

Oh God...I'm fucked.

Before she could even blink, he was on her, pinning her down. "You're going to pay for that."

Annabeth thrashed and screamed.

I have to get away. He's gonna kill me.

His gloved hand silenced her. A single tear slid down her cheek as she writhed under his bulky weight. Her efforts weren't making a difference. Pain and fear had weakened her.

This is it...

Her attacker used his weight to hold her still as he poked around in her pants pocket with his free hand. When he came up empty his hand tugged at her tank top.

"Nooo...," she cried out against his gloved hand. Not that. In a panic, Annabeth brought her teeth down hard on his hand. He yelped, pulling his gloved hand back.

"Help!"

In the blink of an eye he toppled forward, crushing her. Then, he slid off her and onto the concrete. She let in an anxious breath.

"Are you okay?" a familiar voice asked.

When she looked up and his coal black eyes met hers, she cried in relief.

"Fin!"

"Annabeth!" Fin reached down and helped Annabeth to her feet. The pain in her arm shot up through her shoulder. She cradled it as best she could against her abdomen.

On the sidewalk beside her was a blood-stained brick. "You hit him with a brick?"

"Yeah, I guess I did. Hey, you're hurt." He pointed at her arm which had already started to swell.

His normally flirty nature was gone and in its place was a look of genuine concern.

"Yeah, it might be broken."

She shuddered to think what might have happened if Fin hadn't shown up.

God! I'm so stupid! The attacker started to stir—a soft moan escaping his parted lips.

"I should call the police." Annabeth used her one good hand to pull her phone out of her pocket.

"Call campus police. They'll get here quicker."

Fin took a roll of electrical tape out of his book bag and began wrapping it around the attacker's wrists and ankles several times over.

She dialed the campus police and cradled her wrist to her belly as she sat on the curb. After she had given the dispatcher all the relevant information, she hung up and waited. She felt a shiver run through her. Her teeth began to chatter as the sound of the sirens drew closer.

"You're going into shock." Fin reached inside his bag, pulled out a sweater jacket and draped it around her. He pulled her close and rubbed her upper arm. "Need to keep you warm."

Embarrassment washed over her. She didn't like to be perceived as weak and yet she was grateful that Fin had chosen to act when he did. She relaxed against him. He felt good.

"My hero," Annabeth said in a teasing tone that made her cringe. "How did you—"

Fin tightened his hold around her. "I...uh...was going out to get my car when I heard a scream. I thought about just calling the police and going home. I'm really glad I didn't leave."

"That makes two of us." Annabeth pulled the jacket tightly around her to stave off the chill that ran through her.

If he hadn't...

No it was best not to go there. The warmth of his jacket and his embrace calmed her. His palm cupped her cheek and pulled her head so that she was resting on his shoulder.

Why am I so tired...?

His warm breath tickled the hair on top of her head. "Rest. I'll be right here."

I'll just close my eyes for a minute.

* * *

Two hours later, the mugger was in police custody and Annabeth had her sprained right wrist wrapped up in a sling. Fin had insisted on taking her out for a quick drink to help loosen her back up a bit. As they passed the long string of bars and music venues that lined the infamous Sixth Street, a familiar face jumped out of the crowd of college students and came bounding toward them.

Amy. It's like even the universe wants me to protect this girl.

"Oh, look. My favorite faculty couple."

"We're not a couple—or faculty for that matter," Annabeth corrected. The last thing she needed was to encourage Fin.

In a teasing/not teasing kind of way he wrapped his arm around Annabeth and gave a tight squeeze. "I'm working on it, Amy."

In her pocket, her phone buzzed again. It was Marcus. The timing of his call caused her to blush with embarrassment. She had been ignoring his calls all night.

He's gonna be so pissed at me.

She just couldn't bring herself to talk to him. The thought of getting into all of this with him exhausted her. Annabeth shot off an awkward left-thumb-typed text message to Marcus that she was on Sixth Street having drinks with friends. After it had sent, she turned her phone off and let Fin lead her into the Funky Monkey Bar by the small of her back.

Three beers later and she was feeling it. She had always been a lightweight. It was then that she remembered the pills she had taken at the urgent care for her arm. Oops...

Amy looked at her phone. "This has been fun, but I'm going to have to take off, y'all. I have an 8:00 a.m. class tomorrow. Don't forget we are meeting tomorrow to go over my paper, Annabeth."

"I'll be there. Where are we meeting again?" Annabeth felt a little fuzzy-headed about some of the particulars. It had taken a bit of finessing to get the girl to meet up. She couldn't very well keep an eye on Amy if they didn't get close. Following her around campus had not yielded anything useful. Their carefully put together profile had led to almost catching one of the sex-traffic low level operatives in Detroit in the act of taking a girl. They had failed on that front. This was their chance to make things right. Marcus was sure she would be the next one. He tended to be right about those kinds of things.

"I dunno, here look it up."

Amy slid her phone across the table to Annabeth. She quickly flipped through the calendar function on the girl's phone and made a mental note of the girls schedule for the next week. At least this way she could be more strategic about her creeping. She backed out of the calendar and slid the phone back to its owner. "Ten at the fountain."

"Great." Amy hiccupped and took two cautious steps before falling forward—conveniently right into Fin's arms.

He steadied the drunk girl and reached for his phone. "Let me call you a car." Fin pulled up an app on his phone. "My treat."

Amy smiled. "Aw, thanks. You're so sweet, Fin."

Annabeth noticed her phone was off.

She stretched her arms up over her head in an exaggerated motion. "I should get going, as well."

Fin was all too quick on the uptake. "Do you need a ride?"

The suggestive glint in his eye told her that he was offering much more than a seat in his car. And while she enjoyed his company—when he wasn't boring her with Proust—she wasn't looking for yet another relationship. The one she already had was more than enough work for her.

"No, I'm good." Annabeth gave him a quick kiss on the cheek. He had just saved her life, after all. "Thank you, though."

"Any time," he said with a wink. Before she could walk away, he tugged the strap of her bag—reeling her in. His deft fingers weaved through her hair and tilted her head to the side. Her heart thundered as his mouth found hers. The somewhat chaste kiss sent a rush of warmth.

"Goodnight, Anna."

She didn't bother to correct him. "Goodnight, Fin."

Annabeth stumbled out of the bar with her head down and almost ran straight into a large man. When she looked up, she was startled to find the former love of her life standing before her.

"Marcus, what are you doing here?"

"What do you mean, what am I doing here? I'm out looking for you. I don't hear from you for hours and then I get some ridiculous text about you going out drinking. Then all my calls go to voice mail. What the hell is going on Anna?"

His entitled tone bristled her. "Yeah, that happens when you turn off your phone. Maybe you should have taken the clue." Annabeth tried to shoulder past him, but he blocked her with his bulk. He had been a fullback in college; he could block her path until the cows came home.

"Oh no, you don't. We're *going* to talk about this." He reached out and grabbed her hurt arm to hold her still.

Annabeth yelped in pain. Marcus's eyes shot down and bulged when they landed upon her brand new sling. He released his hold on her. A look of concern washed over him.

"Oh, God. Anna what happened?"

"I got mugged." She tried to push away from him but he blocked her again.

Fin emerged from the bar and inserted himself between them. "Anna, is this guy bothering you?"

She sighed. "I'm fine, Fin. He's just my roommate."

"*Just*, huh? And what's he doing calling you Anna?"

"Marcus, you're making a scene."

Marcus glared at her while Fin assessed the man in front of him.

Fin took her uninjured hand and brought it to his lips, "Well, if you're sure you're all right, but... Call me if you need anything or if ya just want to talk."

"Goodnight, Fin." She watched him walk in the direction of where they had parked their cars.

"What the hell is going on, Anna? You were mugged? I told you not to walk alone. You just don't think." Marcus growled through clenched teeth. She had never seen him so angry. "And that guy. I told you he wants to sleep with you."

So what if he does, she wanted to shout at him. She didn't owe him an explanation for anything she did with her personal time.

"This is why I shut off my phone. None of this is any of your fucking business," she spat back.

Marcus towered over her. His nostrils flared and his lips pursed in a look of controlled rage. "Look—I uh—I know you're still angry with me, and I get that. I take full responsibility for everything that got us to this point, but we can't keep going like this, Anna."

"Annabeth."

Her correction seemed to anger him even more. "Damn it! I'm not talking to some fictional version of you. I'm talking to *you*. I love *you*, Anna. Why can't you see that?"

And, just like that, he was kissing her.

No, this was definitely not okay. She shoved him away with her one good arm. "Marc," she said using his given name for the first time in weeks. "If you loved me, then you wouldn't have slept with that bitch at the bar."

His face fell. For a second she thought he might even start to cry.

"It was a mistake, and I can't be any sorrier for it than I already am."

Tears started to spill down her cheeks.

I'm drunk and crying like a fucking idiot.

She took a deep breath in a last ditch attempt to rein in her emotions before they came spilling out for all of downtown Austin to see.

"I'm the one who's sorry. Sorry that I thought I could put all that aside to do this, but I was wrong. I can't let it go, and I don't know that I ever will."

Having said all she needed to say, she gave him one last glare before taking off down the sidewalk—in a hurry to get away from him. At that moment the inner rage she'd kept locked away inside had been let loose. She wanted to smash something. Before now, she had kept her hurt feelings in check, but now it all came crashing down, suffocating her.

"Anna, wait!"

Her eyes darted around for a cab, but there was none in sight. She knew she was too drunk to even try to drive.

I should check into a hotel. There has to be one nearby.

She couldn't go home, that was for sure. There was a bus on the other side of the street. She quickly dodged the incoming traffic to the other side.

"C'mon, Anna. Please stop." Marcus was just a

few yards behind her.

"Go away, Marcus! I don't want to see you ever again!"

She couldn't hold it back any longer. The past few weeks playing the perfect little couple weighed too heavily on her. A small crowd had stopped to watch as their sad drama unfolded, but she was past the point of caring.

Annabeth turned to see Marcus start to cross the street.

Why won't he just leave me alone!

He had gotten halfway across when it happened. The black sedan had turned onto 6th Street from Trinity. The driver had gunned it. Marcus hadn't stood a chance of getting out of the way.

The screech and sickening thud of his head connecting with the windshield would be etched in her mind for the rest of her life.

After that everything happened in slow motion, just like it did in the movies.

"Noooo!" Her piercing scream filled her ears.

A pool of blood began to form around his head like a halo.

The car quickly flew into reverse as it backed into the side street doing a wide U-turn on the narrow road, just missing taking out a few pedestrians along the way.

Annabeth watched in horror as it sped away.

The sound of everything around her had become muffled and far away like she was hearing it from under water.

Her wobbly legs carried her over to him before they gave out and she sank down onto her knees beside his body. She barely noticed the gravel that dug into her knees.

There was so much blood.

Is he dead? He can't die. Not like this. Not when the last thing I said was... No.

His eyes were closed and his body was twisted in an unnatural way but his chest still rose up and down.

He's alive. Thank God.

"I'm calling the police!" yelled someone from the crowd. "It didn't have a license plate... it was black... four door... hurry!"

Her stomach churned as she touched his bent arm. It looked broken just like the rest of him. She watched in horror as his breathing became shallow. The sirens were getting closer. "Marc...hold on."

Please, hold on.

CHAPTER 20

VI

IN the distance Vi could hear the sound of the train that ran along the back side of their subdivision. The familiar *clickety-clack* and whistle blowing soothed her for the moment. In the back of her mind, a little voice told her she needed to talk to someone before she descended so far into the darkness she couldn't find her way back out again.

Ricky. The loss of him left a hollow place inside her that ached like a phantom limb.

When her parents died there had been no room for her to process her grief. So every day she carried it around with her. Each year since their passing, the weight of her sadness got heavier and heavier. She felt the fissures in her sanity widening. The dam of emotions was fixing to burst.

A northern gust of wind carried with it a new sound—crying. It was coming from the direction of the Kings' backyard.

Vi shoved her keys into her purse and went to investigate the crying like some superhero for sadness. The wooden gate that shut off the yards hung ajar. Not bothering to knock, Vi tugged the gate open and trespassed yet again onto the Kings' property.

Her stomach bottomed out at the sight of Annabeth sobbing. The light from the security lamps made her hair look almost crimson.

Vi took a deep breath, her senses assaulted by a strong metallic odor. As she got closer she saw the origins of the smell—blood. Annabeth was covered in it.

Vi rested her hand on Annabeth's shoulder and stooped down to be at her eye level.

"Annabeth, you're covered in blood! What happened? Are you hurt?"

Her head rose slowly from the nest of her bent arm. There were wide streaks of red across her cheek and her eyes were puffy.

What the hell happened?

Vi stumbled back a step. Her breath quickened and her mouth wet dry.

"Annabeth?" A knot of fear gripped Vi from deep within her belly. Maybe Brooke had been right to be wary of the new neighbors.

"Annabeth, please...you're scaring me."

"He... I... we had a fight." Annabeth's flat affect and robotic tone did nothing to ease Vi's unrest.

She twisted her hands together as she debated whether to flee and call the cops. Had Marcus done this to her? He had seemed like such a nice man, but weren't all batterers charming? No one ever really knows what goes on behind their neighbors' closed doors.

"Did Marcus hurt you?"

"What? No!" Annabeth said, almost shouting. Vi let out a relieved sigh. Annabeth reached for a bottle of scotch that rested on the table in front of her. She took a good long drink before she turned back to Vi, nodding with a sullen expression.

"It's my fault. If he dies..." Annabeth began sobbing again.

Vi's heart hammered in her chest. "What?"

Panic began to set in.

Maybe I need to just learn to mind my own business. Hoe your own row, Mama used to say.

Even if she wanted to bolt, she was frozen in place. She just couldn't leave her alone—not like this. So she reached for the lawn chair behind her and sat down across from her.

Annabeth twisted her body toward Vi. The security lamp above them spotlighted the sling that held Annabeth's splinted arm in place.

"What happened to your arm?"

Annabeth looked down at her wrapped wrist like she had forgotten all about it. "I was mugged."

Vi leaned closer in to make sure she had heard correctly. "Wait...you were mugged?"

I'm so confused. What the hell happened tonight?

Annabeth took another drink of her scotch. "After my last class, I was walking alone. So stupid. I know, I know. I should have had someone walk with me...so stupid."

Vi took a sharp breath. "Are you all right? Is it broken?"

Annabeth took another drink before she shook her head no.

Vi sighed. Her patience was beginning to grow thin. As if her life wasn't complicated enough, she has to come home to a barely coherent neighbor crying and covered in blood. Real life wasn't supposed to play out like some Lifetime Movie.

"Okay, so let me get this straight. You were mugged after class tonight and then what happened?"

"Fin hit the bastard over the head with a brick. I don't even know where it came from. If he hadn't come when he did—" She interrupted herself with two successful hiccups.

Vi grabbed her drunken neighbor by the chin and looked her in the eye, just like she did with Joy when she needed her attention. "What happened after that?"

She pouted as she looked at the almost empty bottle. "Marcus came all the way downtown to fight—took a hundred dollar cab ride to get there." Annabeth stared at the amber liquid at the bottom the bottle. "He got all pissy, like he always does—thinking he owns me. I don't owe him a thing. Especially after what he did."

"What did he do?" Vi asked.

Annabeth started to sob again. "He fucked the damn bartender. He says he was drunk...I don't know. We'd been fighting about the case and the law suit all night and he just stormed off to the bar." Annabeth downed the rest of the bottle and grimaced. "He came home hungover and sorry."

Annabeth wiped at the tears that fell in earnest. "A fucking bartender. He didn't even know her name. But I do. *Beth*. Beth the Bitch."

Before Vi could say a word Annabeth started up again. "When we took this job, and had to pick new names.... You should have seen his face when I picked Annabeth. I didn't want him to forget for a minute what he had done to me."

Vi shook her head in confusion. "I don't understand, Annabeth. What job?"

Annabeth paused as if she had just then caught up with processing the words she had spoken. A look of dread fell across her tearstained features as she began to tremble. The woman before her was a stark contrast to the one who had introduced herself to Vi just a week and half ago. Had it really only been a little over a week?

Annabeth sighed, "Jesus, I'm a total fuck-up."

Vi clasped her hands together to keep herself from shaking her neighbor senseless. Brooke had been spot on. These people had some seriously messed up stuff going on. Maybe if she could calm herself then Annabeth would calm down as well. Then maybe they could get somewhere.

After taking in another cleansing breath she reached out for Annabeth's hand and gave it a reassuring squeeze. She couldn't imagine what it would be like to have Ricky cheat on her.

"Annab—"

"I can't do this anymore, Vi. I mean—I thought leaving the Bureau would make things better. I thought…I don't know." Annabeth hiccupped and swallowed hard. For a second Vi thought she might throw up right then and there.

"Sometimes it helps to talk. Have you talked to anyone about what you've been going through?"

Annabeth scrunched up her nose. "Like a shrink? No!"

Vi smiled and let out a tired sigh. "Annabeth, you can talk to me. I want you to know that I'm here for you. You don't have to go through all of this alone. And anything we talk about stays here. I'm bound by my code of ethics to keep all of this confidential."

Annabeth seemed to weigh her offer. After a long pause she wet her lips. "Call me Anna."

Vi relaxed into the chair, mirroring Annabeth's posture. She let the silence fall between them. A simple therapeutic trick she knew that worked to draw out reluctant clients like Anna. It of course worked like a charm.

"When I joined the Bureau I thought I would make a difference. Make the world a better place." Anna fiddled with the ring she wore on her left hand—her wedding band.

"The FBI?" Vi leaned in closer to Anna.

Annabeth met her eye and paused as if she was debating whether or not to go any further. Vi backed off and honed in on the distant sound of the cars on the main highway. The stillness of the night was always a comfort to her. It seemed that her neighbor, however, found no comfort in anything except maybe the liquor she had downed. Annabeth eyed the nearly empty bottle—as if reading Vi's mind—but didn't reach for it. Instead she raised her sleepy looking eyes and met Vi's gaze head on.

"I was with the FBI a couple of years, but the FBI and I decided it was a bad fit for me, for both of us. So we left."

"We?"

Annabeth nodded. "Marc…I shouldn't be telling you any of this. This is crazy." Annabeth pushed off the table like she was going to get up, but Vi reached out to stop her.

"Annabeth, you don't have to talk to me, but you really should talk to someone."

That seemed to work, as Annabeth stayed seated. "You can't tell anyone, Vi. This isn't just some tidbit of gossip that you can run and tell Jesse."

Vi bit her lip and nodded. "No one has to know any of this—least of all Jesse."

Annabeth took a shaky breath. "Okay..." A shiver rippled through her body. "Everything's been a lie, Vi. I'm not married and Marc and I didn't move to Herald Springs just so I could go back to school. I'm a P.I.—a lousy one at that."

Of all the things Anna could have said, that was not at all what she had expected. Though it was a relief, considering the myriad of things she *could* have said. Suddenly the information that she and Brooke had found in the Kings' house made perfect sense. The files of the girls must be related to the case they were working on.

Vi didn't move, afraid to scare her off. "Annabeth, what happened with Marcus tonight?"

Annabeth choked on a sob and looked away from Vi as a fresh set of tears slid down her cheeks.

Vi pulled a tissue out of her purse and handed it to her.

"Thanks." She dabbed at her blotchy face and looked dismayed when she pulled the tissue away and saw blood.

"Anna...Where is Marc now?"

"The hospital," she said, choking on the words. "We were fighting. And I'm just so tired of having the same fight over and over again. You know?"

Anna twisted the balled up tissue with her good hand and bit her lip. When Vi didn't respond, she continued. Her clear, resolute tone barely disguised the underlying anger that was simmering just beneath the surface.

"So I walked away. I didn't think he would follow me. The car... the doctor said there was a lot of swelling and they had to put him in a coma. They don't know if he will make it."

"Jesus," Vi said as she crossed herself. "He was hit by a car?"

"The last words I said to him were that I never wanted to see him again." Her body shook.

Vi hugged Annabeth hard and prayed. As the sobs began to subside she gave her a tight squeeze. "Let's get you cleaned up, okay?"

Annabeth wiped at her face with the wrecked tissue. "Okay."

Her body buzzed with the information she had been given. One thing she knew for certain was that Brooke couldn't know the truth about Annabeth. She would just make it worse. Even if she didn't mean to.

Vi had never lied to her best friend before, but it couldn't be helped. Too much was already at stake.

CHAPTER 21

BROOKE

IT was already Tuesday, and the gala would be here on Friday. Even though there was zero time to spare, Brooke sat on her favorite wingback chair, her legs pulled up into her chest and her iPad balanced on her knees. She held a giant mug of tea between both hands, letting the steam warm her face. Normally she'd be dying from the heat this time of year, but all the extra heat seemed to bring her comfort in a way little else could these days.

Well, little else except for the afghan she'd accidentally stolen from the Abrahamsons the night before. Smiling to herself, she hit refresh on her browser and saw a new article from Jesse pop into the feed.

Attempted Assassination of Herald Springs's Newest Resident, the headline read.

Brooke nearly dropped the mug from her hands in shock. Had something happened to Annabeth last night?

Before she could give it another thought, her phone buzzed with a text message, forcing her to tear her eyes away from the stock image photo of a car crashed into a tree.

> *Auntie B, I'm heeeeeere! When can we get together?*

Ligia, her goddaughter, had just moved from her boarding school in New York to a residency dorm at the university, and Brooke had promised to look after her. As much as she loved her goddaughter, she was duly motivated by the desire to make Ligia's mother Cinthia proud of her. After all, Cinthia was the mother Brooke wished she would have had. Back in high school, she'd sponsored Brooke when she'd done a study abroad—anything to get away from her mother and their humdrum life together.

And Brooke had stayed close with Cinthia even after the year was up, especially since she lived the exact life Brooke aspired to, what with her high end fashion boutique and modeling career on the side. She'd even helped Brooke get started in the industry herself, back in the day.

Ugh. She really needed to text Ligia back, but the sensational headline beckoned her. She needed to know what had happened and to whom...

Okay, so maybe my headline is a little sensational.

Brooke held back a laugh as she read over Jesse's opening sentence. They always had seen things the same way.

After all, what happened was an accident— at least that's what everyone thinks so far— but, regardless, our newest neighbor was plowed into by a hit-and-run driver and is in the ICU at Brackenridge Hospital. Yes, I'm talking about Marcus King, the tall drink of water that moved into town less than two weeks ago with his wife Annabeth in tow.

When asked to comment, his wife was, understandably, quite hysterical and perhaps a bit too drunk to say anything of meaning either. Still, who could blame her, right? I mean her husband is in a coma for chrissake!

Vi Hernandez, who had spoken to Mrs. King earlier that night, said...

Oh my gosh, she had just seen Marcus that same afternoon. He'd been strong, alert, and—yeah—pretty damn hot, and now he was at death's doorstep? A sudden sadness clawed at her insides.

Poor Annabeth!

Not only was her husband laid up in intensive care, but having to drive back and forth to the Austin hospital every day would certainly take its toll. Nobody should have to commute an hour a day in crazy Austin traffic to look after a loved one.

She chewed on her thumbnail, disturbing her manicure in the process. Herald Springs had recently built a state-of-the-art hospital that would be perfect for Marcus to convalesce in. It was only ten minutes away from the subdivision.

A plan began to form in her mind.

If it had been Brian...

No, she refused to think it. Sure, Brian had his rough spots, but at the end of the day she loved him. If nothing else, Marcus's accident definitely put that into perspective for her.

The grandfather clock in the next room chimed, announcing that the morning was officially half through. Brooke had so much to do for the gala, but zero energy to do it. She'd allowed herself to sleep an extra three hours last night, hoping it would rid her of whatever virus had taken over her normally healthy body, but she felt even more tired today, if that was possible.

I need to go take care of this Marcus business. It's the least I can do.

Even though she actively despised Annabeth and she didn't really know Marcus from Adam, she wanted to help. His life sucked enough already, what with getting hit by a car *and* being hitched to Annabeth. Yuck.

Then there was her whole belief that you should keep your friends close and your frenemies closer. How could she continue to dig up dirt on Annabeth if the chick was never around?

Plus, it would be fun to make the staff at Brackenridge jump a little. It had been a while since she'd exerted her influence over the board. High time. Perhaps the whole thing could help rid her of her funk, get her back to work.

She glanced down at Jesse's photo in the sidebar of his blog, taking comfort from his familiar crooked smile and twinkling eyes. How had he even had time to break this story last night after taking care of first Brooke and then Heather? The man never ran out of steam, and she guessed that, between his girls and his thriving blog, he probably didn't sleep anywhere near as much as she did—especially those eleven hours she'd taken last night.

If only she could bottle his Jesse-ness and keep some for herself and spritz at will, she'd have been done with re-planning the gala before that fire had even broken out at the Gables.

She sighed and shrugged into her jacket, then wrapped a pashmina around her neck for added warmth.

"C'mon, Miss Tiara," she called. "Marcus could use your furry little kisses to help him feel better. Yes, he could." She scooped up the pom into her arms, and together they headed for the hospital.

* * *

THE administrative staff at Brackenridge Hospital were delighted to see their favorite therapy animal, scratching Tiara behind the ears, cooing, and offering the miniature doggie biscuits they kept on hand for visits like this.

"Can you keep her with you for a few minutes?" Brooke asked a forty-something woman in magenta scrubs. The ID card that hung from her shirt pocket read *Rayne*. "I have to go see a friend. I won't be long though."

"Of course, Mrs. Fischer. It's time we two get to know each other," she answered in a baby voice and set Tiara on the floor of the small office area behind the glass admission windows.

Once she was certain her fur baby would be fine, Brooke hurried down the hall toward the intensive care unit. It was strange not to hear the *click-clacking* of her heels as she walked, but then again Brooke just hadn't felt up to heels that morning. Instead, she'd laced up her running shoes for the impromptu visit to the hospital. She kept an eye out for Annabeth's shock of fiery red curls as she paced up and down the hallways, but her neighbor was nowhere to be found.

Brooke stopped a woman with a bouncing ponytail before she could escape through the double doors and into another wing of the hospital.

"Excuse me? Doctor?"

"Nurse, actually." She smiled, showing off all her teeth like an over carved jack-o-lantern. "How can I help you?"

"I'm looking for my neighbor, Marcus King."

She bobbed her head. "Of course, of course, such a terrible thing to... Oh, you don't need any of that doom and gloom from me, I'm sure you're worried enough as it is."

"I don't mean to be rude," Brooke said, and for once it was actually true. "But I'm in a bit of a hurry. Where can I find him?"

"You're in luck. Mr. King stabilized last night and is now in room 305 just down the hall and to the left. Can't miss it."

Brooke thanked the chatty nurse, then power walked in the direction she had pointed.

Why am I in such a hurry?

She didn't have an answer for that question, but she knew it would all make sense once she'd had a chance to see Marcus.

A few steps later, she found his room just where the nurse had said it would be. Still no sign of Annabeth. Where was she?

If it had been Brian, I wouldn't leave his side.

Brooke took a deep breath and tiptoed in, as if being careful not to wake Marcus from his coma. This trip was so different from those she'd made with Tiara on therapy animal visits, and from the times she met with the board to plan this or that event. This visit felt sacred somehow.

Marcus lay before her, enshrined in a chaotic mismatch of tubes, wires, and machines. He seemed so small, lying beneath the simple white covers as the heart monitor blipped steadily in the background.

She barely knew the man, yet somehow she felt so deeply connected to him in that moment. All those tubes and wires kept Marcus alive yet also ensnared him within their clutches.

Brooke felt that way about everything in her life—her business, her marriage, her friendships. They all kept her going but also held her down. How could that be possible when she herself was always in charge?

"Oh, good. You found him." The same nurse from earlier peeked into the room, smiled, then disappeared.

Brooke shifted her weight from foot to foot wondering what to do next.

This is ridiculous. Maybe I should just leave.

But then the nurse was back again with that same saccharine smile that somehow made Brooke's teeth hurt.

"They say it helps if you talk as if nothing were wrong. He can hear you, you know?"

"Thanks," Brooke mumbled and turned from the door. "Oh, and excuse me?"

"What can I do for you?" the nurse returned with an eager look on her face, not unlike a dog waiting for its favorite ball to be hurled across the backyard.

"I need to speak with Dr. Vance. Could you send for him please? Tell him Mrs. Fischer is waiting."

"Sure thing. And, seriously, talk to him, okay?"

She listened as the squeak of the nurse's Keds made their way back down the hall, leaving her and Marcus alone in the sterile white room.

"You want me to talk, huh?" Brooke took a step closer, then before she could change her mind, took a seat next to Marcus on the edge of his bed. "Well, I wanted to talk to Annabeth, but since she's not here, I'll have to tell this to you instead. I guess I should just come out and say it, right? Say that I'm sorry, because it's true. I really am. I'm sorry I couldn't even give you and Annabeth a chance, that I immediately jumped to spying on you, assuming that something had to be wrong. Sorry for breaking into your house, too. That was a little over the top, even for me."

She laughed, batting away any lingering doubts. She felt bad enough as it was without flat-out ignoring this wake up call. Was Marcus's accident meant to be a sign that she needed to slow down, to take time to appreciate what she had rather than worry so much about possibly losing it?

Marcus's face remained smooth and expressionless, yet somehow Brooke felt heard.

She continued, "That's how I am. You'll figure it out soon enough. I never feel at home in my own life, so I have to take over others' whenever I can. I'm sorry about that too, but it's just not something I can control. Which is funny really, because control is the only thing that makes me feel as if my life isn't one colossal joke. But I guess I shouldn't complain, seeing as you can't even breathe without this weird machine to help you, and..."

Things were getting too serious. Whether or not Marcus could hear her words, she could and she was embarrassed by them.

Deep breath. Take it back to normal.

She forced a laugh and stood up, smoothing the wrinkles from her dress. "God, Marcus, all that machinery really does clash with that gown they have you in. Maybe it's a good thing you're not awake to see it."

Dr. Vance breezed into the room and gave Brooke a quick peck on the cheek. "Ahh, Mrs. Fischer, so good of you to stop in. Is this man..." He checked his chart. "Marcus, a friend of yours?"

"Yes, and a good one, so you better take great care of him, you hear?"

"Of course." He smiled at Brooke then toward Marcus's still body.

"And you can start by transferring him to Herald Springs Memorial just as soon as he's stable. His wife shouldn't have to drive back and forth an hour each day to visit her husband."

"That's easier said than done at this point. He just stabilized this morning. Things are looking very positive for Mr. Ki—"

"Then what are you waiting for?" She didn't wait for him to answer. The more uncomfortable she could make people, the quicker they would meet her demands. "I expect him to be set up at Herald Springs Memorial by dinner time. Got it?"

"We'll do our best, but—"

"But nothing. Not unless you want the Junior League to hear about this. I'm sure they won't be so keen on supporting your next Fun Run if they find out that you were unwilling to take care of this poor man in the manner he deserves. Don't make an enemy of me. That's one regret you'll never be able to live down."

The doctor nodded and drew a stray mark on his chart. "We'll arrange for it, Mrs. Fischer. Is there anything else?" he asked between gritted teeth.

Her mission a success, Brooke smoothed her face into a smile and returned her voice to its usual chipper tone. "That will be all, thank you. Oh, would you just look at the time? I better get going. Toodles." She left the room with a quick wave toward Marcus then hurried down the hall with a renewed sense of purpose.

Even if she couldn't fix her own life, she could still influence those of others. Regardless of their quirks, she'd done something nice for the Kings, something only she could accomplish, and it gave her the burst of confidence she needed to move forward. She *could* troubleshoot all that had gone wrong with the fundraiser; she *could* make this party one the town would never forget. And, at least for now, these things would have to be enough.

CHAPTER 22

ANNABETH

ANNABETH awoke early the next morning to an unfamiliar snoring sound.

What the fuck? Did I go home with someone?

Whistle—snort—blow.

As she rolled in the direction of the sound, she made out a limp body flung across the overstuffed chair beside her bed. After three hard blinks, the person's face came into focus.

Vi. Why is she in...?

Oh. Marcus.

Just like that, the events of the night before came crashing over her like a tidal wave. She could hear the sickening thud of Marcus's skull coming into contact with the car's windshield, could see the halo of blood forming around his head when he fell onto the asphalt—the violent scene now burned into her long-term memory.

An acidic mix of guilt and anger rolled around in her gut making her feel nauseous...or maybe that was just the cocktail of booze and pills she had ingested. The strangely gratifying pairing—scotch mixed with the Vicodin the doctor had prescribed for her arm—thundered through her veins, leaving her wasted and hungover at the same time.

I should be with him. I deserve all this pain and more.

Despite the crushing guilt, she knew she wouldn't go to Marcus. The thought of seeing him hooked up to machines, a ventilator breathing for him, was far more than she could handle now.

Besides, he wouldn't want her there anyway. He'd want her working the case, not worrying over him. They had already lost too much ground as it was.

I need to prove to him—hell, myself—that I can handle this case. If we fail again I'm going to end up mopping floors for a living.

As it was, this job was one thing that she could have some control over, and she couldn't afford to fail at that. Not when it was all she had left. Especially if Marcus...

Vi choked and sputtered as she began to wake up. Her plump lips formed a tight bow, much like they did when she was awake and on the listening end of a conversation, much like they'd been the previous night.

Fuck...what all did I tell her?

Vi stretched and yawned. A look of concern washed over her. "Hey, Anna. How are you feeling? I was worried about you last night." Her eyes shot toward the floor and she frowned. "You got pretty sick."

She could taste the remnants of this truth, but had no memory of it. Then it clicked in her mind.

Did she just call me Anna?

Her heartbeat quickened, her chest prickled with fear. "Vi, what... What all did I tell you last night?"

Annabeth pinched the bridge of her nose and prayed that she had not messed everything up for them.

I am so fucking stupid.

Vi reached over and took one of Annabeth's hands into hers. "Your secrets are safe with me. I'm a counselor so the information you shared with me is completely confidential. I'd like to think I am your friend, too. I don't mean to be forward, but it seems like, with everything going on, that you might be needing a friend about now." She smiled a sweet Vi smile.

Annabeth felt the panic attack coming. She wiggled her fingers and took slow, calming breaths. "Anna, Anna, Anna." She repeated the familiar grounding technique under her breath.

Vi regarded her actions and she pointed to Annabeth's wiggling fingers. "How long have you been having panic attacks?"

She paused. Vi's choice of words and mannerisms were more of a counselor than a friend, but, hell, she *could* use both those things right about now. And so she went against her better instincts and decided to trust this woman just enough to reveal a few of her more closely kept secrets.

"Ten years."

"What you went through last night, with the mugging and what happened with Marcus, is a lot for any one person to handle all at once. Whatever you might be feeling or thinking is okay. I know you might not feel like it, but you are coping really well."

Annabeth let out a hearty laugh and dug her fingernails into the palm of her hand to keep from breaking down. "Oh, ya think so, huh?"

Vi's solemn nod spoke volumes.

Annabeth hated long silences and had been through enough therapy in her lifetime to recognize it as a drawing out technique, which irritated her. "I never should have told you all of that. I need to go. I'm sorry, I just...... can't right now."

She slid off the bed and looked around for her shoes. Despite her best efforts to hold herself in check she could feel hot tears burning the corners of her eyes.

Where are my fucking shoes?
"Your shoes are over there."

Annabeth's anger deflated when she snatched up her shoes. They had dried blood caked to the soles. Marcus's blood...... She sank down onto her haunches and felt the sobs rack her body.

Vi slid down onto the floor beside her.

Why can't she just leave me alone?

"Do you want me to drive you to the hospital so you can see him?" Her eyes filled with sympathy.

She shook her head. The last person she wanted to see right now was Marcus. She needed something to distract her. "No, I should be working. I can't afford to drop the ball here. Those poor girls are depending on me to save them."

"What kind of case are you working on? Maybe I can help? I worked as a Victims Services Coordinator for a few years with the Austin Police Department."

She'd tell her just enough to satisfy her curiosity. After that she'd keep her mouth shut for once.

"I'm investigating a sex-trafficking ring, but I really shouldn't be talking to you about this. Confidential or not, this is a breach in protocol. Just forget I ever mentioned it."

Vi's face turned chalk white and her jaw dropped. "Anna, I have some information that might be useful to you."

Annabeth tilted her head closer. Maybe one of the victims had come forward and sought shelter. That was just the kind of break that the case needed.

Maybe I won't end up as a fry girl, after all.

"Did someone come to your Center?"

Vi let out a small huff of air. "This is where *I* get caught up in confidentiality issues of my own." A look of shame washed over Vi's features. "Before I get into all that, there's something I need to tell you. I really want us to be friends, and I can't start this friendship with a lie."

Please be something stupid. I don't have the energy for anything else.

"What?"

"As you probably already know, Brooke has been suspicious of y'all from the beginning. She...uh...well, she got the bright idea to break into your home and snoop around. And I kind of went with her."

What the fuck?

She would have expected something like that from Brooke, but Vi? Evidently that friend stuff was just a bunch of B.S. The people in this town were batshit crazy.

We should have just lived on campus and avoided all this pointless drama.

"I'm so sorry, Anna. I didn't want to do it, but I knew she would go for it with or without me. I thought maybe, if I went along, I could keep her from doing something really stupid—"

Was she really that delusional?

That's it, I'm done. These crazy women deserve each other. I want nothing to do with either of them.

"I think you should go now." She jumped up from the floor and headed for the door.

Vi stood and followed close behind her. "I'm so sorry!"

She'd heard enough. She held open the front door and avoided Vi's eyes. To her credit, her so-called friend said nothing more as she walked out the door.

Annabeth slammed the door with a satisfying thud. The satisfaction though soon turned to disgust as she sidestepped a puddle of her own vomit from the night before.

Jesus! How much did I drink?

A text buzzed her pants pocket. Her screen lit up with Fernando's name and number.

> *Hope you are doing okay this morning. I heard about your roommate getting hit by a car. That's crazy! I'm here if ya need me.*

How had he heard about Marcus?

I don't have time for this. I need to meet with Amy.

The more Annabeth looked over Marcus's notes the more she agreed with his assessment that Amy was a perfect target. Her contact at the Bureau hadn't called in a few days. Hopefully she could buy some time before she had to report back to him again.

Annabeth flipped through her calendar app but then remembered she hadn't gotten around to adding the meeting to her phone last night. She shot the girl a quick text asking the where and when before jumping in the shower.

Despite her efforts to push them aside, angry thoughts and questions bubbled to the surface of her overworked mind. What had they found when they were snooping? What all did Brooke know? Did they see Marcus's office? All those notes about the girls. A little knowledge was a dangerous thing...

Annabeth shook her head.

This isn't an episode of Desperate Housewives for fuck's sake. This is my life, my life.

She'd already been demoted to PI. What was next? Getting assigned bozo work like doing background checks or investigating fertilizer permits? She'd rather die than be humiliated like that—again!

The phone rang in the other room, and she shut off the water to rush for it but stopped short when she realized the other caller was probably just her nosy neighbor.

The nerve of her calling me!

Anger radiated off of her in rolling waves.

Amy hadn't texted back while Annabeth had been in the shower, either. No bother, she didn't have any classes on Tuesday but could go to campus anyway and just drop the paper at Amy's dorm room. She had been pretty drunk the night before, too. Maybe she was just sleeping it off.

She might have forgotten that we were meeting.

Annabeth threw on a pair of shorts and a threadbare Detroit Tigers T-shirt that she loved. Five minutes later with her wet hair in a tight bun, she was out the door and on the road.

* * *

ANNABETH walked through the bustling campus in a daze. No one really knew her, which meant she might as well have been invisible. No one in her department even said hello to her as she made her way in and out of the building.

Fuck them! Pretentious bastards.

The gust of air from the opening door blew back a putrid smell.

Oh God, that's me.

Despite the shower she could still smell the booze oozing out her pores.

Well that's a sure fire way to ensure no one bothers me—smell like a bum. Real professional, Anna! A drunk P.I.—how cliché can I get?

She was so far removed from the young, promising agent she had been when she entered the

Bureau five years ago. Now she was little more than a waste of a human being.

She tried not to focus on the failure in Detroit and instead chose to focus on the fact that it had led them to Texas, where the group had their headquarters.

This was their last hope. If the ring got wind of their investigation, they might change their system, their location, whatever it took to evade capture. They had been paid a lot of money to come through and failure just wasn't an option.

Over-caffeinated and wound up, she stalked across campus to the co-ed hall that Amy lived in. Because of Marcus's research she knew the young girl lived on the third floor, so she quickly followed behind a student entering the building. Security sure sucked around here.

Once there, she grabbed the first student she saw—a petite Asian girl with thick glasses and long dark hair wrapped in a messy bun. "Can you tell me where Amy Rangel's room is?"

The girl's eyes narrowed. "I'm her roommate. Why?"

Annabeth pulled out the essay and handed it to her. "I'm her teacher and wanted to give her this."

The girl gave her a look like she didn't quite buy her story, but grabbed the essay anyway.

"Thanks. We were supposed to meet up this morning but I haven't heard from her."

The roommate shifted her weight from one foot to the other. "She's not here. She never made it home last night. Must have stayed over with her new guy friend."

Fin? Did she end up with Fin?

Annabeth's heart beat painfully against her breastbone. "Do you know what dorm he's in?"

"No, he's older. Your age maybe. Look, I gotta go. I'm already late for class. I'll give this to her when I see her."

Annabeth was practically paralyzed by the implications. All she could do was nod like some dummy. Did she and Fin hook up? Or... Shit, what if *they* had gotten to her already? Even when she doubted every other aspect of her life, she'd always been confident in her abilities as an investigator—failing wasn't allowed.

Ever since Marcus had slept with Beth, the bartender, everything had gone to shit. She had been stupid to trust him—let him in. Now once more she'd allowed herself to lose focus on what was really important—saving the girls. If she'd been paying attention to the girl instead of her own problems, this wouldn't have happened.

It's like the incident all over again.

Annabeth tried to push all of that out of her mind as she turned and made her way out of the building. She thought back to the night before and tried to home in on any other details she knew about the girl.

Wait! What if...

Annabeth's mind pinged on a memory of a story she had read about the rise in sexual assaults for women using those paid driver services. Just like the one Fernando had called to take Amy home. What better way to lure unsuspecting college girls into a car? They could have dozens of rotating drivers picking up the girls.

I need to tell Marcus!

She stopped herself just before she pressed send.

Marcus can't help me...I'm on my own.

The thought sent a chill down her spine. Alone. The one word echoed in her mind. She straightened her spine. Well, at least she wouldn't have him distracting her from the task at hand. She pushed down the ache she felt in her chest, compartmentalizing her unspent emotions. A familiar numbness settled inside her. Ever onward.

Annabeth shot off a quick text message to Fin asking him the name of the driving service he had used. She didn't tell him that Amy was missing. She would keep that information to herself. Just as she was jamming her phone back into her pocket, it buzzed with an incoming text message. But instead of Fin it was from Brooke.

I had Marcus moved to Herald Springs Memorial. No need to thank me. It's the least I could do. We are doing event set-up tomorrow, but I understand if you can't make it. I'm sure we can find someone to fill in for you. Ta!

Annabeth felt her face get hot.
What the fuck! Are you kidding me?
The people of Herald Springs had gotten on her very last nerve.

CHAPTER 23

VI

AFTER Vi fought with Annabeth she went straight to church for Tuesday morning Mass and Confession. She was grateful for the partition that saved her from seeing the look of disappointment on the priest's face as she told him about her breaking into her neighbor's home. Five "Our Fathers" and two "Hail Marys" later, she still felt miserable. She wouldn't feel better until Annabeth forgave her, and maybe not even then.

She spent the rest of the day at the shelter, but she was too distracted to get much done. The fight with Annabeth weighed heavily on her. When she got home she did the only thing she could think to do—cook. Thankfully, no calls came in through the hotline. By two a.m. she had a week's worth of meals packaged up and ready to deliver to the Kings. It would mean that Vi had to eat peanut butter and jelly sandwiches for a week, but if it helped repair her relationship with Annabeth, then it would be worth it.

Anna was her first real new friend in years.

Sure, she had Brooke and Jesse, but they were always so wrapped up in their own drama that she often felt invisible in their company. Anna had been such a comfort at the rodeo when she broke things off with Ricky. She hadn't made it all about her like Brooke would have done, or blown it off like it was nothing in true Jesse fashion. She had just listened and offered sympathies. Yes, Anna was the kind of friend she so desperately needed.

Bright and early the next morning, she knocked on Annabeth's backdoor, praying she'd hear her out. No one answered, and the house was pitch black. The car wasn't in the drive, either. Not home.

Of course, she's probably at the hospital with Marcus. Poor thing.

Just as she turned around to go home, Vi remembered that even though it was Wednesday—her day off—she was supposed to help Brooke out that morning. Brooke had emailed all of the volunteers with a list of roles and responsibilities for the event.

I'm surprised she didn't make a PowerPoint presentation.

She didn't know why, but Brooke had been irritating her more and more lately.

Just like last year, she had been assigned to help with set-up. This year was extra challenging since they had moved the venue at the last minute to the Book Cellar. Life would be so much better when this stupid gala was over with. It wouldn't be so bad if it didn't take up so much of her time, especially since she was on call all week at the shelter.

Late hours taking care of victims and long hours each day getting the event ready was taking its toll on her—especially since Brooke assigned her the same boring task each year, pointing out bidders to the auctioneer.

No one ever trusts me to do anything that actually requires thought. A monkey could do this job!

She stopped just short of wondering if Brooke thought she was too stupid to help with anything important. After all, if Annabeth refused to forgive her, Brooke would still be the best friend she had, and, annoyed or not, she didn't need to ruin that.

Vi put away all of the food in her garage standing freezer and put a note on the Kings' door.

> *Dear Anna,*
> *I know this doesn't make up for what I did, but I put together some meals for you. I know you have a lot going on with your*

work and Marcus in the hospital. I'm hoping that this helps take something off your plate.

Sincerely,
Vi

She placed a quick call to the hospital only to find that Marcus had been transferred to Herald Springs Memorial. She made a note to herself to call the florist later and have a planter sent to his room.

She wished she could go visit with him, but between Brooke, Joy, the gala, and her work, that just wouldn't be possible.

Beep-beep-beep.

Vi's phone reminded her that she was scheduled to assist Brooke with event set-up. She had signed on for two full days, and today was just the beginning. Ugh. She really needed to learn to say no to things.

For a brief moment, she allowed herself the luxury to imagine what it would be like to have a partner, someone to help lighten her load. But she shook the thought away—scattering it into the wind and letting it blow away.

No sense going down that road. There was zero time in her schedule for a pity party. She snatched her keys and a bottle of water, then ran out the door. Always running...

THE morning sped by in a rush of activity. Brooke was in full form, which meant she had been shouting orders at everyone all morning.

"Vi, not there! I told you to put that table by the beam!"

To cope, Vi fantasized about putting the table tape around her bossy BFF's mouth. The thought made her giggle a little on the inside, but she instantly felt guilty for mentally turning on Brooke in her hour of need. She made a quick sign of the cross and asked the Virgin Mary for forgiveness for the umpteenth time that day. The poor Virgin was working overtime for her this week.

Brooke smacked a piece of paper down in front of her. "Just follow the CAD design! Damn it, this isn't rocket science, Vi. We have to get the tables set up today so that we can stay on schedule!"

Why does she have to be so mean?

Things had been tense between them ever since the Kings had moved in. She had always been bossy, but she had had never been mean, not like this. At least never to her supposed best friend. Vi looked away just in time to catch a shock of red bobbing toward her.

Sure enough, Annabeth had shuffled inside with her assignment sheet in her good hand. Her injured arm hung in a splint—it looked swollen. She wasn't using the sling. Vi's inner nurturer wanted to run to her and beg her forgiveness again, but Anna flashed her a look that said "stay away."

Brooke turned and charged toward her poor neighbor with a manic bravado that worried her. Something was wrong—and it wasn't just this whole gala mess. She was amped up to an eleven these days, which was frightening to witness. Brooke half-hugged Anna, who stiffened in Brooke's embrace. It was painful to watch.

"Oh good, you made it."

Annabeth nodded. Her eyes looked puffy, her face drawn like she hadn't gotten much sleep. Vi wondered how much rest she'd had since the night before.

Little Miss Queen B didn't seem to notice, which wasn't all that surprising.

"How's Marcus?" Brooke crooned, placing a hand on Anna's shoulder in what Vi assumed was meant to be a comforting gesture—though close contact with Brooke like that tended to unnerve even the most stoic of persons. "I was so sorry to hear what had happened to him. I can't even imagine what you must be going through. If that had been *my* husband, I would be a total mess." Her words ran into one another in an anxious way that was unlike her.

Vi had a fleeting thought that maybe Brooke was on anti-anxiety meds or perhaps she'd had one too many mimosas with her breakfast that morning.

Annabeth let out a tired sigh; Brooke had a way of wearing people out. She shifted her weight from one foot to another. "He's unchanged unfortunately. Um, yeah, about your having him moved—"

Brooke simply beamed, not even letting Annabeth finish her sentence. "Oh, no need to thank me. It was nothing!"

Annabeth squared her shoulders and a look of irritation flashed across her face. "I wasn't—"

Brooke flapped her hand as if to dismiss Annabeth. "Never you mind. Anyway, I am so glad you are here, because Violeta here is in desperate need of your help. Do you have the CAD design I attached in the email?"

She held up a crumpled paper. "Yeah, I have it. I can do this myself if you need Vi to work on something else."

Vi's heart sank.

But Brooke's face lit up like a Christmas tree. "Oh, aren't you the eager beaver? While I do love your enthusiasm, with that arm of yours, I highly doubt going solo would be such a good idea. It's on the schedule that you two are going to work together. That's not going to be a problem... Is it?" she asked with a quirk of her brow.

Annabeth grumbled under her breath, causing Vi's guilt to weigh like the whole of the earth on her shoulders.

She walked over to them with her head hung low. "Anna—"

Annabeth held up her bad hand to stop her, wincing from the pain of the sudden movement. "Don't. I'm just here to help out your sister and the rest of the residents. Let's just get this over with."

Vi bit her lip to keep from crying. Looking down, she nodded in passive agreement. And, despite the tension between them, they worked well together. They even finished their assigned tasks ahead of schedule.

Brooke beamed at their progress. "Well, look at my busy bees! Gold stars for both of you."

Annabeth checked her watch. "Do you need anything else? I really want to get back to the hospital this afternoon before I go back to the University tonight."

Brooke regarded her with a solemn look of understanding. "Of course, you do. You've been such a trooper helping us out as much as you have. Vi can do the rest, don't you worry. Right, Vi?"

She nodded. "Of course. Don't worry about it. I've got everything covered here."

"Good!" Brooke took off, yelling corrections to the team who was working on getting all of the sound equipment set up.

She used the moment to reach across and touch Annabeth's hand. "I really am sorry. I hope in time you can find it in your heart to forgive me."

Annabeth removed her hand from underneath hers and walked away without saying a word. Vi slumped down into one of the chairs and buried her face in her hands.

Hail Mary, full of grace. Our Lord is with you. Blessed are you among women, and blessed is the fruit of your womb, Jesus. Holy Mary, Mother of God, pray for us sinners, now and at the hour of...

"No time for dilly-dallying, Vi!" Brooke shouted from across the room.

She crossed herself and slid out of the chair. A pile of boxed up linen waited for her. She took a pair of box cutters out of Brooke's overly organized supply box. She'd even used a label maker to identify each tool. The girl sure did love her label makers—all three of them.

Vi couldn't help but chuckle as she sliced open the boxes of white linens that had arrived that morning from the cleaners. The lingering chemical smell of industrial laundering wafted up to her nose as she fluffed one out onto the table. She couldn't help but wonder how Brooke got the company to hand deliver them to the venue. Maybe she didn't want to know.

"I think the eighties part of this theme may be missing," the centerpiece volunteer whispered to her partner.

"You don't *actually* expect Brooke to go full on eighties, do you? That would be way too cheesy," the other volunteer responded with a smirk as they unboxed the centerpieces.

Everything had to be just so, she thought as she tugged at the corners of the linens that dressed the head table. The volunteers were right. Of course, Brooke didn't want it to be any old 80's theme. No, it had to be GLAM. Glitter was everywhere and the color scheme of silver and gold made it look more like an after party for a Hollywood awards show.

From the corner of her eye, she watched as Brooke ran the volunteers like a well-oiled machine. She was in her element bossing everyone around. The volunteers grumbled but they all gave their best, because they all knew how well Brooke rewarded all her volunteers—handsomely.

She found ways to cut and skimp on the event so that there was always enough left over in the budget for a volunteer blowout afterward, designer goodie bags and all. Everyone wanted to be a Volunteer Bee, which is what Brooke called her makeshift team. She even had a logo made up with a little buzzing bee.

Just as she was placing the last of the linens down, her phone rang.

Joy.

"Hi, Joy. What's up?"

"Vi, I'm hungry."

Vi looked up at the clock on the wall. One thirty.

Vi sat down with a sigh. She was kind of hungry, too. "Then eat something, Joy."

Joy grumbled. "I want a pizza, and you said to call if I wanted a pizza. Everyone got mad last time. Remember?"

The lack of sleep was starting to take its toll. She rubbed her eyes and pinched the bridge of her nose. "Joy, I'm busy. I can't make you a pizza right now. Don't you have to go to work this afternoon?"

Joy bagged groceries at the store by the home and normally loved her job. "Yes, but I'm really hungry."

"Go to work, Joy. Eat a snack there, or buy one of their pizza slices."

"I can't buy pizza!" her voice rose to a near shrill.

"Why not?"

"You need money to buy pizza!"

Her blood pressure began to rise. "Did you spend all of your allowance already?"

Her sister's voice rose higher. She was heading into a meltdown. "I'm HUNGRY, Vi!"

She checked her watch. "I'll meet you at the grocery store and get you a slice of pizza, okay?"

And grab myself some lunch, too.

Her sister's breath came out in short pants that bristled Vi to the core.

"Joy, I will get you pizza if you go to work."

"Okay," she said as she hung up the phone.

Vi waved to Brooke. "I'll be right back."

Brooke's eyebrows formed an angry "V" but she thankfully didn't say anything. She knew she needed to be more firm with Joy, but was just too tired to parent her these days.

Jesse came bounding up the walk just as she walked out the café entrance. "Hey, gorgeous. Why the frown?"

Vi hugged him hard, and, after a short pause, he hugged her back. "Hey, toots, what's wrong?" he asked.

She shook her head. "Oh, nothing. I've gotta run."

He gave her a tight squeeze before letting her go. "All right. Go off and save the day, Super Vi." He shot her a teasing smile.

Despite her grumpiness, she smiled back. "Later, Jess!"

He stood on the walk outside the café watching her get in her car and waving goodbye.

She *wished* she was a super hero. Instead, she felt more like the bumbling fool, failing at everything and disappointing everyone. At least the pizza was an easy fix. If only all of her problems were that simple to mend. The ache in her heart turned to a pang.

Maybe I'll have a heart attack. Then my problems wouldn't matter.

Joy... she reminded herself. She needed to be there for Joy.

CHAPTER 24

BROOKE

UGH, Brooke's week just kept getting worse and worse. Even Tiara's shiny fur seemed to have lost a bit of its luster as the result of the constant string of disappointments that kept coming their way. They both needed a pick-me-up in order to work well into the night, thus pulling this shit storm together with one beautiful, sparkling bow. Besides Brooke still wasn't feeling like herself, and the pom had noticed.

When Brooke settled the dog into her car basket, Tiara let out the most pathetic whimper and hid her tail between her legs.

"Aww, Ti-Ti......" She reached out to stroke the little dog's fur and noticed her manicure had chipped in several places. She'd even—*gasp*—taken to chewing on her French tips in moments of extreme and utter disaster. Well, that just wouldn't do.

"You want to go see KiKi?" She made her voice high-pitched and cheery to excite her melancholy pooch.

Immediately, Tiara's tail began to waggle and she let out an excited yip. Brooke laughed just thinking about how good a mani-pedi would feel.

Maybe she should schedule a spa day for all the girls in lieu of a larger volunteer after-party for the gala. A party after a party would be far too exhausting. Yes, a follow-up spa day would be just the ticket.

Brooke was able to multitask by making calls through her car's bluetooth as they drove to Nexus Nails in Austin. Sure, it was forty-five minutes away, but KiKi was a goddess when it came to nails, and Brooke happily worshiped at her ethyl acetate-scented alter. She'd have to schedule a primping session for everyone prior to the gala, too. Otherwise, she had no doubt both Vi and Annabeth would show up at the party looking like a couple of cheap Madonna wannabes—not at all what she had in mind for her spectacular event, or for the closest members of her entourage.

There wouldn't be time to get everyone out to KiKi's and back again before the gala's doors opened to their elite guest list, which meant… Trudy's. Brooke shuddered at the thought of the subpar stylists handling her locks, but sometimes sacrifices had to be made for the greater good. And at least she'd have KiKi for her mani-pedi. That had to count for something, right?

When they arrived at the salon, KiKi rushed over to greet Brooke and Tiara at the door.

"How is my favorite customer today?" she asked in a goochy-goo voice, bending down to pat Tiara on the head. "And, Brooke! So good to see you, yes."

She popped up and took Brooke's hand, studying the chips in her polish. "You waited too long this time to come see KiKi. You know better than this, Brooke." She clucked her tongue and led Brooke over to an open station.

"Tina, you take over here." She gestured toward the woman whose nails she'd been soaking when Brooke and Tiara had strolled in. "I need to catch up with Miss Brooke."

Brooke unleashed Tiara, who did a quick lap of the salon before settling at her mama's feet.

As KiKi sat down across from her, a whoosh of her exotic perfume wafted toward Brooke. "So... How are things?" Kiki began to file Brooke's nails as she always did at the start of their sessions. Nexus Nails and Beauty served a dual purpose in Brooke's life: beauty and therapy—the perfect winning combination and exactly what she needed this week.

"You wouldn't believe me if I told you." She let out a long sigh.

The nail tech smiled knowingly. "Try me."

Brooke unloaded all the anxieties of the past week—the sudden change of course for the gala, the charity's overbearing director, her strange new neighbors, even visiting Marcus in the hospital and making sure his transfer would go through. She shared everything—well, everything except for all the recent fights with Brian. That felt too private, too sacred.

KiKi listened, nodding frequently and interjecting occasionally to offer some bit of wisdom that was oddly reminiscent of what one might find inside a fortune cookie.

"You want pedicure, yes?" She asked once the final coat of paint had been applied to Brooke's stunning new metallic manicure.

"Of course."

"Then c'mon back. Want a glass of wine? Coffee?"

Brooke's stomach roiled at the suggestion. "No, I'm not feeling too well today, actually."

KiKi twisted her face into a pout. "Oh, you poor thing. I'll bring you some water. Water is good for the skin, keeps wrinkles away."

She scuttled to the back room and retrieved two cold bottles of Evian. She handed one to Brooke and poured the other into a shiny ceramic dish for Tiara.

"Now you sit back and relax. Let the chair do its job." She pushed a button and the massagers in the back of the chair roared to life. Another button set the foot spa bubbling.

Brooke leaned back into the soothing leather embrace of the chair and closed her eyes. It would be so easy to grab a quick, little nap.

But no. She still had so much work to do, and putting things off would only make it all that much worse. Right on cue, her phone buzzed on her lap. Kim. Of course. Brooke groaned and brought up the text. Just another couple days and this would all be over. She could last another couple days, right?

B, how about clam shooters?

Crazy. This woman was actually certifiable. Not only would clam shooters send them way over budget, but they also clashed horribly with the rest of the menu.

The door pushed open, bringing in some of the warm air from outside and, with it, one of her favorite people in the entire world. Tiara's too. The little dog pranced over to the tall, modelesque, and perfectly tanned teen at the door.

"Auntie Brooke!" the girl cried. "I had a feeling I might find you here."

"Ligia, you have no idea how glad I am to see you. I'm so sorry I didn't call sooner. Is everything going well at college? How's your roommate? Do you like your classes? Meet any cute guys?"

Ligia laughed, but her breasts didn't jiggle with the rest of her, despite being a DD-cup at least. "Too many questions, Auntie B. At least wait until I'm in the chair."

"KiKi, you remember my goddaughter, Ligia, don't you?"

"Ahh, yes, I remember. Liggy, you here for a mani-pedi like your aunt?"

"Please, and I'll also take a bottle of Evian."

Brooke waited for Ligia to get settled into the chair beside her before resuming her interrogation.

"Again I'm really sorry for not calling sooner. I feel like the worst aunt in the world."

"Auntie B, seriously, calm down. I've only been here for like a week, and I know you're busy with that gala thing. I'm on the guest list, right?"

"Of course, you can be my own personal plus-one."

"Won't Uncle Brian mind?"

Brooke studied the fresh polish on her nails. It would go perfectly with the sequined gown she'd purchased for the big event. "Okay, you can be my plus-plus-one. I'm the host, so I can get away with it, right? Enough about me though, do you like the school? How's living in Texas after all that time in New York?"

Ligia shrugged. "Same as anywhere else. I spent the summer in Rio with my folks."

"Oh, yes, I knew that already. Didn't I? So, dish, how was it?" Brooke felt younger and more alive just talking with Ligia. Though they weren't related by blood, she was the spitting image of Brooke—tall, leggy, gorgeous—but Ligia had the added advantage of a natural honey tan and very unnatural silicone enhancements—a graduation gift.

"OMG, I had the greatest time ever. Speaking of which, you owe us a trip, Mom has been asking after you, says you haven't been down in ages. Hey, maybe you can come for Carnival this year! Wouldn't that be fun?"

Ligia was right, it had been forever since she'd visited Cinthia in Brazil, despite the fact that the woman was one of her oldest friends. And even though Rio was a world away, Brooke always felt at home there. From the beaches to the lavish houses, the entire city buzzed with sexuality. With a bit of practice, it became easy to block out the shanty-filled ghettos, to focus only on the posh side of life there.

"I'll definitely put it on my calendar," Brooke said at last. *My private calendar.* Brian had been strangely controlling lately, and she didn't feel like getting into a fight over it. Besides, she was sure he'd be back to his normal, doting self soon enough... Wouldn't he?

Ligia shot her a proud smile then fished her own phone out of her Betsey Johnson bag. "Look at this," she said, waving the phone toward Brooke. "It's my website, at least the mobile version of it. Do you like my logo? I did it myself!"

"Whoa, whoa, whoa, what's all this?"

Ligia beamed. "I'm following in your stilettos, Auntie B, and I'm going into business for myself.

"Into business? But you're only a freshman! Shouldn't you—I don't know—take some time to do the whole college thing first?"

She laughed. "Yeah, right. I've gotta work fast if I'm going to become an international brand before my thirtieth birthday, right?"

Ligia still had a long way to go before thirty. Brooke on the other hand... She frowned, but luckily her companion was too caught up in her phone to notice.

"So, umm, what business are you starting?"

"Pageant consulting, duh." She put her hand on her hip and flashed a dazzling smile.

"Oh, Texas is the perfect place for that. Good thinking." Had Brooke been this enterprising at eighteen? It was hard to remember, but one thing she knew for sure was that Ligia could accomplish whatever she set her mind to and then some. She was like a younger, better Brooke. Brooke 2.0.

"Right? I get to be close to you and make my first million, it's like the perfect combo."

"So how do you—?" Brooke's phone buzzed, interrupting her mid-sentence. "Excuse me one sec."

Brooke, I need to know. Can we get the clam shooters or not?

"Ugh, this woman is driving me up the wall," Brooke growled, flashing her phone Ligia's way.

"Clam shooters? Ewww. That's so tacky."

"You're telling me." Her stomach roiled just thinking about it.

Another text came in.

Could you confirm the plan for the bar? What will we have in stock? Is two drink tickets too much? Maybe we could save money by cutting back to one. K?

Ligia's eyes grew wide. "Seriously, what's her problem?"

Brooke frowned. "Now you know why I've been too busy to be a good godmother this past week."

"Auntie B, seriously, let me help. We can handle this whackadoo together. Besides it will be good practice for me."

Brooke opened her mouth to argue, but pushed the words back down. Why not let Ligia help? She was so much more enthusiastic and—let's face it—

competent than Vi, Annabeth, and the rest of the crew she'd managed to pull together.

Brooke took a deep breath and nodded. Time to put her game face on, to push herself, to push everyone, to get this done and get it done right. Even if it meant ruffling a few feathers or allowing a few of Kim's terrible ideas to slip through. She could do this. After all, that's why she was the queen.

CHAPTER 25

ANNABETH

THE midday sun hung heavy in the cloudless sky. Annabeth had never imagined that she could despise the sun, but somehow she found herself missing the gray skies of the Midwest. Back in Michigan, the trees would be turning about now, but here in Texas fall still seemed a million years away.

Annabeth leaned against the Book Cellar's cool stone walls to catch a bit of shade. With a quick sweep of her thumb she checked her messages. Nothing. She hadn't heard a word from Fin since Tuesday morning. What was his deal?

She shoved her phone back into her pants pocket and put her injured arm into the sling. Her impatience to be done with the injury had caused her hand to swell. It had been almost four days since she'd injured it. When would enough be enough? The doctor had told her to take it easy, but she hated that phrase.

Of all the times to get mugged and injured...

She had a video conference scheduled with her boss that morning. He made it abundantly clear that he was none too pleased with the progress reports she had been sending. They had failed yet again. First the Bureau and now this. Annabeth had somehow managed to convince the boss to give them a little more time. It had only been a few weeks after all. They weren't miracle workers for fuck's sake.

Doubt was seeping in from every corner.

Can I do this without Marcus's help?

Am I going end up spending my days asking people if they want fries with that?

She'd been so busy going over the evidence and researching paid-car services, she hadn't had time to process his accident. The hospital and police had each called a few times, but she hadn't called anyone back. That would mean acknowledging what had happened, and she just wasn't ready to do that yet. Because if she stopped even for a moment to think about how she almost lost him, she wouldn't be able to keep going. Instead, she spent every waking hour pouring over their notes and researching, trying to find something that they might have missed.

The night before, Brooke had sent out an email thanking the volunteers for their hard work and trying to get everyone pumped up about being in the home stretch...as a segue for asking them to come in yet again the next morning to help finish up some last-minute preparations. And even though it would mean two days in a row spent volunteering, she'd agreed to show up. It was just what she needed to give her mind a little rest—busywork. And it was for a good cause. Joy was a sweet woman with a big heart. In their short time together she had seen snatches of the person behind the mask of her diagnosis.

As Annabeth stepped out of her car, several volunteers and vendors bustled past her, heading into the café to deliver last-minute supplies. Mitsy and her crew were carrying in arm loads of desserts. Annabeth jogged up ahead to hold open the door.

"Thank you!" Mitsy called out over her shoulder as they bustled inside.

Annabeth let the door close behind her with a pleasant jingle. The potent aroma of fresh brewed coffee mixed with the comforting buzz of southern chatter. The Book Cellar had become one of her favorite places in Texas, hands down. She loved that they made almond milk lattes and offered her as many refills as she wanted on the house. Probably had something to do with the "friendship" she'd formed with Brooke, but she knew better than to question it.

The barista smiled at her as she made her way up to the counter. "Latte?"

"Yes, please," she said.

While she waited for her drink, she leaned against the counter and flipped through a Proust book of poetry that someone had left on the counter. Inside the front of the book was Fin's business card. He must have left it here when he was working with the crew. Annabeth slipped it into her messenger bag to give to him later.

Why hasn't Fin texted me back?

She really needed to know what company he had used to call the car for Amy. Without that crucial bit of information, the investigation would remain stalled. She had some connections still at the Bureau that could help her get a warrant for the driver records. They still had an open case file on the group. If she could find out the name of the service, she could feed them the information they needed to get the case moving and for her to fulfill her boss's request.

"Here ya go, Miss. Brooke has y'all covered. So enjoy!" The perky barista handed her a perfectly crafted latte.

She didn't want Brooke's charity, but it was a damn fine cup of coffee. Okay, so she'd overlook it...this time.

There wasn't enough coffee in the world, though, to prepare her for the crazy jumble of people that awaited her in the back room. Even though the Book

Cellar often hosted small parties, it had never seen anything like the gala before. Brooke had really done an amazing job in transforming the space to work for her needs. Not that Annabeth would ever give her the satisfaction of telling her that.

The white walls were trimmed with oak and were tastefully decorated with French accents. The cozy room boasted a full kitchen and wood burning fireplace. The French doors to the back were held open by two white wooden folding chairs. They opened out into a large deck that had bar tables and stools spread out around a portable bar.

The volunteers had finished putting the tables together yesterday and had started work on the decorations.

"Becca, that isn't the Fieldstone Company table. They are over there. Pay attention, this is important."

Brooke's face reddened as she charged toward a group of young men examining the electrical system. "What's the problem, gentlemen? I needed this done yesterday."

Her phone buzzed with a new text. Her heart rate jumped as she fumbled to get it out of her bag and wake up the screen. Not Fin. Mic, her friend from the Bureau, who'd been transferred to the Austin field office.

Anna, I heard about Marcus and the hit-and-run. I have a friend in the police department and he seems to think it may be tied to an organized crime group. They have been having similar hit-and-run "accidents." I'll let you know if I hear more.

Annabeth's chest tightened. Could the sex trafficking group be on to them? She dropped her phone back into her bag and searched the sea of faces trying to find Fin.

"Anna?" Vi stood behind her, holding an armful of silver tinsel-like decorations.

She desperately wanted to still be angry at Vi for what she and Brooke had done, but Vi was one of those people it was hard to hate. The freezer full of homemade meals had certainly helped. After all, food was her love language.

She sighed, the decision already having been made. "Hey, sorry I'm late. Are those the decorations we have to put up?"

Vi nodded, her face contorted into a sad grimace. "Yeah, I was just going to do it myself, but the ladder is shaking too much, and Brooke was yelling at me about insurance coverage, and how she doesn't need one more thing to have to deal with, and—"

"It's okay. I can help hold it still. C'mon." She smiled and took the decorations from Vi. "Oh, hey, thank you for the meals, by the way."

Vi's cheeks reddened. "It was the least I could do."

Annabeth sat down on the bottom rung of the ladder to stabilize it. She used her good arm to stretch up and hand Vi the streamers. Vi then fastened them to the ceiling with a special adhesive.

Nearby, a young Latino woman sat tapping away at her laptop, carrying on a distracted conversation with one of the guys from Fin's sound team as he untangled a huge mess of wires. Where was he, and why wasn't he answering any of her texts?

The young man who had turned up looked like a younger hipster version of Fin. His thick, black hair was slicked back into a man bun and he sported a well-trimmed beard. His tight, black jeans hung low on his narrow hips and his T-shirt left very little to the imagination, showing off the sinewy muscles of his arms and chest. All he needed was a scarf and a paper cup and he would look just like all the other pretentious assholes who populated the coffee house part of the venue. "C'mon, baby, tell me your name," he said with a smile that made Annabeth's stomach flip-flop.

The girl who held his attention was one of the most beautiful Annabeth had ever seen. Her black hair fell across her shoulders in glossy waves, and her dark brown eyes popped from the carefully applied eye makeup. Her tight white tank top highlighted other assets as well.

"If I tell you, do you promise you'll let me get back to work? Brooke needs the social media blitz to all go out this afternoon, and I'm already behind schedule."

He sat on the edge of her table with his arms crossed over his broad chest. His wide, charming smile was almost hypnotic. "Maybe."

She sighed and shut her laptop closed. "Ligia." Her eyebrow lifted in a suggestive arch. "Now, I really do need to get back to work."

His smile widened. "Ligia... I like it. Where are you from? I dig your accent."

She tilted her head to the side. "Brazil. And, seriously, later. Okay?"

He touched her arm with the tips of his fingers and let them linger. "Now that I know your name, don't you want to know mine? Isn't that polite thing to do? C'mon, ask me my name."

A faint blush spread across Ligia's face. She pushed the lid of her laptop back up and cleared her throat, but didn't say anything.

"Well, since you aren't going to ask me." He laughed and sat down backward on one of the chairs next to her. "My name is Carlos, and I'm a junior at the University of Austin. And you're a freshman, am I right?"

Ligia looked up at him, her eyes wide with surprise. "*You* go to University of Austin?"

Carlos chuckled "Yeah, I'm an English Major. Not just some uneducated grease monkey." The teasing tone and smile had the desired effect.

Ligia blushed and looked away. "I wasn't implying—"

A smile snaked across his lips until it took up his whole face, dimples and all. "Of course you weren't." His pointer finger ran down her bare arm. "Are you going to this thing?"

Ligia seemed noncommittal to his obvious advances as she tapped on her keyboard. "Yeah." She bit her lip to mask the smile that creeped along the edges of her bow shaped lips.

"Save me a dance."

Carlos's persistence made her think of Marcus and how he had been when they first met at the Bureau. Things had been so much simpler then, back before... The ladder shifted underneath her bottom, breaking Annabeth from her daydream. Her eyes shot up just in time to see Vi lose her footing.

Carlos, who had been only a yard away, reached over just in time to catch Vi as she fell.

"Oh no!" Annabeth cupped her open mouth and sucked in a startled breath. "I'm so sorry, Vi! Are you okay?"

Vi's hand rested on her chest. "Oh my gosh, that was scary! I think I'm okay. Thank you!"

Carlos smiled wide—laying on the charm. "No problem, ma'am. Catching an angel like yourself is all my pleasure."

He was laying it on pretty thick. What was his angle? Did he think he would increase his odds of getting laid by flirting with everyone within a three-block radius?

She narrowed her eyes on him. "I think you can put her down now."

Vi shot her a 'mind your own business' look.

Annabeth stifled a laugh behind the back of her hand. Who was she to begrudge Vi enjoying a little attention from a good looking guy, even if he was at least five years younger?

Carlos placed Vi's feet on the ground with great care. "Let me help you finish this up. I work on ladders all day. I can get the job done pretty quick." He gave Vi a suggestive wink. "And I think the guys can spare me a few minutes while I come to the aid of you beautiful ladies."

Vi blushed. "Thank you."

Annabeth couldn't help but roll her eyes. This guy's act—like too much good cologne—was almost noxious. Vi seemed to eat it up with a spoon, though.

He held up his pointer finger, a sly smile on his face. "I'll help save the day, but only if you agree to hold the ladder for me. Your friend is in no position to do this, but I bet the beautiful Ligia can use her help with that computer she keeps hiding behind," he said, this time tossing a wink back across the room toward Ligia.

Good Lord, enough with the winking already.

Ligia frowned. "I really could use some help if you don't mind."

She plopped down onto one of the chairs at the table. Ligia handed her a stack of papers. "I know you're a little limited with your injury, but do you think you can tri-fold these brochures?"

"Yeah, I think I can handle that." Annabeth took the stack and soon got into the groove so that she could do it without even looking. In the center of the room, Brooke and Jesse stood suspiciously close to each other. As a trained profiler she couldn't help but analyze their micro-expressions and body language.

What's the deal with them?

If she didn't know better she would think they were an item.

Vi walked over to the table and sat down next to Annabeth and Ligia, letting out a deep sigh. "It's been a long day. I can't wait to get home and put my feet up." She rotated her head making it pop and crack. Before Annabeth could respond, Brooke stepped up to the table with a plastic pageant girl smile. "Ladies, y'all have been such a help the last few days. The place looks amazing. I really couldn't have done it without you."

Vi, ever the eager beaver, chimed right in. "We're happy to help."

Annabeth gave Brooke a half smile. It was all she could muster.

Brooke clasped her hands together in a classic OM pose. "So... I was thinking that since y'all are going to the event, we should get our hair and makeup done up together tomorrow afternoon."

Annabeth generally avoided all things primping. Messy buns, band T-shirts, ripped jeans, and Converse tennis shoes were her usual go-to. Even when she had to go into the Bureau, she had worn simple pants suits.

With everything on her mind, this little detail of what to wear to the event had slipped her mind. "Shit," she said under her breath.

Brooke hugged her clipboard to her chest and looked each of the girls in the eye. "I won't take no for an answer. Trudy is expecting us at three p.m." Brooke straightened her spine and looked down at them over the tip of her nose. "Oh and you need to be here at the Book Cellar no later than six for last minute instructions and to man your post."

Annabeth stifled a laugh. She wasn't asking. No, the queen had made a decree—hear ye, hear ye. Go forth and get pretty.

Brooke about-faced on her three inch heels and took off in the direction of Carlos, who had returned to work on the sound equipment with the rest of the team. They still hadn't finished the job.

Ligia elbowed Annabeth. "What was the 'oh shit' about?"

"I just now realized that I don't have anything to wear to this thing."

Ligia oozed excitement. "Oh-oh! I can help you out with that. You look like you're my size. I have the perfect dress for you. I was going to drop it in one of those donation bin thingies, but I can see you need it more than the homeless do. It's totally last season, but you strike me as a girl you doesn't care too much about that. Am I right?"

Annabeth chucked. "Yes. Thank you. That would be a real help."

"No worries. I'll go get it now so I don't forget. I have a class in an hour." She got up and stretched.

"What's the class?"

"Women in Politics. I want to major in business but maybe minor in Women's Studies. My dad wants me to go pre-law and my mama just wants me to find a nice guy, settle down, do the whole wifey-wife thing."

"What do you want?"

Ligia paused for a moment. Her long eyelashes fluttered and her lips pursed. "I'd love to have my own business, but my mama said no man wants to marry an entrepreneur." The girl shook her head and smiled.

"Anyway, let me get that dress for you. Hey—are you a size six shoe?"

Annabeth nodded with surprise. "Yes, actually I am."

Ligia squealed. "Oh what fun. You can be my little project. I know I have some shoes for you as well."

"Wow, thanks." Annabeth let out a breath of relief, choosing to ignore the whole project business.

As Ligia took off, Vi slid into the seat beside her. "I'm sorry."

Annabeth let out a loud exhale. "I know."

Vi wrung her hands in her lap. "I don't have a lot of friends. Except for Jesse and Brooke and—"

Annabeth held up her hand. "I'd like to be friends with you too, but things like that take time... I mean... I don't know. This whole experience has been so surreal. Why did she want to break into my house?"

"Well technically we didn't break in since I used the key you gave me."

She couldn't believe her ears. Was she really trying to split hairs with her over the semantics of breaking in? She could have both their butts in jail by day's end, if she wanted.

"Wait a minute...The false alarm that the police officer mentioned to me was about my house!"

Vi turned bright red and looked away. "Yes. We didn't know you had an alarm and we must have tripped it. The cops came. It was awful. I got sick. Brooke felt up the cop and gave him my number. He's called me like three times."

The people of this town were a few fries short of a happy meal.

I need to get the fuck out of here before I become one of them!

Whenever the shit hit the fan, her first instinct was always to flee, but she'd been running for far too long. Maybe that was the real problem. The big girl panties needed to come out. After all, if she couldn't face this mess head-on, how could she even hope to bring down a multi-million dollar sex-trafficking ring?

Annabeth took a deep breath. From the facts at hand, it seemed Vi had nothing really to do with it. No, Queen B herself had orchestrated the scheme. To what end was anybody's guess. The real question, of course, had not been answered.

"Vi, what I don't understand is—why are you friends with someone who makes you do something you don't want to do? I mean—."

Vi held up her hand to interject. "You don't know her like I do. I know she can be really high-maintenance and half the time she is dragging me into one drama after another, but she's Brooke." As if that was all the explanation needed.

Annabeth stood up and looked down at her. She couldn't help but feel sorry for her. "I think you can do better. I know I haven't known any of you for very long, but I can see that you are a good person. I hate to see someone like Brooke holding you back."

As Annabeth walked away she could swear she heard the faint sound of Vi crying.

CHAPTER 26

VI

How is it Friday already, Vi wondered as she sat in her car outside Trudy's. She slipped off her hands-free device. She had just come off an overnight shift at the shelter and had already gotten two calls from work during the short drive over. The midday heat and the greenhouse effect going on in her car made her sweat, but she couldn't hear properly over the noisy, clanky air conditioner, which meant she was stuck. Besides, she needed to be on her A-game. The other advocates were worried about Anjali, the Indian girl who was part of the sex trafficking ring—and, of course, Vi was, too. The poor thing wouldn't speak with anyone but Vi, but Vi couldn't exactly be there 24/7. She had other clients to look after, and a life of her own.

Vi tossed her keys into her purse. She wasn't in a hurry to get out of the car, but the oppressive heat was beginning to make the outside unbearable. On the flipside, spending an hour or two in a small shop with Annabeth and Brooke would likely be every bit as miserable.

Out of habit and reverence, she did a quick, sloppy sign of the cross and pleaded with the Virgin to give her strength. For extra measure, she kissed her St. Rita Medallion. The patron saint of the impossible was definitely someone she needed on her side.

St. Rita, I ask for your peace and guidance. Be with me now.

The sound of her own voice in her head sounded foreign, since it was usually drowned out by the sound of everyone else's needs and concerns.

She walked into the beauty parlor, where Brooke sat under one of the hair dryers with a sangria in one hand and that month's new Vogue in the other. Brooke's goddaughter sat beside her, entranced by her phone. She didn't even notice that Vi had arrived. Brooke, however, lit up like a Polish Church on Christmas Eve the moment Vi stepped through the door.

"Yay, you're here! Mani-pedis, makeup, and hair. All of it, my treat. Prepare to be pampered, Violeta."

Brooke looked positively radiant. She had always been gorgeous, but lately—despite everything going on with the gala—she had a sort of glow about her. The effect made her even more devastatingly beautiful than ever.

"Yup, I'm here. Though I don't know why you are. You already look amazing!"

She flapped her hand theatrically as if to brush the compliment away. "Aww, c'mon. You know I can't resist a pampering sesh."

"Miss..." A technician took her by the elbow and guided her across the room to the row of pedicure chairs. "Sit here." The man's commanding voice comforted her. It was nice to not have to think and just be told what to do.

Well, sometimes.

Vi sat obediently and closed her eyes in an attempt to shut out the chaos of the outside world. But the world, it seemed, was not to be deterred. The door shot open again, bringing with it a hot gust of late summer air. And also Annabeth. She had a purple U of A T-shirt on and a pair of ripped 7s jeans. Brooke's complete opposite.

Vi watched in amusement as the technician greeted Annabeth and attempted to guide her over to the last chair, the one directly beside Vi.

"I can sit on my own, thanks," Anna barked at the poor man, who had made the mistake of trying to help her sit down into the cushiony massage chairs. She looked like a cat who was being made to take a bath—obviously not the type who enjoyed being told what to do.

Vi stifled a giggle behind her hand.

Anna glowered at her, but soon a smile cracked across her face and she laughed too. "I guess I'm not in the best mood today."

"Yeah, me either."

"Would you ladies like some wine? Champagne?" the owner asked with a pleasant, obviously practiced smile.

"Coffee," they said in unison, making them both break out into another fit of giggles—this one even more robust than the last.

She could feel the tension between them begin to dissipate. Maybe their new friendship was salvageable, after all.

The owner gave them an amused smirk and went off in search of coffee.

"What is so funny over there?" Brooke asked with a look of jealousy.

She had only seen Brooke ever look jealous a few times in their ten years of friendship, and every one of those times had ended badly.

Anna had no idea just how out of hand Brooke could become. The whole breaking-and-entering thing was child's play compared to some of the stunts Brooke had pulled over the years. Much to Vi's dismay, a part of her had enjoyed a few of their reckless adventures.

Through the mirrors that lined the wall, she could see Brooke reflected back at her, and she couldn't help but smile. While her friend could be a handful, she was also fiercely loyal and protective. The day they met had been branded into her memory.

Joy had decided to throw an epic fit in the new posh grocery store that had opened up next to their subdivision. It didn't take long for Joy's antics—screaming and crying while slapping Vi—to draw a crowd of spectators.

"Ma'am, if you and your friend here can't control yourselves, I'm going to have to ask you to leave," the manager had threatened.

That was when Brooke sprung into action, pushing her way through the throng of people like Wonder Woman there to save the day. Brooke had gone nose-to-nose with the manager and used her lanky stature and bellowing voice to her advantage. He really hadn't stood a chance against the mighty Queen B, and the bastard had actually cried! By the time Brooke was done, he'd not only apologized, but also offered to deliver the groceries to Vi's home for free.

Vi had never been so grateful to another human being in her entire life. Over the years she had fought for Vi and Joy with an intensity that was both a blessing and a burden at times. At the end of the day, she loved Brooke and couldn't imagine her life without her.

She flashed another smile at her BFF in the hopes of reassuring her. "Oh, nothing. I think we're both just a bit slap-happy."

Brooke's eyes narrowed. "Well you had better wake up. We have a long night ahead of us. I can't have you two cackling like a bunch of hyenas."

Vi and Annabeth shared a quiet, amused look before settling back into their chairs. Now that the tension had leveled out for the moment, she fiddled with the massage settings until she got it just right.

One of Trudy's assistants filled the basin in front of her and placed Vi's feet inside. From the corner of her eye, she could see that three people were attending to Brooke, who was holding court. This was her element. Vi, on the other hand, felt horribly awkward as the woman assigned to her scraped layer after layer of calluses from her feet. Every swipe of the tool made her twitch.

"Hold still!" the tech grumbled and clamped down on her foot.

"Sorry, it tickles."

The woman muttered something under her breath, and Vi was grateful that she didn't know what had been said.

Brooke shot her an admonishing look. She was no doubt embarrassed by Vi's overly sensitive feet. Her BFF was all about social protocol.

Anna reached across and touched her arm. "My feet are ticklish, too."

Vi smiled back.

Ligia put away her phone and got up from the chair. "I'm going to get my eyebrows done. Umm, you should too, Vi."

Brooke didn't hesitate. "She's right. Your brow—because let's be honest, I can't really say brows, now can I?—well, it looks like an angry caterpillar. Excuse me, could I trouble you for another drink?" Brooke handed one of the techs her empty glass.

Vi sank further into her chair. Did she really look that bad? She flipped her phone's camera over and saw herself reflected back.

I do look terrible.

She angrily tossed her phone back into her bag and slumped over to the side. The chair no longer had the power to relax her, so she shut it off. The three women sat in an awkward silence with only the sound of the technicians chatting back and forth to each other.

By the time Ligia came back, Trudy and her three assistant stylists were ready to start on everyone's hair and makeup.

"Martinique, you will have your hands full with Annabeth there. Her hair is long overdue for some work. I was thinking maybe a Brazilian blowout. Spare no expense. I want these ladies to be the stars of the gala."

Martinique smiled back at Brooke, but Annabeth's jaw dropped. Her piercing green eyes glared at Brooke through the reflection of the mirrors. Vi—caught in the crossfire—didn't know what to do. She knew Brooke meant well. If only Annabeth knew her like Vi did.

"Rita, a little help here," she whispered, a short prayer of intercession.

"You're in really good hands," she said louder so that Anna could hear, while the stylist ran her fingers through Vi's glossy black hair.

"What are we doing with you today, Miss Vi?"

Before she could answer, Brooke spoke up, "Excuse me. Yoo-hoo. Didn't you get my text?"

The stylist scrambled for her phone and pulled up the message.

"Don't I get a say in this?" Vi said under her breath.

"Really, Vi. Trust me. You know as much about style as I do about bull riding. Let me handle this. Okies?"

Vi felt her cheeks get hot, but did her best to bite the anger back down. Brooke didn't know that she'd finally broken things off with Ricky or how much her comment was like a knife to her heart.

The stylist put down her phone and started to cut large sections of Vi's hair, and all she could do was sit there in horror and watch as black ribbons of hair fell around her at an alarming rate. She kept her eyes down to hide the glassy sheen of unshed tears that threatened to spill at any minute. Then came the dye, and lots of it. The noxious smell of chemicals made her stomach turn, while the too loud crinkle of the aluminum foil being wrapped around the strands of painted hair boomed in her eardrums.

Time passed, she was sure of it, but she had kind of stopped paying attention. A warm hand reach across and grabbed onto hers.

"Vi, are you all right?" Annabeth asked, just barely above a whisper.

"Yes… I'm fine."

Anna's eyes narrowed in disbelief.

"Hello! Earth to Vi!" Brooke's expression implied she'd tried more than once to get her attention. "I'm leaving. Can you drop Ligia off at my house when she is done?"

She nodded. "Yeah, sure. Of course."

Brooke rolled her eyes as she spun around to take off, which added to her feeling of violation.

The three women who remained were all put under the dryers and then back into the chairs for makeup. As Vi's stylist took the foil off, she couldn't help but gasp at what she saw. While she was definitely still angry at Brooke, she was also stunned by the sight. Her hair, which had always been plain black, was now a rainbow of reds, blondes, and browns mixed seamlessly together.

"Wow," she said under her breath.

"Yes, Miss Brooke picked the perfect look for you. And I like to think I helped a little, too." The woman smiled, obviously proud of her work, as she grabbed two threads and set to work on Vi's eyebrows.

Anna glowered and crossed her arms. "Gorgeous or not, it doesn't take away from the fact that she didn't give her a say in her own hair."

The stylist clucked her tongue and motioned for Annabeth to hush. "I don't hear Vi complaining, so there's no need for you to. Anyway, Mrs. Fischer has settled all your bills, so y'all can leave whenever you feel ready."

She watched in embarrassment as her stylist walked off in a huff to the customer who had just walked in. Her newest neighbor tended to shoot straight from the hip, which might have worked well and fine back in Detroit, but this was Texas. Respect was non-negotiable here.

"I'm sorry if I caused more trouble, Vi, but this was just wrong. She treats you like a child."

Ligia walked up to the women with her bag in hand. "Are you girls ready?"

Just then Vi's phone rang with the shelter's ring tone. "Excuse me, I have to take this." She stepped over to the side for privacy. "Vi speaking."

"You need to come. Now. Anjali's parents won't let her come home. She's really distraught and will only talk to you."

"All right, I'll be there in a minute."

I can't even get a few hours away from that place.

"Sorry, Ligia. I have to go to the shelter. A client needs my help."

Annabeth perked up. "The same girl you told me about earlier?"

"Yeah, she's upset and will only talk to me."

Ligia fluffed her hair. "Don't worry about it. I'll just order a ride," she said, pulling her phone out from her purse.

"Don't!" Annabeth put her hand over the girl's phone to stop her. "Call a cab instead."

Ligia rolled her eyes. "Jeez, calm down. It's perfectly safe."

Annabeth grew flush. "No—no, it's not. One of my students went missing. The last I saw of her was when she got into one of those paid-car service cars. Haven't you read about all the sexual assaults, too?"

For a second, Ligia's face took on a ghostly pallor. "You're joking right?"

Annabeth shook her head. "No, I'm really not."

"Fine, I'll take a cab."

"I'll call ya one, sugar," Trudy said as she grabbed her phone.

Vi felt some tension leave her chest, which had felt tight all week.

"Do you think your client would talk to me?" Anna asked with eyes full of hope.

Her breath quickened as the many sources of her stress piled on top of each other and pushed her down. "I can ask her, but I can't promise anything. She signed a confidentiality agreement that gave me permission to talk to the police, but I don't know how she would feel talking to a P.I."

Annabeth held up her hand to stop Vi. "Don't worry. I know what I'm doing. I won't push her. But if she has information that might save these girls from being taken...well, how can I not at least try?"

CHAPTER 27

BROOKE

BROOKE ran around the empty house, alternating between quick phone calls and shouty all-caps texts. The gala was tonight, and she needed to be sure it would go off without a hitch, even if that meant pushing all her contractors—and even her volunteers—to the brink of madness. She hadn't become the best in the biz by putting everyone's feelings before the work that needed to be done. They could all hate her for now. She knew how to win them back.

Just a couple more hours to go.

God, how will it all get done in two measly hours?

The garage door rumbled, and she shot to her feet in search of the kitchen clock. Dizzy, so dizzy. She sunk back onto the couch and took a few deep breaths, then reached for her phone. Brian wasn't due back for another hour and a half, but...

"Honey, I'm home!" His voice boomed across the threshold. What, did he think this was a 1950's sitcom, and why was he in such good spirits anyway? His moods were becoming impossible to predict.

Still, he had promised he'd make it home in time for the gala, and even though she'd set herself up for disappointment, he'd actually made good on his word. That had to count for something.

She stumbled to her feet again, slower this time, and went to greet her husband.

Just keep swimming. Just keep swimming.

"Hi, baby," she chirped, kissing his cheek. "You're home early."

Brian tossed his briefcase into the corner, then placed a firm hand on each side of her butt and squeezed. He attacked her with a deep, hungry kiss.

"You know how delivering closing arguments gets me all worked up. God, I could hardly make it home. I need you so bad." He rubbed his erection against her thigh. Did he even notice that she was all dressed up? Did he remember that tonight was one of the biggest nights of her career? Have any idea how much still needed to be done?

"Mmm," he hummed and leaned in for another kiss.

She returned his kiss for a moment, but then pushed him away. As things were, she'd already need to touch up her makeup and make sure there were no palm imprints on her ass.

"Bri, I can't."

He laughed. "You can't? C'mon, Brooke baby, just give me a little quickie. Believe me, I earned it today. If you could've seen me in that courtroom, you'd be just as hot as I am." He began working the buttons on his shirt and pressed his hot mouth to her neck.

"Brian, tonight's the gala. Remember? And I'm kind of running the whole thing. I don't have time to…"

"Don't have a few minutes for your husband? C'mon, Brookey B. Don't be ridiculous. Tell you what, no foreplay. It will be the quickest of quickies." He reached around for the zip on her gown, but she wriggled loose. The last thing on her mind right now was sex. Why couldn't he understand that?

"Brian, I really don't have time for this. I would if I could, but there's still a lot to do, and I don't have time to redo my hair and makeup. I *promise* when I get home tonight, we can—"

He silenced her with a kiss and pushed her up against the counter, lowering the straps on either side of her dress.

She pressed hard against his chest, but he was much stronger than her and very determined to get his way. Should she just give in? They were married, and they were trying for a baby. It's not like Brian was wrong to expect sex from his wife. Shouldn't she just take one for the team?

No. Because this was America where no still meant no, or at least it should.

She just couldn't afford to lose any more time from her schedule. She still was feeling a bit woozy, besides. Who knew what the rush of an orgasm might do to throw her even more off-kilter.

She turned her head away, so he would have to stop kissing her—at least on the mouth where he was smudging her lipstick. "Brian, I said no."

"Yeah, but you didn't mean it, now, did you?" He grabbed her hard and forced her face toward him. His other hand clenched down on her wrist. Not only was this decidedly not sexy, but it hurt.

"No means no, jerkface," Ligia said stomping into the room.

Brooke hadn't even heard her come in, but her timing couldn't have been better.

Brian laughed nervously. "It's just a game we play. No harm done." He turned away from Ligia and shot Brooke an irritated look, daring her to say otherwise. "I need to get back to the office anyway. Have a great time tonight, girls!"

Her husband put on his most endearing smile, gave Ligia a quick hug, then headed back out the door, forgetting to do up his buttons first or to grab his discarded briefcase. "Good to see you again, Liggy," he called before slamming the door and disappearing entirely from the house.

"Ick. What happened, Auntie B? That did *not* look good."

Honestly, Brooke didn't know what had just happened, and didn't really want to waste any time trying to figure it out, either. Brian's excuse would work for the time being. "C'mon, you don't want to hear about Uncle Bri's and my sex life, do you? Unless you want to know about the time he tied me to the bedpost, and I—"

"No, no, dear God, no."

Brooke forced a laugh, and Ligia's demeanor softened a little. "Hey, where are Vi and Annabeth? Didn't they give you a ride back?"

"Nah, they kind of ditched me, but it's cool. I took a cab."

"What? They ditched you!" Suddenly all of Brooke's anger shifted toward her so-called friends.

"It's fine, Auntie B. I'm a big girl, I can take care of myself. But yikes!" She came closer and lifted Brooke's hand into the light. "Did he do this to you? This is not okay."

Brooke looked down and saw the ring of bruises blossoming around her wrist where Brian had clamped down. Damn her sensitive skin. She laughed, but not before Ligia caught the growing horror in her eyes.

"Game, my ass. And, oh my God, your face." She put her phone in selfie mode then thrust it toward Brooke. An angry bruise was spreading across her jaw as well.

She laughed again. "Calm down, Ligia. You know how popular all that *Fifty Shades of Grey* stuff is. Brian and I just wanted to try it out. I should have known better than to do something so kinky this close to the big event, though. You know how I bruise up like a peach."

Ligia frowned, but then laughed too. "Auntie B, I had no idea what a slut you were."

Thank God.

"Could you help me touch up my makeup some? I don't want all of Herald Springs to know I like it rough." She winked, and Ligia winked back.

"Your secret's safe with me. Just make sure I never walk in on that again, okay? Oh, I have the best new MAC lipstick. The shade will look great on you. Wanna try it out?" Before Brooke could answer, Ligia had already started rummaging about in her clutch.

"Shoot!" the girl exclaimed. "I forgot to pack some tampons when I switched over my purse. Got some I can borrow?"

"Sure, be right back." Brooke jogged upstairs to her master bathroom, and on the way it hit her. How long had it been...? She brought up her period tracker app, and a giant red 7 greeted her.

No. It couldn't possibly... Could it?

She grabbed the box of tampons from under the sink, and fired off a quick text to Jesse before returning to Ligia.

"Here you go," she said, handing them over. "Jesse is heading over to the gala early to direct volunteers. Would you mind if he picked you up and took you over early while I finish up here?"

"No probs."

She gave her goddaughter a tight hug. "Thanks for being so awesome through all this, L. You know how much I love you, right?"

"Of course. And you know how much you owe me, right?"

Oh, she has no idea.

"Well, Jesse should be by to grab you any minute. I'll let you go take care of business."

Speaking of business, it was time to pee on a stick and hope like hell no little blue lines popped up to greet her.

CHAPTER 28
ANNABETH

ANNABETH wiped her clammy palms on her jeans. Even though she had her doubts about questioning the victim, she continued to reassure Vi on the drive over to the shelter. Interrogation had never been her strong suit when she was with the Bureau. Marcus was the one who excelled at getting the information they needed. She'd been avoiding the hospital every time they called to provide an update. He was in a coma, she got it, but... There was only so much she could handle right now.

Things had not been going well for her these days, and she desperately needed a check in the win column. Getting some forward momentum on this job would definitely be a step in the right direction. Her billionaire boss only had so much patience. He wanted results sooner rather than later. Coldhearted or not, there just wasn't time to focus on problems she had no control over. She couldn't pull Marcus out of his coma, but she *could* put her all into her work and maybe—if she was lucky—even save some lives.

Annabeth swallowed hard as she followed behind Vi into the crowded crisis center. It was time to act like she knew what she was doing even if she didn't.

Annabeth wet her dry lips and grimaced at the chemical taste of the lipstick the salon had forced on her. *Everyone* commented on Vi's new look.

"Oooh girl, you look fierce!" one of the advocates exclaimed.

Vi blushed and looked away. "Ginnie, where's Anjali?"

"Out back smoking. And where might you be headed, hot stuff?"

Vi frowned. "The gala, remember?"

"Oh, lord. Is that tonight? Wish I could make it, but duty calls." She eyed her chart with a frown. "You will take pictures for me, won't you? Let me be there Vi-cariously." She snorted and put a playful hand on Vi's shoulder. "I slay myself sometimes."

Vi wriggled out from under her coworker's touch. "Of course. I'll fill you in on all the details tomorrow."

"Alright. Have a good time."

Annabeth and Vi walked down a long corridor lined with half-open doors. Women and small children bustled about, in and out of rooms. They all flashed looks of distrust at Annabeth, who tried not to take it personally. These women had been in horrific situations, after all. Trust wouldn't come easily to them.

After what seemed like forever, they reached the large, metal door that led back outside into the tiny courtyard. The afternoon air hit her like a slap to the face. It was the kind of heat that took your breath away. The locals claimed it wasn't so bad—a "dry heat," they called it. But hot was hot no matter how anyone tried to justify it.

Her thin flip-flops clacked across the patio behind Vi to where a young Indian woman was camped out at a picnic table smoking a cigarette. From the looks of the overflowing ashtray, she had been there awhile.

Vi and Annabeth slid onto the bench across from the girl.

"Anjali?" Vi asked with a look of concern. "You asked for me?"

She glanced at Vi before looking out toward the distant horizon. She shook loose a new cigarette and placed it between her shaking fingers. It took her several tries to get the lighter to flicker to life. When she finally succeeded, she took a long drag, then let it out with a sideways smile.

"So, tell me, why are you looking like a Miss Universe contestant?"

Vi gave the girl a half-hearted smile. "I'm going to a gala benefit tonight for my sister's group home."

Anjali's right brow arched up. "They should have applied more kohl. Your eyes look a bit squinty, *na?*"

"Do you want to talk about me and my personal life or do you think it might be a better use of our time to talk about what is going on with you? Why did you want me to come down tonight?"

"I'm having a hard time here. The other girls aren't at all nice, and, to be honest, all their troubles seem so small after what I've... Anyway, there's no one here I can talk to, and then I get stuck inside my thoughts. Sometimes it is too much, *na?* And that's when I call you." She took another slow drag. "You help put my anxieties to sleep, at least for a little while."

Vi sighed, "Okay, but there are other advocates here that can help you. They care about you and want to help. I'm sorry that the women here aren't being kind to you. This all has to be so hard and frustrating for you."

Long pause.

"*Arey,* this talk is much too serious." Anjali exhaled a plume of smoke and nodded her head in Annabeth's direction. "Who's this person? Your date?"

Annabeth extended her hand in greeting, and Anjali took it with some reluctance.

"Hi Anjali, I'm a Private Investigator."

Anjali's face paled and her eyes narrowed.

"I was hired by a man whose daughter was taken and murdered by the same organization that took you."

Anjali's face fell and the tremor in her hand worsened. "Absolutely not! This has gone too far already. I will not talk to the police. Mummy-Papa will never forgive me for bringing such shame to our family."

Annabeth nodded. "I'm not with the police, Anjali, and I'm not asking you to press charges." Annabeth sucked in a nervous breath. "I'm just trying to stop these men from hurting any more girls. None of what we talk about here needs to leave this room... Well, this table." She laughed, but it did nothing to relieve the tension. "I just need whatever information you can give me so that I can stop this."

The girl took in a trembling breath. "So, what, you can hand them over to the police*walas*? They will hunt me down and kill me. No thanks."

Annabeth felt her heartbeat quicken. What this girl must have gone through. The sadness and injustice of it all enraged her. She had to stop these men. Make them pay. She took a deep breath, trying to keep the desperation she felt out of her voice.

"No one has to know that you had anything to do with this investigation." Annabeth leaned in closer to the girl. "Is there anything you can tell me? Anything at all? They took another young woman this week—a friend, actually."

Anjali's eyes began to well with tears. "I just can't. Please understand."

This was the hardest part of the job, and she hated that it had become necessary when Anjali was obviously already so close to the edge. She would need to push this victim to get what she needed. The greater good and all that.

"You know you will never be free until they are stopped. You'll always be looking over your shoulder. Help me stop them from ever hurting another girl, and free yourself in the process."

After a long pause, Anjali took another puff of her cigarette. "You can't ever let them know I told you anything. They can't find me."

Annabeth nodded even though she knew it was a promise she might not be able to keep. "I won't."

"You don't know what you are saying. They are everywhere. They work at the University and sign up to drive those private cabs, too."

So, I was right about the car services! Finally, I'm getting somewhere.

"Do you know which specific service they used?"

Anjali nodded. "1-2-3-Ride."

Annabeth let out a sigh of relief. Finally, she had a lead to get the investigation jump-started again. She needed to keep the girl talking, to see what else she could find.

"I know this may be hard to talk about, but how did you get taken into the organization?"

Anjali's eyes watered as she looked away from Annabeth.

Vi cleared her throat. "Anjali, you can trust Anna, she's here to help you and all those other girls."

Anjali huffed as she twirled the lighter in front of her. The tremor in her hand was getting worse. She abandoned the lighter and brought the cigarette up to her lips and held it there for a moment before taking a short puff. The smoke leaked out the side of her mouth.

"He was the teaching assistant for my Intro to Lit class. He often held bonus study sessions to help students prepare for the exams, and I always attended them because I liked the way he spoke about words and the written language." Her wan face suddenly blushed at the memory.

"He liked me too, said I was the smartest in the class and encouraged me to pursue my poetry. My parents wanted me to study engineering or to become a doctor, but he continued to tell me what a great poet I could be if I kept trying, that I could do anything I wanted because I was the smartest and most beautiful woman he'd ever met."

Annabeth let out a short breath, afraid to move or speak, lest she stop talking.

Vi offered her hand and the girl took hold of it like it was a lifeline.

"I was his special girl. He spoiled me with fancy gifts and showered me with compliments. He even wrote poems for me. Always the gentleman, that one. And I fell for his drama display, thought maybe we could be married one day, that maybe Mummy-Papa would even give their blessing for the match. My whole world became about him. I stopped coming here and quit going to class. Our first time together was like my wedding night," she said as her tears fell in earnest.

Vi let go of the girl's hand and pulled a tissue out of her purse.

"Thanks," Anjali said as he dabbed at the tears.

"Take your time," Annabeth whispered with a nod of encouragement.

"I just need to finish it fast."

"All right, what happened next?"

"After we were together the first time he got really possessive. Then one night he...got us a hotel room—penthouse. A friend of his was waiting for us. It was his first time...said I was to practice on. They...I didn't want to. When I tried to leave they tied me up. They gave me drugs. I don't really remember most of it. I was there three days. After that I was taken to some house somewhere. They kept us locked up in the back. There were twelve of us."

The wealth of information Anjali was providing was just what Annabeth needing to push forward with the investigation. And as much as she hated putting the girl through the trauma of reliving the worst time of her life, it was a necessary thing in order to save these young girls' lives. Twelve!

"They always made sure that we had lots of drugs—it kept us numb. Or at least they did at first." Anjali's body began to shake, but she took another puff of her cigarette. "They took us to posh hotels, different ones each time. One day I lost count after fifteen men came to...to use me." Anjali's shaking turned to sobbing. "I can't talk about this."

Annabeth bit her lip, steeling herself against the guilt that bubbled up inside. "You are very brave, Anjali. I know this is very hard, but I need to ask you for just one more thing. I need to know his name. Could you please tell me?"

Anjali looked up at Annabeth with tear-stained cheeks. They had washed away some of her makeup, revealing harsh purple bruises on her face. Had the men been responsible for the marks or the accident? What horrors were yet to be revealed? Annabeth almost didn't want to know the answer.

"Whose name?" Anjali asked, obviously avoiding the question.

Annabeth wet her lips and leaned in toward the girl. "The man, your TA?"

Anjali's face paled and she looked away. Her body trembled. She needed the name and she was prepared to do whatever it took to get it. "Anjali, it's very important that I have his name. He needs to pay for what he did to you."

The young girl let out a shaky breath. "Even if it makes a dead woman out of me?"

Annabeth nodded. "Please."

"Anna!" Vi exclaimed. She turned to the girl, her face softened with concern. "She doesn't mean that. You don't have to share anything you aren't comfortable with."

Annabeth bit her lip to keep from objecting. A long, awkward pause followed.

Anjali brought her splayed fingers to rest on her abdomen.

Long sleeves... In this heat?

When Anjali finally broke the silence, goose flesh broke out on Annabeth's bare arms.

"Fin. That's what he called himself, but I don't remember his full proper name."

Annabeth's stomach bottomed out, and the air left her lungs in an anxious woosh. Fin. Fernando.

He's a part of all this! How could I be so stupid to not have seen through his act?

Annabeth's eyes welled up. She wasn't the only one who had been charmed by this man.

"Now, please, just leave. I want to be alone," Anjali said, turning away.

Annabeth looked over and met Vi's eye. It was time to go. She had gotten what she needed.

They stood in unison.

Anjali avoided looking at them.

"Thank you for everything, Anjali. I know this wasn't easy. But I'm going to do everything in my power to keep you safe and to save those other girls." Annabeth slid one of her cards across the table. "Please call me if you think of anything else that might help."

Anjali fingered the card but said nothing.

They walked back through the center and out the front door in silence. Annabeth had never seen her neighbor look so mad.

"Was that necessary?" Vi's perfectly shaped eyebrows formed a hard angry line.

Annabeth bit her bottom lip before answering, "Yes. I'm sorry I had to push her, but I needed that name."

Vi shook her head and mumbled something under her breath.

She wasn't surprised that Vi was upset. It was her job to protect the victim, not to bring the perpetrators to justice.

"You knew her before all this, right?"

Vi looked both ways before crossing the street to where they had parked her car.

"She was a volunteer at the shelter two years ago. One Monday she just didn't show up." Vi paused with her key in the door. "Two years, Anna. How can she ever hope to recover from that? And to have to bring it all back up again. She shouldn't have to do that. No victim should."

Annabeth swallowed back the ball of emotion that choked her. "I...don't know if she can come back from what she's been through, but if what she told us can help save those girls, I have to believe that it was worth it."

Vi unlocked the car and let out the rush of heat that had been trapped inside. Her quietness was disconcerting. She finally broke the silence. "Did you at least get what you needed after all that?"

Annabeth rolled the question around in her mind before answering.

If Vi hadn't been there I could have pushed her harder and gotten even more...but at what cost?

The seatbelt buckle burned her hand as she tugged it over her body and clicked it in place. "Yeah, I got what I needed. For now."

As they pulled out onto the road, Annabeth recalled something Anjali had mentioned about the abundant supply of drugs the organization had provided. She didn't look to be detoxing so she must still be using. "You might want to have her room checked for drugs. Most likely heroin. I think she's been shooting up. She had a long sleeved shirt on. Might be to hide track marks."

Vi took her eyes off the road and met Annabeth's with a look of defiance. "She's not using drugs, Anna."

Annabeth frowned. "Don't be naive."

Her normally meek neighbor sat up straight and squared her shoulders like she was ready to go to war. "I'm not naive. I know this girl."

You knew this girl, she wanted to say, but Vi was obviously in denial about this whole thing. No sense pushing it now.

"Well, let's hope you're right."

Annabeth took out her phone and dialed Mike, her contact at the Austin Bureau. They had gone through the academy together and still kept in touch. He had been the first one she and Marcus had called when they got the job.

He answered on the third ring. "Hey Anna, ya got something for me?"

"Yeah, I've got a lot for you to work on. I have a source that gave me a name of one of their mid-level operatives."

Mike sighed. "It has to be good Anna. I can't act unless it is solid intel."

"One of the girls got away and I got her to talk."

Mike paused on the other line, making Annabeth anxious.

"Will she testify?"

Annabeth bit her lip. "No."

Mike sighed. "All right. Give me what you got and I'll see what I can do without arousing too much suspicion." He paused a beat before continuing. "Some of us like our jobs, Anna."

Annabeth bristled at his comment, but chose to shake it off.

"Okay, His name is Fernando 'The Fin' Reyes. He's approximately five foot ten, one-hundred and eighty pounds, twenty-nine years old, works for the University. He's of Filipino descent and has light brown skin. He is the one who took my source into the group. He didn't just sell her off to the dons to use. He repeatedly raped her himself."

Annabeth felt flush with anger.

She cleared her throat. "They are meeting the dons in hotels and are using the 1-2-3-Ride App to get at the girls. See if you can get a judge to issue us a warrant so we can petition for their driver information records."

"Okay, but on what grounds am I petitioning for this warrant?"

"I have a victim statement that I'll shoot over to you as soon as I can."

"All right, but it had better be good. Judges in this county are tough to get warrants from. How's Marc, by the way?"

Annabeth's gut twisted into a tight knot. She knew she was going to have to face it sooner or later, but for now, later was the better option. "No change. I'll let you know if I have anything else... I'll shoot that victim statement to you later tonight."

"All right. I don't think it's enough to act on, but I'll do a little poking around. If you could get one of their men to turn that would be the ideal. Just be careful, okay."

Annabeth ended the call and put her phone back into her bag. It was already four o'clock and they still hadn't gotten dressed yet.

As soon as Vi put the car in park, Annabeth jumped out.

"I'll see you at the gala."

Vi nodded as she walked with her shoulders hunched over. The toll of everything must be getting to her.

Hell, it's getting to me.

She didn't have time to explore all the implications, though; she had a party to go to.

Annabeth rushed inside and threw on the dress Ligia had given her—careful not to mess up her hair and makeup in the process. As much as she didn't want to admit it, she was pleased with the outcome. Maybe Brooke really did have her best interests at heart. Hmm. That was a frightening thought.

Her phone ringing broke her from her train of thought. The hospital. "He-llo?"

"Is this Mrs. King?"

"This is she." Her palms dampened and her breathing became shallow. She had been doing such a good job at pushing Marcus out of her head.

"Ma'am, your husband is awake and asking for you."

Annabeth let out a short laugh of relief. "What? He's going to be okay?"

"Yes, ma'am."

Tears slid unbidden down her cheeks. He was going to be okay. This amazing bit of good news made all of their problems seem insignificant. She'd almost lost him, but she hadn't. He was going to be okay, and maybe—just maybe—they would be okay, too.

* * *

ANNABETH stood, paused outside his open door. Her last words to him, *I never want to see you again*, bellowed in her mind. *Please forgive me*. The mantra played over as she walked slowly into his room.

She rested her trembling hand on his chest. The rise and fall of each new breath and the beat of his heart against her palm gave her immense comfort.

"Marc...I'm here."

His long eyelashes fluttered and after a short pause he opened his eyes and smiled up at her. He wet his lips and his smile widened. "Anna."

Annabeth fell forward against him, resting her head on his chest in an awkward embrace. "Oh,

Marcus!" She squeezed him tight and nuzzled against him. "I thought I'd lost you."

"Takes a lot more than a little hit-and-run to take me down." His raspy voice, so different from the honeyed one she was used to, was still him.

He brought his arm up and enveloped her into his protective embrace.

Tears ran down her perfectly put together face, but she didn't care. All the hurt she had been holding in had finally found a way out and she was powerless to stop the tsunami of emotions that washed over her.

He wiped away her tears with the pads of his thumbs. "Look at you! Maybe I died after all. My Anna doesn't get dolled up for nothing."

My Anna. There was a time when such a possessive remark would have irritated her, but not now. She had Marcus back. *Marcus,* not Marc, because with Marcus there was no sordid past, only the hope of a better future. They were together again—nothing else mattered.

Anna smiled as a sudden feeling of shyness washed over her. "Yes, well...it's for a charity event. I—"

Marcus slipped his hand behind her head and pulled her down to him. His soft lips touched hers tentatively at first, but soon demanded more.

Annabeth acquiesced to his kiss. She could feel the stress of the day slough off her and onto the floor.

As much as she hated to admit it, she needed this, she needed him.

The beep of his heart monitor going off made her smile, breaking the kiss.

"If I'd known that a little makeup would get this reaction I might have done this sooner."

"Oh, Anna." His dark brown eyes softened. "You are always beautiful to me. With or without makeup."

His words warmed her heart. Maybe they could move past the whole Beth debacle and go back to the way things had been in the beginning. "I love you, Marcus. I'm sorry about what I said that night—"

"You don't have anything to be sorry about." He smiled up at her with glistening eyes then took her hand and brought it to his lips. "I want you to know that you don't have to worry about me going anywhere. You're the only girl for me. I'm yours, that is, if you'll have me."

Annabeth inched away from him. She wanted to commit to him then and there, but just couldn't. She wasn't ready to have this discussion with Marcus, not when so much was still up in the air with the case, with Amy, with Fin. She needed to deal with all of that first, then she and Marcus could figure out the best label for what they had together. Annabeth looked up at the clock on the wall—she had to leave now or she would be really late.

"Can I take a raincheck on this discussion?" She stood and straightened her dress. "Brooke is already going to be mad at me for being so late."

He flashed her a sad smile as he raised the top of the bed so he was in a sitting position. "Speaking of Brooke, the nurses told me that she's the one who got me moved to this hospital. Is that true?"

Annabeth checked her reflection in the paper towel dispenser. Her makeup and hair had somehow managed to hold up just fine.

"They said she even visited with me when I was in the coma. Weird, huh?" He smiled as if the revelation were no big deal, as if Anna's head weren't spinning.

She gave Marcus a quick peck on the lips, choosing not to acknowledge any of his Brooke talk.

He tried to grab hold of her but she managed to wiggle out of his arms.

"I have to go, but I promise I will come back tomorrow and we can talk."

Marcus gave her a sleepy grin. "Okay, but I'm holding you to it."

Annabeth placed her hand on her heart, then blew him a quick kiss. She flew down the halls feeling like Cinderella before the ball. They had a suspect, a real lead, and she and Marcus were back on track. But, also like Cinderella, the clock was ticking. She needed to find out what happened to Amy and how she could use Anjali's information to stop the ring before the clock struck, and it was game over.

CHAPTER 29

Vi knelt down on her bathroom rug and began to rummage through her cupboard in search of her rarely used makeup bag.

One of these days I'll clean this mess out! When I have time… That's never gonna happen. Like the world is just gonna stop because I need to do a simple thing like clean out the clutter under my sink.

She'd gotten the Clinique bag back in high school when she'd still had the time and inclination to put effort into her looks. She took out her ancient eyeliner and repaired the damage her tears had made. She didn't want to incur the wrath of Brooke over some smudged eye makeup.

Waterproof my ass.

So not worth the trouble.

Her new cut and color reflected back at her. She didn't know the person in the mirror. All she knew was that the woman underneath all of the glitz was dying inside.

Vi bit her lip to stop herself from crying again. She'd been a social worker long enough to recognize the signs of secondary trauma. Anjali's story had deeply disturbed her. Vi enjoyed her bubble world where things like that just didn't happen—especially to someone she knew. But, sadly, she didn't have time to process all she and Annabeth had just learned.

The dress was already laid out and ready for her. Brooke had insisted she buy the thing two years ago at Nordstrom's Off the Rack. Her robin's egg blue pashmina—a gift from Brooke—would add a little bit of color and keep her warm if the air conditioning got cranked up too high. For the finishing touch she put on her floating pearl necklace with matching earrings—a gift from Ricky during their dating years.

Looking at herself in the full length mirror that hung from her bedroom door, she let out a long sigh. She looked stunning, but that just didn't matter. Not with Ricky being long gone from her life…

She fiddled with the pearl as the memory of their last kiss still lingered on her lips. The thought alone made her pulse quicken as if somehow she could relive that special memory. Come Sunday, he'd pack up with the rest of the rodeo and head to the next town. For a moment, she let herself imagine she might go with him, thus leaving all of her commitments behind. How freeing life on the road with her lover would be! How wonderful!

Ricky had always gone with her to the annual gala. Every year he would stay at her side the entire night, helping her manage her anxieties. Tonight she would be on her own and the thought terrified her.

I'd better get used to it since I am going to be alone for the rest of my life.

The rest of her life... It had been so long since they'd made love, but she remembered the feel of his chest pressed against hers with aching clarity. The need to be touched—a loving touch that asked for nothing—threatened to devour her.

Like it always did, the fantasy quickly gave way to a crushing guilt. She had responsibilities—people counted on her. She couldn't just up and leave.

Thankfully, the doorbell interrupted her inner critic's harangue. She stumbled downstairs, practically tripping over her heels in the process.

A flower delivery man stood on her porch balancing a huge arrangement of purple roses. "Are you Violeta Hernandez?"

Vi nodded, not trusting her voice.

The man handed her the flowers. "These are for you. Have a nice evening, ma'am."

Vi smiled, a little stunned. "Thank you. You, too."

She closed the door and leaned against the wall of her foyer, taking in the intoxicating perfume of the unexpected gift. A gift that, apparently, also came with a card:

Violeta, my sweet.
Promise me you'll think about it.

Ricky

Vi's chest tightened as she choked back a sob. Her fingers brushed the soft petals as she wished again that Ricky could be there with her. The flowers would have to be enough.

Her phone rang with the familiar chords to Beethoven's Ninth Symphony. She placed the bouquet down on the table and raced to get it before it could switch over to voicemail.

"What's wrong, Joy?"

"I'm sick. Come get me."

Vi sighed. Of course she was sick and wanted to be picked up. Her high maintenance sister seemed to have a radar that went off whenever Vi was the busiest and most overwhelmed. "I'm sorry, but I can't. I have to work."

"I hate you, I hate you, I hate you!" Joy screamed her favorite verbal tick into the phone.

Well, I guess the speech therapy is working...

Vi had reached the end of her rope. She didn't have the patience to put up with this for a second longer. Didn't Joy realize that sometimes things happened to Vi that didn't revolve around her every whim? That sometimes there were even bigger problems to be dealt with? No...the reality was she didn't, but this realization didn't make dealing with her any easier.

Vi huffed and clicked the big red "end call" button.

But Joy called right back. Again. And again. And again.

And Vi' rage grew with each new ring. Finally, so angry she could've spit, she put her phone on silent.

She gathered everything she would need for the night including a flask full of whiskey. She had a feeling she might need a little help to get through the evening.

Shit, the flowers!

She grabbed a vase from the cupboard in the kitchen and filled it with water, her hands trembling as she tightened the spigot.

Too much, too much, too much.

A knock at the door startled her. Jesse. When she had mentioned that she would be going alone, he had kindly offered to be her escort. And his good-natured, easy-going attitude was exactly what she needed to get through this whole ordeal. Now here he was, decked out in a designer tux.

"Well, Mr. Abrahamson, don't you look dapper this evening."

"And you, Ms. Hernandez, are a vision," he said with a mock bow before offering her his arm. "Your chariot awaits, m'lady."

She giggled despite herself. Maybe the evening would make up for the crappy day, or rather week, she'd been having.

"What's up, Vi?" Ligia popped forward from the back seat and squeezed Vi's shoulder in greeting.

Of course, Brooke would be too busy to actually take her own goddaughter to the event. She really had no idea how easy she had it. She had everything Vi yearned for, and then some. Everyone always catered to Brooke and her needs. No one seemed to notice how Vi was barely treading water these days.

She could drop dead and no one would blink an eye.

CHAPTER 30

BROOKE

As soon as Jesse swung by to pick up Ligia, Brooke rushed to the bathroom to take another in a seemingly endless string of at-home pregnancy tests. Every other time she'd wanted the test to turn up positive, but this time she wasn't so sure.

Brian had always been under a fair deal of pressure at work, but these past couple of weeks he'd gone from merely a crab to outright hostile, and earlier that night... She shuddered remembering how afraid she'd been of her own husband. What would have happened had Ligia not arrived when she did?

And what would she have done? Would she have allowed Brian to take her in whatever way he wanted even though she'd said no? Would she have cowered as he hit her rather than fighting back?

Vi always yammered on about how much she admired Brooke's strength, but she was so, so wrong. Brooke wasn't strong. No. She was the worst kind of coward, and a fraud, and...

And *pregnant.*

She let the positive test fall onto the marble floor. The sound of its contact both soft and deafening. A baby? It hadn't been much more than a week since she'd taken the last one, and it had said she was *not* pregnant. Maybe this was a fluke. She decided to take a third test, let it be the tiebreaker, let it decide her fate.

And it declared that she... and Brian... were going to have a baby.

Instead of a rush of excitement, she felt anger overtake her from the inside out. Blood surged through her veins as her pulse quickened. *Why now? Why?*

Vi would say everything happened for a reason, that God had a plan. Well, it seemed God's plan for Brooke was to fuck her life up as much as possible. Great, just fucking perfect—and on one of the biggest nights of her career, too.

The gala, shit.

She just had to focus on making it through tonight. The rest she could figure out later. She sucked in a deep breath and held it in her diaphragm.

Normally, she'd place a hand on her belly to feel the air enter and leave her body in order to calm her nerves, to ground her. But she couldn't do that tonight. That would make all of this feel far too real.

Sometimes fake was for the best. She composed a smile and headed toward the big event.

* * *

SHE made it to the gala early, though not as early as she would've liked. Kim spotted her right away and ran through a list of inane questions, to all of which Brooke answered "yes, absolutely" with the fakest smile she could muster.

"Should we get started then?" Kim asked once they had been over everything, taking a half hour of Brooke's life she'd never get back.

"We still have twenty minutes to go. Let me run my checks before everyone gets here at eight." Brooke hurried away from Kim and went to hide in the bathroom.

Vi was there, washing her hands.

Brooke breathed a deep sigh of relief. "Vi, thank God! You'll never—"

"Brooke, I'm sorry, I can't talk right now. See you after your big speech, okay?" She smiled and it appeared genuine, but Brooke couldn't help feeling betrayed. Her best friend was supposed to be there for her, no matter how inconvenient the timing—and especially when a number of personal crises converged to make for one fuck-tastic evening.

The door slammed behind Vi as she hurried away, waddling awkwardly in her unpracticed heels. Brooke wanted so badly to cry—about the stress of all last week, about the baby, about the way Brian—

Shoot! Brian was supposed to play MC for the night, yet he'd stormed off to the firm after his and Brooke's squabble. And Kimberly would ruin the party before it started if Brooke were stupid enough to let her go up.

Jesse. Jesse would save the day. She took another several minutes to calm herself before returning to the party. It didn't take long to find Jesse at the punch bowl, chatting with Mitsy Grazier about God knows what. She didn't have time to feel jealous about the attention he was lavishing upon her nemesis, and, besides, he excused himself from that side conversation the moment he spotted Brooke approaching.

"Let me guess, Brian bailed?" He took a sip of his punch, a little bit of red residue remaining on his upper lip until he sucked it away and smiled.

The expression on her face must have said all he needed to know.

Jesse tossed his cup in the nearby trash and rubbed his hands together. "He doesn't deserve you, B. But don't, worry, I've got this."

"Thank you so much!" she cried and wrapped him in a hug, enjoying the scent of berries that clung to his breath. If she could just stay wrapped in Jesse's arms forever, she wouldn't have to face her problems. She was safe as long as he was there to hold her, to take care of her.

But forever wasn't an option, not when they had a show to put on. And Kimberly was right there tapping at her wrist and then pointing to the stage as if Brooke could forget that it was go time.

She shot the director a thumbs-up—although she'd much have preferred a bullet—as Jesse strode toward the makeshift stage, ascended its steps, and switched on the mic.

"Welcome, welcome, all you rad dudes and dudettes!" He pumped his fist in the air, and the audience cheered. Everyone loved Jesse. What wasn't to love?

"We're here tonight to get our party on—*Whoo!*—but we're also here for a good cause. A great one. So I ask that you all be generous with your pocketbooks, and..."

Brooke let her mind wander as Jesse continued to wow the crowd with his touching and totally on-theme speech. He'd obviously had a speech prepared, knowing Brian would let her down. Did he know about their other problems too, or did he at least suspect? Did everyone?

Ligia came up and hugged her from behind, placing a quick kiss on her godmother's cheek. "Hi, Auntie B! Thanks for inviting me, I'm having the best time!" she chirped as the DJ did a quick sound check then fired up a song by the Bangles.

"Who knew the eighties were so cool! This is like my favorite oldies jam."

Brooke turned and watched Ligia dart off toward the dance floor then join up with a good-looking Hispanic guy, who couldn't have been much older than her. She thought maybe she recognized him from somewhere, but couldn't recall where. Anyway, the two looked like they were having a blast. She could at least take solace in that.

A dark presence loomed to her left, and she turned to see Vi approaching in her midnight dress with her long sheath of black hair. "Sorry about before," her ex-best friend said. "I just needed some time to..."

"Shove it up your ass," Brooke hissed. "I'm not interested in your excuses, okay?"

For really, what excuse would make it okay for her to suddenly be besties with a woman they suspected for pornography, pedophilia, and possibly murder? Then to abandon Ligia on top of it? Oh, hell no.

"But, Brooke, we're best friends." Vi whispered then bit her lower lip to keep from crying.

"If that were true, you'd have known how much I needed you to be on point tonight. Not caught up in your own drama or—"

A waiter passed by with a tray of those damn clam shooters Kim had insisted upon and waved it in front of Brooke's nose to offer a taste.

The mix of liquor, tomato, and smelly seafood was too much for Brooke to bear. She had to book to the bathroom before her guts came spewing out.

Of course, Vi followed after her like some lost puppy, unwilling to accept the fact that Brooke wanted nothing to do with her. But Vi had made her choice when she'd decided to laugh and gossip with Annabeth over nothing then blown Brooke off on top of it. Brooke had actual real problems, and Vi hadn't been there for her.

Stupid Annabeth King. All of this was her fault, everything. Even Brian's strange behavior, the baby… Her stomach churned at that particular recollection, and she threw up whatever hadn't made it out of her stomach the first time.

"What do you want?" Brooke groaned, swiping at her face with her forearm, only too late realizing that it was the same arm she'd covered with foundation in order to hide her bruises.

And Vi didn't miss a beat. "Brooke! Oh my God, what happened?"

"I threw up." She flushed the toilet with the toe of her shoe and went to wash her hands, hoping she would just drop it.

"Did you get hurt? Did Brian do this to—?"

"I told you to leave me alone!" Brooke thundered. "God, just drop it, okay? Maybe if you weren't so obsessed with me, you'd realize what a joke you are, that your whole God-forsaken life revolves around being a martyr. Well, nobody asked you to do that. So grow up and move on."

Tears welled in Vi's dark eyes.

Brooke hadn't wanted to hurt her, but she couldn't have Vi prying with all her counselory questions forcing the truth out of Brooke before she was ready to tell it.

Luckily, Kimberly burst through the door before either woman had a chance to say anything more.

"Yoo-hoo, Brooke!"

If she noticed the vomit clinging to Brooke's lips or the bruises visible along her jaw, she certainly didn't let on. "Your registration workers never showed up, and I can't man that table forever. Do you have someone who—?"

"I'll do it," Vi said, keeping her eyes fixed on Brooke. "At least *someone* appreciates my help."

As soon as the others had left, Brooke tore her compact from her clutch and set to reapplying her makeup to cover the bruises. If she covered them for long enough, maybe they'd finally stop hurting.

CHAPTER 31

ANNABETH

ANNABETH pulled up to the bustling café. The venue was already getting crowded despite the fact that it wasn't supposed to start for another fifteen minutes. The valets were hard at work parking the cars in whatever free spaces they could find. Annabeth tossed them her keys and made her way inside. She was a little late according to Brooke's timeline, but whatever. Some things were just more important.

Madonna's *Like a Virgin* blared through the Book Cellar's kitschy speaker system. The eerie sound made gooseflesh break out on her arms, putting her a little on edge. When someone laid a hand on her bare arm, she jumped back in surprise.

"Wow, look at you!"

Jesse and Vi both wore huge grins on their faces.

"Trudy sure has outdone herself," Jesse said. "You look amazing, both of you do."

"Thanks. Sorry I'm late, I was at the hospital."

Vi shot her a look of immediate concern. "Is Marcus okay?"

She let out a gigantic sigh of relief. "He's perfect. He's awake and breathing on his own."

"Oh, thank God! What wonderful news!" Vi gave her a tight hug, then whispered into her ear, "I was praying for him."

Jesse glanced distractedly around the room. "I've got to head over to my post. I'll chat with you lovely ladies later. Make sure you both save me a dance. K?" Rather than wait for a response, he shoved a hand into the jacket of his designer tux and walked away.

What's up with him?

Annabeth turned back to Vi. "Where's Brooke? Is she mad at me?"

Vi turned in close and whispered in Annabeth's ear, "She—uh...she's having a hard time right now. So just be patient with her."

Annabeth shrugged. She wanted to ask for details, but something in Vi's expression told her that would not be okay. Whatever had happened had to have been pretty major to bring Vi back on the team

Brooke bench. Especially after the appalling way she'd treated her that afternoon at the salon.

"Please, for me." The sincerity of her plea pulled on Annabeth's heartstrings.

Annabeth held up her right hand like she was pledging to tell the whole truth and nothing but the truth. "I'll be on my best behavior."

Vi's eyes narrowed as if she didn't quite believe her. She couldn't really blame her for that though, could she?

Speak of the devil. The high and mighty Queen B had come out of the bathroom and caught Annabeth talking to her best friend. She charged at them like an angry bull. Could Annabeth pull off Brooke's signature fake friendliness? Only one way to find out...

"Brooke, so sorry I'm late. I was with Marcus in the hospital. He's awake." She smiled, but Brooke did not smile back. "I, uh, knew you would understand."

Brooke slowed her charge to a full and complete stop. She seemed taken aback by the rapid fire news just as Annabeth had hoped.

"Oh, that's wonderful. You're late. Thankfully Vi here stepped in for you. Guests are arriving. Keep in mind that we want to make sure they feel, you know, *welcome.*"

Annabeth rolled her eyes a little, but Brooke was so wrapped up in herself that she didn't even notice.

"Here's the sign-in. Make sure that only the people on the list come in. We can't afford to give away free food and drinks to people that haven't paid. Do you understand?"

Annabeth narrowed her eyes at Brooke. Was she serious? "Yeah, I think I got that, thanks." She couldn't hide the sarcasm from her tone.

Brooke spun on her heels and stalked off in the other direction. Heaven help the person who messed up or got in her way tonight. The woman was half-cocked and ready to fire.

* * *

WHEN she had signed up to do the welcome table, she had thought it would be a simple job. Boy had she been wrong. The majority of the party-goers barely acknowledged her as they came in. They would toss their names her way like they might their coat to the coat check. Then there were the irritable ones that became irate if she didn't find their names right away. One woman had the nerve to yell at Annabeth for the event being moved to the Book Cellar instead of the country club, as if it had been all her doing—elitist bitch! Through it all, she managed to keep her cool and smile politely despite their abhorrent behavior.

Even though the theme was Glam in the 80s, everyone looked more glam than 80s. The dress Ligia had given Annabeth was perfect for the event—a mix of glam and 80s style. She had her wrist brace on, but had forgotten her sling as part of her mad dash to get out the door.

A few men had hit on her—hanging around the table while their wives shot her hateful glances. During one of the lulls she got a text message from Marcus.

> *Sneak into the hospital tonight, babe. Let's make things official, if you know what I mean ;-)*

The solitary time spent at the welcome table gave her lots of time to think. It was getting harder and harder to push thoughts of Marcus out of her mind. Especially since she saw couples everywhere.

I need a drink, she thought as a waiter passed her with a tray full of champagne flutes. She snagged one before he could get away. Brooke's rules for volunteers were clear—no drinking—but after her week, a drink was definitely needed.

As she sipped her champagne and watched the decked out couples dancing on the makeshift dance floor, her mind began to wander back to Marcus and his promise to be faithful to her this time. She wanted to believe him. They would have to wait until the case was over before they could tackle their relationship woes head-on. They had made that decision when they took the case. At the time it had been a simple thing to agree to, but now...

"Can you believe they have clam shooters? I would've thought Brooke would have better taste than that," said a woman in a hushed tone to her friend as they passed by Annabeth's table.

Is that what those were? They smelled awful!

Annabeth shifted her weight from one foot to the other. She wasn't used to wearing heels and her feet had already begun to ache. She wished she could dance to help get her mind off Marcus, the case, and her sad little feet. Too bad she'd already exhausted her Vicodin prescription.

Even though her time was up at the welcome table she had no desire to mingle with anyone at the party.

The music shifted from a slow song by the Cure to an upbeat Duran Duran song. That got the crowd out on the dance floor. One couple in particular caught her eye. The young girl was a vision in white. Her cocktail dress flared at the bottom in a puff of multi-layered taffeta. On her arms she wore white lace Madonna-like gloves and her wrists were covered in shiny bangles. The outfit on its own would have been ridiculous, but on the girl it looked dazzling. When she spun around, Annabeth saw her face and recognized her at once—Ligia.

Her graceful partner wore a classic ruffled blue suit and shades. His feet moved in long graceful strides as they glided together in precise steps that looked almost choreographed. Their elaborate moves drew a crowd that cheered them on. As the song came to an end, he lowered his shades and winked. Annabeth recognized him immediately, too—Carlos—the charming hipster from Fin's sound crew. So Ligia had saved him a dance, after all.

Annabeth's skin prickled as his eyes met hers and he gave her one of his signature winks. What were the odds that he wasn't part of the trafficking ring? As far as Annabeth could figure they had to be pretty slim. Was he trying to lure Ligia? She was a very young and beautiful college student all alone in the country just like the other girls had been. If she could just get him in for questioning she might just have a chance at saving all of those poor girls. She, of course, had no weapon—hadn't thought it would be necessary for a charity event. Damn. But, gun or no gun, she couldn't just let him go...

As the DJ transitioned the music back to a slow song, Annabeth left her station and walked over to the young couple. She tapped Carlos on the shoulder with her good hand. "May I?"

Ligia wrapped her arms tighter around him and moaned, "Carlos, make her go away."

He gave her butt a squeeze and laughed. "The night is young, and it is just one dance of many."

Ligia yanked away, mumbling something about trading in a Mercedes for a pickup truck, then stalked off—no doubt in search of Brooke.

Carlos seemed unmoved by the outburst and took Annabeth into his arms. He glided her across the dance floor with a measured ease. "You look exceptionally beautiful tonight. I can see why Fernando is so infatuated with you."

Annabeth met his eye and held it. "Where is he? I was hoping to see him tonight."

Carlos smiled and pulled her in more tightly against him, making her heart hammer. Adrenaline surged through her veins, bringing her to a new level of alertness.

What was I thinking? I have no plan...

His lips grazed her bare neck all the way up to her ear. "You'll see him soon enough. Don't you worry. My brother has big plans for you."

His touch and the whispered words against her skin sent a chill down her spine. Wait...*brother?* Carlos was Fin's brother? Annabeth bit her lip to steel herself against the fear that bubbled in her gut.

"Oh?" she said at last. The deep husky sound of her voice sounded foreign to her ear.

Carlos chuckled. The strong, sure hand on her back slid a little further down and his pelvis shifted—

pressing against her in a suggestive manner that frightened her. Of all the times to be without a weapon.

"He isn't the only one with ideas for you."

Annabeth's breath quickened as his hand slid even farther down, coming to rest on her ass. The rough point of his tongue grazed her neck, and she realized then what she needed to do. "Maybe we should go somewhere a little bit more private to talk."

Carlos turned his head so that they were nose to nose. His enchanting brown eyes studied her with interest. "Talking isn't what I have in mind."

Annabeth took in a slow breath to steady her voice. "Let's go outside."

Carlos nodded with a sly smile. She led him off the dance floor and toward the back entrance.

She gasped as a well manicured hand clasped hold of her wrist.

"Hey!" Carlos called out.

Brooke shot him one of her practiced smiles. "I'm going to need to borrow Annabeth here for a sec. And I think *your date* would like a word with you."

Carlos nodded. "Yes, of course." Then headed back into the pulsing crowd.

"Wait—" Annabeth called out after him, but it was too late—he was already gone.

Brooke grabbed Annabeth and pulled her into a quieter spot by the kitchen—cornering her with her tall, commanding presence.

"What the hell are you doing? You're a married woman! Or have you forgotten that?" Brooke's overly white teeth were bared, and she was clearly out for blood.

Annabeth stepped back against the wall, and Brooke stepped with her in a frightening dance.

"What the hell, Brooke!" Annabeth tried to step to the side, but Brooke blocked her.

"Oh no, you're not going anywhere until you explain yourself." Brooke rested her hands on her hips and leaned into Annabeth like a parent scolding a child. "You may have everyone else fooled, but not me."

Annabeth crossed her arms over her chest—resting her injured arm against her breasts. "Brooke, you need to mind your own business for once. None of this has anything to do with you."

"After everything I've done for you, this is how you thank me?"

Her snarl startled Annabeth.

"I'm not going to let you drag Ligia into whatever perverted porno-rape-murder business you've got going on over there. It's bad enough you've turned Vi against me."

Annabeth tried not to laugh. Was she really being serious?

"All that you've done for me? Yeah, okay. As for Vi, she'd be better off without you, and I think you know that. The rest of that stuff? You're beyond crazy."

Brooke paled.

"I don't have time for your crazy bitch routine right now, okay?" Annabeth stepped forward to walk away.

The hard slap across her right cheek stung.

I should have seen that coming.

"Damn it, Brooke." She gritted her teeth and cupped her stinging cheek with her palm.

I will not hit her, I will not hit her, I will not hit her.

She repeated the mantra over and over until she felt her body relax a little.

Brooke tightened the hold on her hurt arm, causing a rush of pain to radiate up her arm and across her chest.

"Ugh. Fine! I'll tell you what's going on." Annabeth would have said anything just to get a moment of relief. "Even though its none of your goddamned business," she said under her breath.

Brooke turned her head and a dim light cast a shadow across her jaw...no, not a shadow, a bruise. Vi had said something about Brooke having a bad day. Had Brooke been in a fight?

"All right, start talking and make it quick. It's all your fault that I'm missing the party." Brooke pursed her lips in irritation.

Annabeth wet her lips. If talking would end this charade then she would talk. Maybe if Brooke knew the truth she would back off.

Walker Texas Wife

If I don't, she is going to keep getting in my way every chance she can get.

"Look, I know you've been suspicious of me from the moment I moved in and I know all about how you and Vi broke into my house—"

Shame washed over Brooke's pinched features for a brief moment, but then her indignant Queen B persona took over once more. "We did no such thing! How dare you accuse me—"

Annabeth held up her good hand to stop her. "Brooke, just stop. Vi told me everything. You know I could have you both arrested for what you did."

Brooke's mouth clamped shut.

Annabeth exhaled slowly to the count of six. Once she had calmed herself a little more she continued. "But I'm not."

Brooke's eyes narrowed in suspicion. "Of course not, because we didn't do anything."

Annabeth shook her head. "Play it like that if you want, but I know the truth."

Despite her words, Brooke's shoulders dropped in obvious relief.

"There's something you should know. I'm not who you think I am. I'm really a Private Investigator."

Brooke exploded with laughter. "Oh...my...God! You can't come up with a better story than that?"

Annabeth clenched her jaw and swallowed down her growing frustration before she continued.

"It's not a story. It's the truth. I'm here investigating a sex-trafficking ring. That man, Carlos, is a part of the operation. And while we stand here having this pointless discussion, Ligia might be in real danger."

Brooke's entire face turned bright red as she continued to laugh. "That is the most ridiculous thing I have ever heard."

If only she had her ID on her. In her rush to get out the door and see Marcus she had left her ID and gun at home along with the damned sling—not that anything she said or did would have convinced Brooke anyway.

Annabeth grasped Brooke's hand, hoping to drive home the seriousness of the situation. "Brooke this isn't a joke. If Ligia is as important to you as I think she is, then you will make sure she stays far away from that man."

Brooke shook loose from her grasp. "Why? So you can have him all to yourself? Marcus's dick not enough for you?"

Annabeth closed her eyes and took a deep breath before opening them again. "Ugh, I give up."

Brooke didn't stop her from leaving this time, but instead followed hot on her heels. Annabeth returned to the hall and scanned the room for Carlos and Ligia.

Damn it, they were gone.

Walker Texas Wife

Fuck.

Annabeth swallowed back the panic that threatened to take over.

She raced to the silent auction table where the other volunteers had gathered. An angry Brooke stalked behind her.

"Have any of you seen Ligia?" Annabeth's words tumbled out.

"She and her date went out the back. They wanted to know where they could smoke," one of the volunteers answered with a worried look. "Is...everything okay?"

Annabeth muttered a quick "thanks," and turned toward the exit. She needed to hurry.

But Brooke grabbed her hand and spun her back around. "You can't really be serious about all this?" Her words came out in a hiss.

"Yes and if we don't hurry up and stop him, you may never see Ligia again." She left off the part about how if Brooke hadn't snatched her away from Carlos earlier, they wouldn't be in this mess in the first place.

No time to point fingers.

All that mattered was making sure that the girl was safe and to take Carlos in for questioning. God, she hoped they weren't too late...

CHAPTER 32

Vi stepped outside to check her phone. Thirty-two missed calls. What the hell?

The majority were from Joy but there were also quite a few messages from the shelter, despite the fact that she had just been there. One was from her executive director, urging her to call immediately.

That can't be good.

She stumbled over to a parking stump and sat down as ladylike as she could given the short skirt. Perhaps a drink would help take the edge off.

Her mouth watered as she unscrewed the cap of her flask and took a long burning gulp before calling back the director.

Her boss, Lauren, answered on the first ring. "Vi, I need you to come in tonight. We've had a..." Vi could hear her boss sniffle like she'd been crying.

Her breath caught in her throat and her vision began to blur. "What happened?"

"Anjali died... she killed herself."

"No." Vi wasn't sure whether she'd said the word out loud or just thought it.

Lauren let out a loud sob. "I knew she was upset after talking with her parents, but..."

This is my fault. If we hadn't pushed her.

Angry tears began to slide down her perfectly put together face. "I talked to her just a few hours ago. I never would have thought... What happened?"

"She called her parents, and they had a fight. She didn't come to dinner. When one of the girls went outside for a smoke, she found her. Overdosed on drugs. I don't know where they came from or if she did it on purpose, but... I think she did. I know you had a big night planned, but, Vi, we need you here."

Vi began to tremble. She couldn't help but second-guess everything she had done. Taking Annabeth to the shelter had been a mistake, a fatal one at that.

"I'll be there within the hour."

"All right, thank you."

Vi jammed the end call button and took another swig of whiskey. She hadn't lost a client before.

Despite some serious cases she had always managed to save the girls that came to her in their darkest hour.

Why didn't I listen to Anna? She'd been right about the drugs. If I had warned the director...

Hot tears streamed down her cheeks. The last two weeks had been hell, but this...

She wiped away the tears with the back of her hand and looked up to see Ligia and some guy getting hot and heavy up against a parked car. She watched as he slid his hand down her side and then up her skirt. It seemed like ages ago since she had been that young, that free.

The smell of the roses Ricky sent were still fresh in her mind. She no longer had his shoulder to cry on, his strength to draw upon. And then her quiet tears turned to all-out sobs. As she buried her face in her hands she felt her necklace fall away and land on the concrete. Vi picked it up and examined it. The clasp had broken. She remembered the day Ricky had given it to her like it was yesterday.

They were celebrating their first anniversary at a nice sit-down restaurant. He had just gotten his first big check from bull riding and had blown the whole thing on their dinner and the matching necklace and earrings. He'd told her it was meant as a promise that he would make her his wife one day. After dinner they had driven out to the Hill Country and made love in the back of his pickup truck. And, two weeks later, while she and Joy were watching Ricky ride at the Rodeo, her parents had died in a four-car pile-up.

Now, with the necklace lying broken before her, all she had left was her memories. Her days of making out in parking lots were over.

She couldn't pull her eyes away from the young people. It was easier to watch them than it was to think about all that had been lost. The soundtrack of their heated moans and heavy breathing seemed all wrong for the anguished feeling wreaking havoc inside Vi's heart.

The guy pushed up Ligia's short skirt and unbuckled his pants. Were they actually going to just have sex standing up in the back end of the parking lot for all to see?

The ping of a new text message broke the spell of her voyeurism.

What the hell does Joy want now..?

Red hot with embarrassment she scooted further into the shadows before she pulled up the new text message.

It wasn't from Joy, but rather Brooke.

> *Annabeth has completely gone off the rails! Have you seen Ligia? I really need to talk to her. And where are you for that matter? The auction starts in 20 minutes. You'd better not bail on me!*

Vi took a deep breath before texting back.

Ligia is in the back parking lot with some guy, and I actually do have to bail on you. I'm sorry. You know I wouldn't leave unless it was important.

Vi took another swig of her whiskey before she called for a cab. While she waited her phone rang yet again. This time it was Annabeth, whose uncharacteristically high-pitched voice screeched in her ear.

"Vi, where exactly *is* Ligia? The guy she's with is part of the group I am investigating. Part of the group that took Anjali. She's in real trouble, Vi. I have to get to her before they can hurt her, too."

Vi stopped breathing.

No!

"Vi, are you there?"

She whispered into the phone in the hopes that the young couple didn't hear her. "Yes, I'm here. They are making out in the back of the building where the overflow parking is."

She looked up to see Ligia's tanned legs disappear into the passenger side of the car they'd been groping each other against.

"They are getting into a car. What should I do?"

"Stop them, Vi!"

Vi dropped her phone into her purse and shot up from her spot in the darkness. "Ligia! Wait!"

The girl spun around and looked surprised to see Vi running toward them. "Vi, what are you—?"

The young man bent to kiss her—silencing her.

"We're kind of busy here." His sinister eyes glowed in the light of the street lamp.

Wait...I know him! Carlos.

The doors to the back lot swung open. Brooke and Anna rushed out into the parking lot.

I can't let him hurt her!

Vi crept closer to the young people, keeping her eyes on Ligia who looked confused and a little frightened.

"Vi, what the hell is going on?"

Carlos wrapped his arm around Ligia's neck and pulled a gun out of his pocket.

Vi's body vibrated as adrenaline shot through her veins. Her hands shot up and she stopped in her tracks, mid-step. "Please don't hurt her."

Ligia stood stone still. Her eyes widened and her chest rose and fell. A single tear slid down her cheek and over the lips that just moments before the boy had been kissing.

"Come any closer, I'll kill her." His coal black eyes trained on Vi.

Time slowed down. Vi's crisis training had never prepared her for a hostage situation, and she was equally compelled to stay and try to talk to him and to run in the other direction as fast as she could. Instead she stood there, paralyzed by fear.

CHAPTER 33

BROOKE

How far was Annabeth going to take this little farce of hers? Normally, Brooke would tell her to take her drama elsewhere, but she didn't play around when it came to Ligia. If her goddaughter really was in danger, she'd put an end to that real quick. And if Annabeth was lying about the whole thing? Not even God could save her from the hell storm Brooke would unleash.

"They went outside for a smoke," one of her Volunteer Bees had said.

"She really is in danger. We need to hurry," Annabeth said next.

And that brought them to this precise moment in time. There she and Annabeth stood facing down what could only be described as Brooke's very worst nightmare—that is, if Brooke would have descended to such silly things as nightmares. But there was nothing silly about the tangle of limbs and cold hard steel that greeted them from across the parking lot.

Annabeth had been right. Ligia was in danger. And now so was Vi. If anything happened to either of them... Especially with the way she had left things with Vi earlier that evening.

Oh my God.

"Come any closer, I'll kill her," the gunman growled at Vi.

Vi inched closer. She probably thought that if she could move slowly enough, he wouldn't notice. But she hadn't factored in her heels or the junky gravel drive of the back lot.

She slipped.

He sighed exaggeratedly and wrapped his arm tight around Ligia's throat. "A shame your friend here refused to listen." He kicked Vi who lay splayed across the ground at his feet. "You'd have been *such* a good lay."

"Stop!" Brooke shouted, the word tearing from her throat without waiting for her permission.

"Auntie B, help me," Ligia sobbed between gasps for air.

"Hush. Go to sleep, go to sleep."

Brooke watched in horror as Ligia's face went from tan to pink to mauve. She struggled and kicked, but he was much stronger.

"No!" Vi screamed as Ligia's eyes rolled back in her head and her unconscious body slumped to the ground.

"I don't have a gun," Annabeth mumbled without moving her lips. "We're going to have to talk him down."

"Carlos, we can talk this out. No one needs to get hurt," Annabeth said with her hands out in front of her. "I'm sure we can all work this out."

The gunman cackled and shook his head. "Is this really the best you could do, *Anna?* Sending an unarmed bimbo to take me down? You're going to have to try much harder than that. As for you…" He grabbed onto Vi's hair and yanked her up to a standing position. "Who the fuck do you think you are, intruding on our nice little evening like this? You're what? Twenty-eight? A bit past your prime, but you'll do."

Vi's voice shook, but she did not cry. "Anna—"

"Don't talk to her," the assailant spat. "You've got something to say, you'll say it to me."

"Carlos," Vi pleaded. "Do what you want with me, but let Ligia go."

"C-Carlos," Annabeth inched closer. "Put the gun down. It doesn't have to go any further than this."

WALKER TEXAS WIFE

Why was everyone so insistent on talking? Why weren't they acting? Words were pointless, but a well-aimed bullet might do the trick. Annabeth didn't have a gun, but...

Vi kicked her heel back and connected it with Carlos's knee, startling him just long enough to get out of his grasp.

"You bitch!" He slammed his fist into her nose.

"Carlos, stop!" Annabeth further closed the distance between her and Carlos. What was she going to do?

It would be up to Brooke to end this. Typical.

"Oh, for fuck's sake." Brooke reached into her handbag and pulled out her Lady Smith & Wesson. It was pink, the perfect match to her heels and the perfect solution to this situation.

"Brooke, what are you doing? Why didn't you tell me you had a gun?" Anna tugged at Brooke's arm.

Yeah, like she would actually give it up.

Now what was the stance the instructor had taught her back when she'd taken her CPL certification? Legs shoulder width apart, check. Arms straight out at chest height, check.

"Brooke, give me the gun," Annabeth urged, but Brooke knew she had to act fast.

She unhitched the safety and...

Steady, steady...

Bam!

The .38 caliber bullet whizzed through the night air—and took Vi down.

Fuck, fuck, fuck! She squeezed the trigger again, and watched in equal parts satisfaction and horror as Carlos stumbled back and fell to the ground, part of his body trapping Ligia's beneath him. Blood bloomed from Carlos's chest. It came fast—gushing like a geyser.

She couldn't move, couldn't look to see what had happened to Vi. Was blood draining from her chest as well? Would Vi die? Was Ligia already dead?

That bastard! Look what he had done. Look what he had made her do.

"Nobody hurts my friends," she said so quietly that probably nobody heard. Then she was charging forward, the gun held at arm's length.

Click. Bang. Plop.

She'd shot the bastard again, right in his dirty, fucking head.

Annabeth waved her arms wildly, her lips moved furiously, but Brooke couldn't hear anything. It was all over now.

Annabeth reached for the gun again, and, this time, Brooke let her take it. As the cool metal switched hands, Brooke's senses blazed up once again.

A sour, metallic smell wafted by, and Brooke realized it was blood, blood *she* had spilled.

Annabeth yelled at her about overstepping *this* and not thinking enough about *that*, while Vi sobbed violently from across the way.

Vi…

Vi!

She was alive and clutching at her shoulder as thick, dark blood flowed over her fingers.

Ligia, though.

Oh, God.

CHAPTER 34

ANNABETH

SHE could hear the sound of sirens in the background, getting closer. Someone must have called the police. She had been too numb to notice. A switch flipped in her mind, cutting off the flood of emotions coursing through her, keeping them from reaching her conscious mind. Years in the criminal justice system had left an imprint on her. Her body could go through the motions of what needed to be done even as her heart burned with grief and anger over the events of the evening.

Brooke's actions had destroyed whatever chance they had of bringing down the group. They were back to square-fucking-one. Annabeth's heels made a crunching sound as she crossed the parking lot to where Vi lay. Squatting down as best she could in her dress, she checked Vi's vitals. She was unconscious but her chest still rose and fell.

Annabeth let the relief wash over her. Thank God!

She ripped off Vi's pashmina scarf and wrapped it tightly around the wound to slow the bleeding. It wasn't the best but it would hold until the ambulance showed up.

"AHHHHHHHHH!!!"

Annabeth started at the shrill scream. Ligia. Annabeth stood slowly and began to walk over to where the poor girl sat shrieking. All of the air in Annabeth's lungs was sucked out like she was in a vacuum. The girl was trapped underneath Carlos.

Ligia's horrified expression broke through Annabeth's false calm exterior. Brain matter and blood splatter covered the girl like a Jackson Pollock painting. Annabeth felt her gorge rise.

Brooke's third shot had hit the man's right temple. Blood oozed out of the open wound in the middle of his chest. He was most definitely dead. Brooke had seen to that. Thankfully she had handed the gun over before she did any more damage.

Before Annabeth could help the girl, she needed to record the crime scene for the cops. She quickly took out her phone and took a couple of snapshots before getting Ligia out from underneath the body.

"I'm sorry. It's a matter of protocol," Annabeth said, hoping she would understand.

Ligia clung to her, breaking through Annabeth's protective wall. Full of grief and anger, she squeezed the shivering girl back. Shock was setting in. Annabeth walked her over as best she could to the stoop where Brooke sat trembling. Annabeth squatted down again, pushing the limits of the fabric of her dress.

"Brooke?"

Brooke's glazed-over eyes rose to meet Annabeth's. "Is she dead?"

Annabeth noticed a slight tremor ripple through Brooke. "She's alive, Vi's going to be just fine."

Annabeth walked back over to Carlos's body. She had to act fast before the police came and all the information was lost to her. During the scuffle his phone had fallen out of his pocket and onto the ground. She pulled up the recent calls and took a snapshot of the screen with her own phone. She quickly flipped through the dead man's phone taking as many photos of information as she could before using the hem of his jacket to wipe her prints clean and place it back where she had found it.

People from the party had started to file out the back to see what was going on and a cacophony of gasps and screams filled the night air.

Annabeth was relieved to see Jesse push his way to the front of the crowd. His wide eyes met Annabeth's. "What the fuck happened?"

Annabeth stepped over the parking stump and pulled Jesse off to the side. "I need your help? Can you help me?"

Jesse's wide eyes darted around taking in the scene. "Yes."

Annabeth nodded and held out her hand. "Your jacket."

Without question, Jesse removed his jacket and handed it to her.

"Thank you. I need you to try to get everyone back inside and see if you can scrounge up some blankets or something. Brooke and Ligia are going into shock. We need to get them warm. Can you do this?"

Jesse bit his lip. She could see the control start to unravel. He could lose it at any moment. "They need you Jesse. I need you to keep it together. Okay?"

"I can do that," he said with a grim determination.

Annabeth watched as he charged toward the crowd with a confident look of authority.

"All right everyone, let's get back inside."

Annabeth could hear the combined voices of concern and worry from the party-goers who wanted answers that Jesse couldn't give, but everyone knew and loved him and did what he asked.

Annabeth took a mindful breath as she tried to calm her body.

She covered Vi in Jesse's jacket to keep her warm. She checked her crude tourniquet and tightened it again for good measure. The sirens blared as the fire and police departments and ambulance pulled into the front lot. Annabeth squeezed Vi's hand. The next couple of hours were going to be a circus so she breathed in the last quiet moment.

The back door flew open. Jesse was leading the cavalry.

Annabeth squeezed Vi's hand one last time. "Hang in there Vi, the ambulance is here."

* * *

ANNABETH lost all awareness of the passage of time. She dutifully answered the police questions. She informed her contact at the FBI and texted a quick update to her boss. Vi had regained consciousness just before they put her in the ambulance.

Annabeth stood in the middle of the lot with her hands on her hips, looking up at the night sky. A hand touched her bare arm. She turned to see Jesse standing behind her. The sleeves of his tux had been rolled up to the elbow. He looked as tired and drained as Annabeth felt. In his hands he held one of those emergency car blankets.

WALKER TEXAS WIFE

"Here," he said handing it to her. "It was in my car."

Annabeth took the blanket and wrapped it around her shoulders. "Thank you."

Jesse gave her a weak smile. The air of confidence that normally hung around him was gone. There was no pretense left.

"The cops took Brooke's statement. Since it matched the one you gave they are going to let her go. I'm going to go and take her home. She's refusing to go to the hospital."

Annabeth nodded. Brooke had to be the most stubborn woman alive. Of course she would refuse to go to the hospital. "Okay."

Jesse turned to leave but paused and turned back to her. "Anna."

"Yes?"

"You were robbed." He paused with a sly smile on his face. "You had that other girl. It should have been you at the Olympics."

Jesse turned to leave, letting his statement hang heavy in the air between them.

He knows who I am!

Jesse turned his head and winked at her from over his shoulder.

"Your secret's safe with me."

I am the worst P.I. ever!

A simple Google search had unearthed her identity to the town gossip of all people.

"Miss, can I give you a ride somewhere?"

Annabeth started and turned to face the plain-clothes detective behind her.

"Yes, can you take me to the hospital?"

The detective held out his hand to where his car sat idle. "After you."

Annabeth walked over to the car and slid inside. It felt so good to finally sit. Her feet ached from walking around the parking lot for hours in three inch heels. Slipping off her shoes and wiggling her toes she let out a deep sigh. The detective got into the driver's seat and laughed a little at her. "You ladies and your shoes. Why you put yourself through that is beyond me."

Annabeth let out a little laugh through her nose. As she settled into the seat she felt the rush of adrenaline start to die down, replaced with exhaustion. The effort to keep her eyes open had become a losing battle and before she knew it, the detective was shaking her awake.

"We're here."

Annabeth stretched and wiped the sleep from her eyes. "I guess the day finally caught up with me."

"Take some advice from an old man who's been doing this since before you were even born. Go home, get some rest, and leave the crime scene at work."

Annabeth smiled. "Thank you, officer. I will."

The man smiled, a slow one that didn't reach his eyes. She could tell he didn't believe her. They were all the same at the core. The work was their life, and, despite any good effort on their parts, there was no leaving it behind.

Annabeth lifted her sleep-laden arm and opened the car door, letting the rush of heat wake her. She watched as the cop drove away.

As she stood in the ambulance bay of the hospital where Marcus and now Vi lay, she couldn't help but think about how epically she had fucked up.

Her phone beeped with an incoming message. Annabeth fumbled for her phone and pulled up the new text message. Fernando!

> *The voyage of discovery has just begun. Now with new eyes you will see what you failed to see before. This is just the beginning, Anna Blackwell, P.I. <3 Fin*

Annabeth recognized the bastardized wording from Proust. A well-educated nemesis who taunted her with archaic lines from literature. Great. Taking this job had been a mistake, but now there was no turning back. Things had gotten personal. She had almost lost Marcus, a victim was taken, one almost taken, and poor Vi had been shot. They deserved to pay for their crimes.

Fin's words chilled her. He knew her name and would blame her for his brother's death. She had never been in more danger in all her life, but now she had no choice but to see it through.

With the blanket Jesse had given her slung over her arm, she walked through the hospital's automatic doors and went straight to the third floor to Marcus's room. He was asleep. Dropping her things on the chair beside his bed and laying her shoes down underneath the chair, she sat on the edge of the bed. His eyelids fluttered open and a look of surprise crossed his sleepy features.

"Anna?"

Annabeth reached for his hand and squeezed it. Marcus lifted his free hand and touched her cheek with a reverence that broke her. Tears slid down her cheeks and he pulled her down into the crook of his arm. With her head nestled against his warm chest, she let the sound of his heartbeat calm her frayed nerves. He didn't ask her anything and for that she was grateful. The words and explanations would come later. For now, she would let the tears fall and find a small bit of comfort in the arms of the one person who loved her.

Tomorrow would come soon enough, carrying with it the problems of yesterday.

DYING TO KNOW WHAT HAPPENS NEXT?

Be on the lookout for *Texas & Tiaras* coming soon.

ALSO MAKE SURE YOU'RE SUBSCRIBED FOR UPDATES AT:

www.MelStorm.com/subscribe
&www.KMHodge.com/subscribe

* * *

As an added bonus, you'll receive a free short story as our way of saying "Hey, thanks!"

ALSO BY THE AUTHORS

By Melissa Storm & K.M. Hodge

The Book Cellar Mysteries
Walker Texas Wife
Texas & Tiaras
Remember the Stilettos
Ladies, We Have a Problem

By Melissa Storm

The Cupid's Bow Series
When I Fall in Love
My Heart Belongs Only to You
I'll Never Stop Loving You
You Make Me Feel So Young
Total Eclipse of the Heart
Tainted Love
I Want to Dance with Somebody
You Belong with Me
She Will Be Loved
Somebody Like You
All I Want for Christmas is You

The Pearl Makers
Angels in Our Lives

Diving for Pearls
Love Forever, Theo
Shackle My Soul
Angel of Mine

Stand-Alone Novels & Novellas
A Texas Kind of Love
A Cowboy Kind of Love
A Wedding Miracle
Finding Mr. Happily Ever After
A Colorful Life
My Love Will Find You
The Legend of My Love

By K.M. Hodge

The Syndicate-Born Trilogy
Red on the Run
Black & White Truth
True Blue Son

Stand-Alone Novels & Novellas
Summer of '78

About Melissa Storm

Melissa Storm is a mother first, and everything else second. She used to write under a pseudonym, but finally had the confidence to come out as herself to the world. Her fiction is highly personal and often based on true stories. Writing is Melissa's way of showing her daughter just how beautiful life can be, when you pay attention to the everyday wonders that surround us.

Melissa loves books so much, she married fellow author Falcon Storm. Between the two of them, there are always plenty of imaginative, awe-inspiring stories to share. Melissa and Falcon also run the business Novel Publicity together, where she works as publisher, marketer, editor, and all-around business mogul. When she's not reading, writing, or child-rearing, Melissa spends time relaxing at home in the company of her three dogs and five parrots. She never misses an episode of *The Bachelor* or her nightly lavender-infused soak in the tub. Ahh, the simple luxuries that make life worth living.

* * *

Melissa loves hearing from readers.
Please feel free to reach out!
www.MelStorm.com

About K.M. Hodge

K.M. Hodge grew up in Detroit, where she spent most of her free time weaving wild tales to spook her friends and family. These days, she lives in Texas with her husband and two energetic boys and once again enjoys writing tales of suspense and intrigue that keep her readers up all night. Her stories, which focus on women's issues, friendship, addiction, regrets and second chances, will stay with you long after you finish them. When she isn't writing or being an agent of social change, she reads independent graphic novels, watches old X-files episodes, streams Detroit Tigers games and binges on Netflix with her husband. She enjoys hearing from her readers, so don't be shy about dropping her a line.

* * *

Connect with K.M.
www.KMHodge.com

Made in the USA
Charleston, SC
05 March 2016